Praise for C. L. Moore

'A pure romantic whose fantasies remain some of the most vivid and engaging of their kind'   Michael Moorcock

'With icy, expert fingers, C. L. Moore paints a chilling portrait of tomorrow'   *Astounding Science Fiction*

'She combined elegant yet colourful prose with a distinctive emotional flair'   Fantasyliterature.com

'Varied, imagination-stretching, written without cheapness or shallowness'   *Galaxy Science Fiction*

Also by C. L. Moore

Doomsday Morning

C. L. MOORE

This edition first published in Great Britain in 2019 by Gollancz
an imprint of the Orion Publishing Group Ltd
Carmelite House, 50 Victoria Embankment
London EC4Y ODZ

An Hachette UK Company

1 3 5 7 9 10 8 6 4 2

A CIP catalogue record for this book is
available from the British Library.

ISBN 978 1 473 22326 4
eBook ISBN 978 0 575 11938 3

Typeset at The Spartan Press Ltd,
Lymington, Hants

Printed and bound by CPI Group (UK) Ltd,
Croydon, CR0 4YY

www.gollancz.co.uk

CHAPTER I

After a while the lurching of the transport bus hit a rhythm I could adjust to. Every time I moved dust came up out of my denims, and even in the hot dark there was light enough to see the dirt from the Ohio orchards under my fingernails. I am in mourning, I thought. Ask me why I wear black. I am in mourning for my life. That's . . . what? Oh yes, Masha in *The Sea Gull*.

The bus rattled and stank. It stank of sweat and insecticide. The insecticide was provided by the government to stop plant pests from moving into the Illinois orchards with the Croppers. It also discouraged fleas and lice among the passengers – not that most of us cared. If we had, we wouldn't be Croppers.

I had got used to the lurching and the smell, I had settled back a little, shut my eyes, turned myself off, and started to think about nothing when a minor riot suddenly exploded in the bus. Somebody seemed to be kneeling on my chest. People were all over me, laughing and yelling. I woke up fighting.

But the pressure of the crowd pinned my arms down until I could hardly move. I felt window glass sticky against my cheek as the uproar jammed me sidewise. I was flattened against the wall by men crowding across the seats to peer out the windows on my side. The bus canted to the left. Most of the seats across the aisle were empty. I struggled to get my arms free.

'Get the hell off me,' I said.

'Take it easy, Rohan,' somebody told me.

'I said get the hell off.'

'Shut up. Take a look at that.'

The pressure eased a little, and I looked out through the smeared glass into the hot, dark night. Half a mile away was a big outdoor movie screen, big enough so the girl on it looked larger than life even this far away. For just a minute, seeing her alive and moving over there, I thought I must still be dreaming.

'Miranda!' somebody said, and whistled shrilly.

'Look at that! Look at her!'

'What a dish she was . . .'

I thought, Yes, what a dish. A morsel cold upon dead Caesar's trencher, that was Miranda, and who would have thought it? Until the day she died, who would have thought it?

'Slow down,' somebody else yelled to the driver. He didn't pay any attention. The bus kept on rolling, fast. It couldn't go fast enough to suit me. The screen as we passed it seemed to turn sidewise, but slowly, too slowly. I knew the picture I was watching. I knew the scene. I knew what was going to come on in the next moment or two, and I didn't want to watch, but I couldn't help it. Even if I'd shut my eyes, the colors and motions of those moving shadows a quarter of a mile away across the fields would have gone right on moving between my eyelids and my eyes. I knew the film that well.

Now an enormous door behind the larger-than-life Miranda opened and a man came into the brilliantly colored room a quarter of a mile off. He had heavy shoulders and a thick neck and a quick, intolerant way of moving. He wore his black hair cut so short it looked like a skullcap painted on his head, which all the critics agreed had a very fine shape. Too bad there was nothing inside it.

Somebody in the crowd piled around me yelled, 'Hey, Rohan, that looks like you!' and somebody else said in a fierce, low voice, 'Shut up!'

I paid no attention. I watched the young Rohan of four years ago come up behind his wife and rest his hands on her waist, one on each side, like a belt. She laid her head back on his shoulder. It was like watching two gods make love, beautiful, gigantic, more vivid than life, and a long way off in space and time. The colors and shapes were brilliant in the magical room

2

where they stood, untouched by the hot night air, untouched by time or change.

The screen turned sidewise as we rolled along the dusty road. The pair in the bright-colored room grew narrower and thinner until they were nothing but a dazzling vertical line, and then they were gone.

And then *they* were gone.

But not me. Miranda, yes. She was out of it, and a good thing, perhaps, considering how she died. But, as for me, I was trapped on a bus that traversed time, held down helpless while the wheels turned and my old, remembered world narrowed and thinned until it was nothing but that dazzling line. A line that went out, carrying Miranda with it.

'It's all over and done with,' I told myself. 'It happened three years ago and nobody remembers now. Not even you . . .'

I heaved savagely against the press of bodies around me. They began to break up, groaning and catcalling. The man who had been jammed against my shoulder lost his balance as the bus lurched. I saw him begin to fall toward me. He tried to catch himself. One hand slapped against the window and the other came down heavily on my chest.

I hit him.

I hit him as hard as I could from my sitting position, and the numbing jolt against my fist was like a spotlight flashing out suddenly on a dark stage. I put all the weight of my shoulder into it. There was a bright, clear certainty in my mind. I felt very eager, very good. We'll fight now, I thought. This is the easy way.

But it didn't work. He caught the back of the next seat and scrambled out into the aisle. He stood there rubbing his jaw and staring down at me. He didn't say a word. But there was a short, confused babble from the men around us.

'What's up?'

'It's Rohan again.'

'Hey, Rohan, why don't you cut your throat?'

I looked at the man in the aisle. I was braced and ready and eager. The bus hummed on. Slowly the spotlight faded in my mind. I knew he wasn't going to fight. My brief sense of relief ebbed.

I shrugged and sat back. The man went away. I reached into my denims and got out my bottle. I broke the seal and had a drink. It tasted like rat poison, but the first one always does, of course.

'How about it, Rohan?' the man in the next seat suggested.

'Isn't enough,' I said, recapping the bottle.

'Sure there is.'

'It's a long haul to Springfield.'

'You can't drink all that.'

'Watch me.'

He gave up. There was still a good deal of clamor from the other men, and the driver gave a bored groan and switched on the TV screen at the front of the bus. A cops-and-robbers film came on, all the cops noble in red Comus coats, and the heroine wearing her hair in a wide halo of curls imitating the way Miranda had worn hers in *Bright Illusion*. Slowly the Croppers calmed down.

You don't stay excited very long if you're a Cropper. You haven't got the energy. Or the interest. For most Croppers life is a closed circle. Once that contract's signed, you know what's ahead. The regular term is five years, but long before it's up you owe the company so much in liquor bills and food that you never get out again. So nobody signs – sober. I couldn't remember signing up myself. But my signature's there in the company files, staggery, sprawling, but a valid Howard Rohan scrawled on the dotted line. I was in for life, or as long as the company wanted me. I couldn't say I cared. Much. Oh, I thought about getting away sometimes. I wished there was a way out. But even if I found it, what then? Here at least I knew I'd always eat, always get the liquor I needed to shut out the world. And, except for work like this, what could I do in this life, outside the one thing that wasn't for me any more?

I took another short drink. The second is never quite as bad as the first. But I nursed the bottle. I hadn't meant to start this

4

soon, but the sight of Miranda – and myself – had shaken me. I needed to turn myself off.

So I worked my way carefully into a warm and pleasant buzz, building a wall around me that hummed like happy bees in summer. Things blurred. Outward and inward things. I looked at the window and it turned into a TV screen with my reflection on it, my head with the uncut hair making the outline unfamiliar. The dirt, the dark, the unkempt hair blurred the image so you couldn't see what three years had done to Howard Rohan.

I gazed through my own reflection, ignoring it, watching the summer night go by. Once or twice another bus exploded past with a roar. A few private cars slid along, little glowing glass bubbles riding the automatic hookup, their drivers dozing. Now and then a big red Prowler went purring by, teardrop-shaped to house the gadgetry in its swollen aft section. I always thought when I saw a Prowler of the propaganda the anti-Comus underground circulates. Big crimson teardrops running down Liberty's face. Or big blood-drops labeled poison circulating through the arteries of the nation. Obvious stuff, but it sticks in the mind.

The only other thing to look at along the dark road was the series of Raleigh posters, one to the mile, regular as clockwork, fluorescing in full color when the headlights hit them. It's irritating, having them come so fast. The image hasn't had time to fade before the next image hits you in the face. But Comus never does anything by halves.

Like Howard Rohan, I thought. Miranda always said you didn't know how to do things the easy way. But I never knew an easy way. 'And that's exactly why you're sitting here now,' I told myself. 'Dirty, itching, smelling unpleasantly of sweat and disinfectant. It ought to be easy to stop thinking. Stop feeling. And you might as well get used to it because you're a Cropper for life, Rohan.' But it isn't easy at all.

The TV screen interrupted itself to give a progress report on the President's health. I looked blurrily down the bus, trying to focus on Raleigh's face. It was an old news clip, Raleigh with

5

the big square chin pushed forward and the big face firm and ruddy. But it's been a long time since Raleigh really looked like that. He must be well past seventy now and he's been re-elected President six times. Powerhouse Raleigh, the man who moved the nation after the Five Days' War. But the powerhouse was running down now. He'd had his second stroke a week ago and nobody really believed he'd pull out of this one. He saved the nation. He founded Comus. That could be his epitaph.

Comus. Communications of the United States – Com. U.S. It got shortened into Comus within the first month after it started. Good old Comus. God of mirth and joy, he used to be. In his oldest meaning he was Greek and he meant carouse. Well, times change.

I thought what a strange new world we would have when Raleigh finally died. He brought us through bad times, the worst of bad times. I can't even remember it, but my parents lived through the days when there was anarchy in America for a while, in the long aftermath of the Five Days' War. And then Raleigh stepped in.

Maybe times make the man. Raleigh took on a gigantic job and he did the work of a giant. Whatever means he had to use, he used. He made no mistakes in those days, and afterward he seemed to get the idea that he couldn't make mistakes at all. He had to pour skills and money first of all into communications to get supplies rolling because the survival of the nation depended on it, and afterward because the survival of the Raleigh regime depended on rigid control of the same communications. By the time he was finished he'd set the limits within which he could operate, and the limits were the borders of the nation. Later on he set up internal walls, not quite so high, shutting off areas within the borders, for the good of the nation.

He was our savior, thirty-odd years ago. He's a benevolent dictator now. Oh, sure, benevolent. Maybe some of the men under him aren't quite as popular as Raleigh, but while he lives we all know things can't get really bad. And if society is stiffening at the joints just the way Raleigh is, well, anyhow, our way of life is pretty good, taken all in all. Up at the top it's very,

6

very fine. I know. I was up there. And at the bottom – well, nobody goes hungry. Not even Croppers.

Raleigh has stopped time. But time, all the same, is having his way with Andrew Raleigh. Slowly, slowly the calcium goes on thickening in his arteries, just as it thickens in the arteries of Comus. The joints stiffen, the mind lags. And even after Raleigh dies, Comus will be with us. Comus is a god. And his name once meant carouse.

I liked that. I had a drink on it. *You know, my Friends, with what a brave Carouse I made a Second Marriage in my house...*

Good old stiff-jointed, paternalistic Comus.

And took the Daughter of the Vine to Spouse.

CHAPTER II

The bus slowed down and light beat on my closed lids. I opened them. We were going through a small town. The bus had stopped at a crossing light and a theater marquee was shining right in my face. Know what its lights spelled out? That's it. *Howard and Miranda Rohan.* A revival of the picture made from our biggest stage hit, *Beautiful Dreamer.*

Even through the buzzing in my head I began to wonder a little. Not very much. It had nothing to do with me. Three years can be longer than you'd believe. They have quietly turned me into somebody else, and I didn't care, then. But it did come to me dimly that I'd been noticing a good many revivals of old films lately. Some of ours, many of others. All of them, of course, are propaganda – opinion readjustment, they call it. Some skillful, most heavy-handed. In *Beautiful Dreamer* I'd argued the Comus boys out of the worst of their ideas. In those days I could get away with it. I was a big name. Actor-manager and half of the top theater team in the country. My name in lights. My word law in the theater – within limits. Riding the crest of the wave . . .

Well, if Comus was reviving old pictures it had a reason. It was probably worried about something. Things were going on in the world. Probably trouble. I didn't want to know. I shut my eyes again as the bus picked up speed. The nameless little town went away, carrying Miranda's lovely and incorruptible image with it into a small dot on the horizon and then into oblivion.

Think of something else. Think of Comus.

I rather like to think of Comus. It's so big you have to pull

8

up and back high in the air, miles high, to see it as a whole. That gets you away from people and things and close focusing. I like it up there, high above the world.

Looking down, I can imagine Comus visible in an intricate network like a spiderweb that touches every human being and every building in the United States. You can see it wink and sparkle everywhere it touches a human mind. Little crackling nerves of electromagnetic energy giving life to the complex machines that run the country for Comus. Chicago Area, St. Louis Area, with high walls between, miles and miles high, tenuous as air, real as granite. Within them, Comus, shaping public opinion among its other deific duties. Maybe different opinions in Baltimore Area and San Francisco Area. That's only natural. Comus knows best, I suppose.

So we went jolting on through the hot night. I nursed my warm buzzing that blanketed thought. Cropping isn't bad. You eat. You sleep. You get whiskey very cheap. You're told what to do and you do it, and everything goes along fine and easy. You never think. You never remember, if you keep the bottle handy. You go rolling along in your own little magical room which the whiskey builds around you, its walls as far on every side as the buzz extends. Inside it, pleasant anesthesia. Inside it also dirt and dust and discomfort. I itched. I needed a shave. I didn't care. I didn't have to in my portable magic room.

But then the bus slowed again. We were pulling into the bright, clean, richly colored belt of a check station and the top signal was on, so I knew Comus was combing the roads for somebody or something. Or else it was just feeling inquisitive about things in general and wanted to take a random sampling of how people feel about things. You never know with Comus. The bus got in line. I hoped my bottle would last.

Somebody called, 'All out. Stay in line. Follow the guard.'

I put the bottle back in my pocket and shuffled out with the rest. If I took things easy the buzz ought to stay with me. I balanced it around me like a big intangible balloon. When the line stopped so did I, trying not very hard to keep my eyes open.

The check station was big and bright and flashy. It probably dated from the height of the Raleigh regime, about fifteen years ago, when the fad first came in for ornateness and ostentation. I'd seen even flashier places than this, with even more colored glass and even bigger Raleigh emblems, shield-shaped, with the AR monogram in neon tubes full of moving bubbles. And if the AR looks like ANDREW, REX, a man can't help the initials he's got, can he?

The light shining across the highway was blue and yellow and purple around its edges from the colored glass that bordered the windows of the station, but a strong, clear glare beat down on the cars before the door, where interrogations went on. I could hear the music of a dance band playing from some far-off ballroom, the sound turned low inside the station. I could hear the metallic voice of Comus inside, too, talking with the voice of authority from some central ganglion to this peripheral nerve ending out here in the dark on the highway.

A couple of the big Prowlers were drawn up in the parking lot beside the station. You could see how red they were even with green and purple light from the colored windows bathing them. Two or three hedgehoppers stood quivering a little on their long bent legs with a queasy motion I hate to watch. They are dishonest little cars. They can go wherever a tank can, and they slip through the grass almost without leaving a track. Antennae whipped gently above them, feeling out messages with a sort of senseless, inanimate eagerness.

Overhead as the line shuffled on I thought I could hear a helicopter hum, a heavy buzzing that could be right in my own head. Comus monitors every Prowler squad with a helicopter, so taking side roads or cutting across country gets you nowhere if the call is out and Comus really wants the traffic sampled. In my mind's eye I climbed a little higher than the helicopters and watched how their blood-red backs caught the starlight from a long way up, looking deep black-red in the darkness. I gazed down on them and they gazed down on their little broods of Prowlers, and there was a controlled, orderly feeling about it all. Everything in its place. Everything predictable. I was safe and untouchable in my little buzzing room floating high up in the middle of the air.

But while I waited a hedgehopper came rocking up the road and pulled into the pool of colored light beside the station. A man got out and went into the station, bright and immaculate in his red coat. The cross-country 'hopper stood there rocking like an uneasy spider. I was thinking about sneaking another drink.

Then I heard my own name called.

I felt a familiar, automatic response run out along my muscles at the cue. But I didn't answer. I just stood there swaying a little.

'Howard Rohan. Step forward.'

Heads turned toward me. I stepped forward. A guard came down the line, neat and authoritative in his red uniform. He looked me up and down, taking in my faded denims, my dust, my stubbled chin. He took in my breath too.

'Right,' he said. 'Follow me, Rohan.'

Inside the station everything seemed very bright and busy. My guard took me up to a counter with an imitation marble top made out of some synthetic. 'We've found Rohan, sir,' he said to the man behind the marble.

The man was looking at my identification card. He bent it back and forth between his fingers. The plastic snapped every time he did it. Finally he said, 'Better use a Prowler, I guess. It's faster.' He stamped a plastic disc and handed it to the guard with my card. 'Straight through by fast plane,' he said. 'Priority. Check the prints first.'

So we went away to another counter, where my finger and retina prints were taken. I could have got mad. I could feel the anger hovering up inside me, waiting its cue. This was part of the life I had got away from, at a cost nobody but I could know. I had sunk without a trace into the particular oblivion I had chosen. I liked it down here. I couldn't see that they had any right to haul me up again. But they had the power to do it. I didn't doubt that. I decided to save the anger for somebody near the top, where it might do some good. These boys were just following orders. So I did what I was told, and not a thing more. I made my arm limp when they took the prints. I focused on nothing when they flashed the retina pattern. Then they looked at me and I looked at nothing, carefully balancing the anger in me to keep it from spouting up and getting me into trouble.

'Think we ought to clean him up first?' somebody asked.

'They want him fast,' somebody else said.

I just stood there breathing quietly, not even wondering. Of course they'd made some kind of mistake. They wanted some other Howard Rohan. (With my fingerprints and retina patterns? Never mind. It's got to be some other Rohan...)

We got into a Prowler. I leaned back and shut my eyes. When I opened them the lights of an airfield shone into them. We got into a plane, not a jet, so we probably weren't going very far. I felt my stomach complain when we took to the air. I had another drink. My guard looked at me uneasily, but he didn't interfere. He had his orders. I didn't wonder what they were.

We sat near the tail of the plane, with a couple of seats between us and the other passengers. So I wouldn't contaminate anybody, I thought, admitting that they had a point there as I scratched myself. The TV screen at the front of the plane showed us a comedian whose timing was lousy. I used to think I was pretty good myself in comedy. I had a long run in the lead role of the new Shakespeare comedy they dug up in '94, though just possibly the author's name contributed something. Miranda always said—

Never mind. Don't think about Miranda.

But, going back to civilization, here in the clean-smelling, gently humming plane, in the flowered plush seats, is it possible not to think of Miranda? God knows I didn't think enough about her when she was alive. Maybe she still would be if I'd listened when she wanted to talk to me. If I'd thought more of her as a woman and less as a beautiful puppet to act as I wanted her to on stage.

Don't think about Miranda.

My image in the window beside me caught my eye. I seemed to be flying along out there effortlessly, keeping pace with the plane, transparent though I was with the stars shining through me. I looked at myself out there and tried to think of anything but Miranda. It wasn't any good. The thought of that last day was moving up on me inexorably, smooth and relentless, and how could I stop it? Once it starts, there's nothing you can do.

It's funny how quick a memory can be. I couldn't get the bottle to my mouth fast enough to keep that last day, that last night from flashing back through my mind, completed from start to finish, the end simultaneous with the beginning and everything in between as clear and perfect as if I'd just finished living them, every detail there.

Life and the drowning man. That's what they mean. The whole picture can flash by that fast. While the whiskey ran down my throat it went by again, retracing the well-worn groove of memory I had spent three years trying to wipe out.

Scene, backstage at the Andrew Raleigh Theater, New York's best and newest. Characters, the cast and crews that were staging *Beautiful Dreamer* for a rerun, starring, of course, Howard and Miranda Rohan. Lead character, Rohan himself, husband, director, and co-star of the beautiful dreamer. Curtain rises on Rohan projecting frenzy better than Stanislavsky could have done it. Louder, anyhow.

Absent from stage, Miranda. Desperate search going on. Her understudy rehearsing hopefully while the search grows more and more desperate. No luck. Miranda missing from morning appointments, missing from her matinee, missing from rehearsal, missing from the night's performance. Rohan going on with half a dozen drinks in him, too frantic to feel them. Rohan snatching drinks every time he steps off stage. Rohan, sober as a judge from start to finish.

Finish – phone call just after the second-act curtain. The police have found – them. Them? Them? There must be some mistake. Who could Miranda be with that she'd miss two performances in a row without a word to me? I forgot about the play. I walked out on the last act. That's me, never-do-anything-by-halves Rohan. Drive yourself and your cast crazy working for impossible perfection, sure, but drop it flat and leave the audience buzzing and be all husband, desperate and bewildered, when word like this comes in. I guess I never was as good as I'd thought as actor, director, or husband if I could turn in a performance like that.

Actually I really did forget about the last act. Our two understudies struggled through it in front of a house full of whispers and rumors while Rohan in a police car, with the siren making the kind of noise he felt like making, headed for the Saw Mill River Parkway and the wreck that had killed both of them. Miranda and her lover. The man I had never heard of.

Sometimes, now, I wonder if I'd ever really seen or heard of Miranda. The real one. If this could happen without my guessing, had I ever known her as she was? Thinking back over and over and over, I could remember times when she was moody and withdrawn, times when it seemed to me she was about to say something she never quite got out. Because I was busy and preoccupied. Because there was never a time for relaxation between jobs and the job at hand filled my whole mind. I can remember now the many times she almost told me – something. But she put it off too long.

The photographers hadn't got there yet when the police car and I arrived. I saw her as they found her. She was lying half out of the smashed car, and except for the back of her head there was hardly a mark on her. She had nothing at all on except a Japanese kimono I had never seen before in my life. Why she had gone out that way, what unknown apartment they had left, where they were going, I never knew.

She looked beautiful. She always did look beautiful. Even when there was nothing remaining any more to control her body and arrange her gestures, she lay against the hillside in her flowery kimono as if a portrait painter had arranged her to show her beauty best. The kimono covered her very decently, considering. You had the feeling that Miranda's ghost must

14

have paused, looked back, and stooped to twitch the brightly colored silk into place, wanting her to look her best even now.

Did they ever find out who the man was? I think so. I'm not sure. It didn't matter. Just a man of no special importance in the world to anyone except – perhaps – Miranda. I don't remember how he looked at all.

What I remember is standing there wondering just when Miranda had made the decision that had led to this moment. It might have been any of the times when she had been on the verge of saying – something – to me and I hadn't waited to listen.

What I remember is the feeling that I might have saved her – could have saved her – and I had not saved her. There would never be another chance. The curtain went down then.

The curtain never rose again.

You see how fast it goes through the mind? You can remember in no time at all. From the moment the rot-gut hit my throat to the time it began spreading around the walls of my stomach I lived the twelve tours over.

I drank the rest of my pint in a couple of gulps. There wasn't much, but enough. The Rohan who had stood on the grassy bank above Miranda and the Rohan who floated easily along outside the plane window and the Rohan inside on the deep plush seat all got blurry together. They all passed out at the same moment.

CHAPTER III

I woke up in bed.

I was sober and it felt terrible. Everything around me had clarity too explicit to endure without my buzzing walls to filter out reality. The room was an average bedroom, a little on the luxury side. I sat up and began to shake all over. My head felt groggy and there was a sore spot at the inside of the elbow where the vein comes to the surface. Some kind of injection? I couldn't remember a thing but a dream I'd just been having stirring uneasily around in the back rooms of my mind, insisting it was important. I tried to remember.

It seems the whole population of the United States had shaken me by my shoulder and said they were in grave danger. No, it was President Raleigh, and he told me he'd never meant things to come to this, and after he died there'd be some changes made. No, after all, it was just a man in a red uniform who said his name was Comus. He was just about to kill himself and he wanted me to help. He planned to use a – what was it?

An antic.

That much I remembered clearly. He also told me. I was on my way to California, where I must be sure to look up a Mr Heiress. I was to give his love to somebody whose name I didn't catch at all. And he also advised me to collect swans. Even in a dream I rejected this kind of logic. I told him to go away.

But he was persistent. He told me a long, complicated tale in a hoarse whisper that tickled my ear, all about what an important man I'd once been and the big things the future might still hold in store if only I— But here a touch of irrational night-mare came in. Whatever it was he wanted me to do scared me. The whole country seemed to go unstable when I thought about it. He said I didn't need to think about it, but he had to have help in killing himself on account of the antic. And don't forget the swans.

I said I had nothing against the Secretary of Communications personally – and how *he* came into the conversation isn't clear – and the man in the red coat kept whispering about *you know what*. Only I didn't, and this was the part that scared me. He said I didn't need to think about it now, because I'd remember when the time came – but he had to tell me while he could.

That part was pure nightmare. I wanted to yell at him that he was only a dream and to shut up and get out, but I was too groggy and he kept right on. When I put my hands over my ears he began to talk in letters of fire that hung in the air over his head. Luckily I couldn't read. 'And be sure you ask for the swans,' he said intensely, and vanished into thin air at the sound of approaching footsteps, leaving the letters of fire behind him. Just in time I reached out and pushed them into a bottomless pit which had been there all the time. They dropped, circling, getting clearer the farther they fell until I could almost read them. But not quite, thank God.

Just before they got too clear to escape, I woke up.

I was sitting there trying to make sense out of all this when a door opened and a man in a white coat came in. I looked up sharply, thinking for one irrational moment it would be a man I knew. The man who had sent for me. Ted Nye. I knew it had to be Ted. Nobody else had quite such connections as this, though the Howard Rohan of three years ago had known a lot of important people. None of whom would remember me now.

It had to be Ted Nye. Which was why the Secretary of Communications played a bit part in my dream. That cleared that much of it up, anyhow. Ted and I started out together a long time ago. I rose high. Ted topped me by a long shot and he was still up there, in the Communications chair in Raleigh's cabinet, and slated to go even higher, for all I knew, when the old man died.

Much too important to be coming into my bedroom in a white coat, of course. The man in the doorway was a stranger. And a doctor, if the white coat meant anything. He took my wrist in a professional grip and looked searching at me. 'Feeling all right?'

'I feel terrible. What I need is a drink.'

'You'll do,' he said. 'For now, anyhow. Get dressed.'

'What about that drink?'

He just shrugged and walked out, shutting the door. So I got up, shuddering a little. There were ants crawling around just under my skin. I went to the window and looked out. New York Area, Manhattan. Very familiar. By stretching my neck slightly I could probably see the roof of the Raleigh Theater, scene of my rise and fall. I didn't try.

My clothes, neatly laundered, hung ready. In the bathroom was everything I needed to get myself clean and shaved. I settled for brushing my teeth. I felt grimy, but I wasn't going to make concessions to anybody. Whoever had sent for me was going to get me just as I stood.

A guard in a red Comus uniform stood outside my door. Oddly enough, it all tallied with the dream. This was the door the population of the country had come in by. Here on the threshold the bottomless pit had opened. I looked down to see if the letters of fire had left any marks on the floor.

'Good morning, Mr Rohan,' the guard said.

'I need a drink,' I told him. 'See?' And I held out my hands to show him my shakes.

'Will you come with me, please?' he said politely. 'Uh – would you like to clean up a little first?'

'No,' I said.

'This way, please,' he told me, shrugging.

Five minutes and three floors later he paused in front of a door, spoke briefly into his lapel mike, and then said, 'In here, Mr Rohan.' I went in.

It hadn't changed much, Ted Nye's office. At first glance you think you've walked into a picture gallery, and then you see all the pictures are live action. Ted's desk is in the middle with all the banks of buttons on it that connect him with their nerve endings of the nation. There's a small bar against one wall, a lot of deep chairs around, a glass tank full of tropical fish, and hanging from the ceiling a round brass cage with a round pale yellow canary inside.

A small man stood at the bar with his back to me. He wore knee-length shorts and a striped shirt. He was clinking glasses. Above him in heavy, ornate gold frames the United States unrolled itself across the walls. Clouds floated lazily in one frame over blue mountains marbled with snow. Next to that San Francisco stood dazzling against her green bay, tiny boats moving slowly over the water. Next to that a doll-sized tractor dragged a broad swath of harrows across a stretch of farmland, scoring the brown earth into patterns. And all of it merely the outward and visible background for the inward, invisible webs of Comus, drawn taut and singing with tension as Prowlers policed the roads of the nation, sifting the population man by man through psycho-polling research. They kept the electronic computers humming day and night, straight around the clock. I could imagine I felt them now, vibrating under my feet, for here was the heart of the Comus administration. And here before me in a striped shirt was the man who controlled Comus.

I was surprised at the sudden surge of bitter resentment that rose in me at the sight of him. We started out level. Look at us now. A wave of the intolerable itching which all Croppers are heir to swept over me and for an instant I could smell the sweat and disinfectant that halo all Croppers like a cloud. I probably carried it with me now, but mostly I was too used to it to notice. Resentment said, 'What right has Ted Nye to stand here clean and happy and powerful, while I—' But reason broke in, 'You asked for it, Rohan. Calm down.'

Without turning, Ted Nye said, 'Come on in, Howard.'

I walked fast across the flowered carpet and reached past his hands at the bar. I grabbed the first bottle within striking distance and tipped it up to my mouth, hearing the gurgle, feeling the bottle jump in my hands a little as the whiskey poured down my throat. It was strange to taste good scotch again. Ted pulled the bottle away after a moment.

'That's enough for now, Howard.' He looked up at me searchingly. 'It's been a long time,' he said.

I tried to return his gaze objectively. He was clean, all right, but this little dark wizened face had heavy shadows under the eyes and something was badly wrong somewhere in the back of his face. Trouble. Ted Nye had his problems too.

I said coldly, 'I don't know you.'

His deep-set eyes darted anxiously at mine, the focus shifting rapidly from left eye to right in a ridiculous little dance. I felt better after the whiskey. I felt better than he looked.

'Having trouble with your memory?' he asked.

'No trouble. I like it this way.' Again the itching swept me, more a ghostly itch than a real one since my clothes at least were clean now. I held every muscle tense until it passed.

Still looking closely at me, Nye walked over to his desk and punched one of the shiny-faceted buttons under the little intercom screen. A greenish office with a greenish-tinged girl about two inches high came into focus in the greenish glass of the intercom. It occurred to me very briefly that every living thing here was scaled down to smallness to match Nye's.

'Give me the file on Howard Rohan, Trudy,' he said to the minuscule girl. A musical humming and then a faint pop sounded, and from a slot on the desk a red folder came out like a tongue from a thin mouth. The canary moved uneasily on his perch, looking sidewise at the source of the musical sound. He tried a tentative chirp and then gave up and settled down into himself, closing his eyes.

Nye flipped the folder open, handed me the single sheet lying on top of the stack inside. I took it without much interest, glancing down casually. Then I shook my head to make my eyes come into focus, and my hand shook too. I couldn't quite believe what I saw, but there it was – the staggering 'Howard Rohan' scrawled on a dotted line, and the ironclad Cropper contract above it, the contract that said five years and meant the rest of my life.

Ted Nye twitched it neatly out of my hand as I stood there gaping. I made a futile grab. 'Not so fast,' he said. 'I've got a job for you. Howard. Do it and you can have this back.'

I said warily, 'What kind of a job?'

Watching me, he said, 'Theater. We're setting up something new. Maybe a little bit dangerous. I need you, Howard.'

For a moment a shock of excitement flickered like lightning through my mind. I was back very briefly in the old, bright, shining days when Miranda was alive and Rohan was himself and all the lights were dazzling. But then I remembered. Rohan was washed up a long time ago. I thought of all the times since Miranda died when I'd blown up in my lines and had the curtain rung down on me. I remembered the times I'd gone on stage too drunk to be sure what play I was in. I thought of all the friends who'd lent me money until I couldn't seem to find them any more.

I glanced around the office. 'How do I get out of here?'

'Don't act like this, Howard,' Nye said.

'It's not acting.'

'You still hold a grudge, don't you? I did everything I could for you when you cracked up, Howard. You must know that. At the end it wasn't I who revoked your license. It was Comus. Maybe you think I control Comus. I don't.'

I felt like laughing. Ten years Secretary of Communications, and he didn't control Comus? But all I said was, 'I'm not holding any grudges. I get along fine.'

'The hell you do.'

'Do I make trouble? Have I pulled any reports?'

He rubbed his face nervously. 'Howard – we used to be friends. I'd like to help you if I can. And you could help me.'

I turned my back on him and looked up at San Francisco and the little boats streaking the bay on the other side of the continent. Yes, we'd been friends once. Very good friends. We'd shared an apartment a long time ago, when he was only an assistant to an undersecretary and I was still haunting the

Comus offices for a license to walk the boards. Even in those days the worm had been eating at Ted Nye. Maybe because he was so small. But he'd always been a man to grab tigers by the tail. He looked now like somebody hanging on to too big a tiger, afraid to let go. But that was his problem, not mine.

I said with my back to him, 'Why can't you leave me alone, Ted?' I shut my eyes and focused on the faint buzzing the scotch I'd drunk was setting up around me. 'You've got what you want.' I said. 'Can't you let me have what I want too?'

He said gently, 'What's that, Howard?'

'To be let alone, damn you.' The words came out firmly, but they didn't quite ring true. Not quite. I made a frantic clutch at the walls of my buzzing room, in terror because they might stop buzzing. I could hear the sound grow thin, and it was Ted Nye's fault. He had breached my only bulwark, and I wanted suddenly to kill him.

I thought, Maybe you don't know it, but the world is dead. Everything's dusty and still out there beyond the buzzing walls. The people aren't real. They're clockwork. You're clockwork too. There are clockwork birds in the trees and clockwork mice in the walls, but nothing has been breathing flesh since Miranda stopped abruptly, glared at me, and then turned to slap at the green, and all voices terrify me because they sound that single monotone keynote of despair.

Nye said, his voice shaking a little, 'Don't try me too far, Howard.' He was under a lot of tension, holding it down with an effort. 'Maybe I know what you want better than you do.' He slapped the red folder with my name on it. 'I've got your psychograph here, every damned thing in it right up to date. Up to last night, when you spilled your guts under Pentothal. I know what makes you tick. I know more about you than you know yourself. If you don't—'

The intercom on the desk burst into its musical hum. He stopped abruptly, glared at me, and then turned to slap at the button as if he were slapping my face. He was very near some kind of breaking point.

The little greenish secretary said thinly, 'Dr Hall wants me to remind you about your rest period, Mr Nye. And the senator from California says he can't wait much longer. What shall I—'

'I don't care what the hell they say,' Nye broke in sharply. 'I'll be busy another ten minutes. If Morris can't wait, give him another appointment. I've got enough to worry about.' He struck the button again and the green protesting face dwindled to a dot and vanished. Nye swung around to me.

'Look,' he said. 'You used to be a good actor once. Maybe even a great one. Right now you're a drunken bum with nothing ahead of you but hard labor in Cropper camps until you get too beat to carry. Then they'll dump you. I'm offering a chance to pull out of it. I've bought up your contract. I've got a job you may be able to do. I need you. I'd like to help you if I can. But it's all up to you, Howard.'

I said desperately, 'I'm washed up in the theater, Ted. Remember?'

'You think you are. Suppose we give it another try. I need actors, Howard. I'm scraping the bottom of the barrel. There aren't enough qualified men in the country for the work I have in mind. Once we get the alcohol soaked out of you and the medication you need pumped in, you can do the job. I'm not asking you, Howard. I'm telling you.'

Something of his urgency vibrated a little through the thin drawn walls that protected me from the world. I knew I shouldn't listen. But somewhere in one of those back rooms of the mind a wild, irrational Rohan who could still believe the impossible began to stir. Maybe there still was a chance for me. To get free of the contract, to be my own man again, to try once more for the old, wonderful, glittering life . . .

For a moment the protective wall ceased vibrating. In that moment there came flooding back over me in one enormous wave the memory of the past. Miranda. The life we lived together. All the things we had known and shared in that vivid world there was so much to buy, so much to enjoy. I let the parties we went to swirl around in my mind like smoke. The wonderful parties. The music by the finest orchestras in the country. The magnificent gowns the women wore, the jewels

23

like big drops of fire, the perfume, the glow. The dazzling talk, because the finest wits of the nation congregated right where we all did, around Andrew Raleigh. The old man himself, tall, ruddy-faced, in those wonderful, spotless, creaseless uniforms he wore once and then gave away. His air of majesty. That whole tremendous feel of being alive and functioning in the very center of the world while the universe revolved around us because we were ourselves making it turn.

'You can do the job. I'm not asking, I'm telling you.' Nye's words echoed themselves in my mind. Tremulously, in hope and terror, I thought, Maybe he's right. Maybe I still have a chance.

'What – what kind of a job is it?' I asked, my voice sounding thin and distant. 'What kind of theater, Ted?'

And I heard his answer remotely, too, filtered through swirls of doubt and hope. 'I want you to handle a traveling theater troupe. I'm sending out several to – to one of the areas. Open-air, ring performances they'll be. I need somebody who can act, manage, direct, every damn thing they need.'

I said doubtfully. 'I've never done theater-in-the-round, Ted. And – traveling? Like the old-time circuses? You know that won't pull. Nobody's interested in legit any more except in the biggest cities. I don't get it. I—'

'Let me worry about that, Howard. Will you do it, or do you want to go back where I found you?'

While I hesitated the intercom sang musically again and Nye slipped it on to receiving so hard the image in the screen jiggled as it dawned. The greenish secretary was already talking, throwing all her biggest names in first to catch Nye's attention before he cut her off.

'—Vice-President,' she was saying, 'and he's *got* to talk to President Raleigh before—'

Nye shot me a quick glance and then punched the earphone button hard. The little voice went silent. Nye snatched up the earcup and pressed it to his ear, his eyes going unfocused as he listened. When he stopped looking at me and his face was unguarded, somehow the fullness and the color under his skin

24

seemed to drain away, leaving him just a little withered, just a little like the way he might look the day after he died.

'Trouble,' I said to myself. 'Bad trouble. At least in the Croppers I'm safe. Do I want to stick my neck out this far?'

A motion in the round cage where the canary hung caught my eye. Roused by the rival music of the intercom, the canary shook himself and then dived suddenly under one wing and began tousling his feathers fiercely in search of mites. The sight of him sent a ferocious wave of the old itching in surges over me. I could smell the sweat and disinfectant again, feel the weariness and the stupor and the itching like ghostly fire so strong that sweat broke out on my forehead with the violence of my effort not to scratch.

I looked at Nye's face and his thin, tense shoulders under the striped shirt. I looked around me at the rich, hushed office. I felt the vibrations under my feet of the vast activities below us that cupped the whole nation in the hollow of one man's hand.

And suddenly I hated Ted Nye, and envied him fiercely, and in a way felt love and pity for the driven little man I had once known so well. A sudden, furious storm of feeling swept through me like cold sleet. I knew I had to live again. Act again. Move and feel power and make the world turn. No matter how hard the work might be, no matter how much it cost me, no matter what the dangers – I had to do it. My safe little magic room built out of alcohol wasn't my room any more. Ted Nye had shattered it from the first moment he called me back to life.

I hated him for that. I hated him for his success and power. I felt a deep, continuous tremor of sheer terror start to vibrate inside me high up under the rib cage, where the seat of emotion is. Scared, resentful, hating Ted and the world and myself, I drew a breath as deep as my chest would hold and said in a flat voice, without any emotion at all,

'Okay, Ted. I'll take your job.'

CHAPTER IV

They had this marble slab in the steam room, with white clouds hissing out all around it. The nurse said to stretch out my back and relax for a while. I shrouded myself decently in the sheet and did as I was told. It felt good. You can feel the vertebrae relaxing and all the bones and muscles along the rib cage readjust when you lie out flat on a hard surface.

A figure loomed up over me in the fog. Ted Nye's voice said, 'Awake, Howard?' and I peered up to see him larger than life among the clouds and togaed like a Roman in his sheet.

'Here comes poor Brutus, with himself at war,' I said. I'd had twenty-four hours of treatment, and I was feeling much better now. 'This is a surprise. I didn't expect to rate any more of your valuable time.'

'What do you mean, with myself at war?' he asked, looking down at me suspiciously.

'Something's eating you,' I said. 'Anybody can see that. Maybe I should have started off with, "Tell me, good Brutus, can you see your face?" It's obvious.'

He rubbed a hand over his face and looked at it vacantly, as if he hoped the expression would come off so he could inspect it on his palm, like dirt. 'Yes, I've got plenty eating me. The whole country has. When Raleigh dies all hell is going to break loose, or try to. Don't tell me you haven't heard rumors.'

'In my social circles,' I told him, 'we haven't kept up with the news.'

He sighed, let himself down stiffly on the adjoining slab, and then grunted with satisfaction as his vertebrae went through the same procedure mine had. He rolled his head sidewise to look at me.

'I don't need to see my face,' he said. 'I know I've got problems. I want to talk to you, Howard. I've briefed the other theater managers myself. I'll give you the same, and a little more.' But he paused there, looking up into the steam. Abruptly he said, 'Do you ever think about the old days, Howard?'

'It was a long time ago,' I said noncommittally. 'Why?'

'No reason, no reason.' He paused again. 'I'm glad you're going to work with us, Howard. We need all the good men we can get.'

Well, that wasn't the way I'd been hearing it, but I didn't say anything. He was right on one question, anyhow. After Raleigh died all hell *would* break loose unless a lot of changes got made. The yoke of Comus was getting pretty heavy. And Comus, according to the rumors I'd heard, was frightened by the prospect of change. New values, new concepts that might supersede the old ones. To hold the country safe, Raleigh had had to hold it rigid. The ferment of new ideas might so easily undermine our hard-won stability.

So Comus maybe needed good men more than it really knew, but it wasn't trying very hard to find them. Comus was trying instead to stop all change, all time. The young men and women with new ideas had to be controlled. No matter how high they might test on the school creativity scale, if they could threaten, even latently, the social order Raleigh and Comus were founded on, then they must never receive training or acquire skills. Sooner or later the psychographs would click through the big computers and directives would emerge.

John Smith has failed his entrance exams at Cal Tech.

Mary Jones is ineligible for training at John Hopkins.

And even if John and Mary knew they hadn't failed, what could they do about it? Well, I thought, nobody ever claimed the system is perfect. On the other hand, let's not pretend we're trying very hard to get the men and women we need into the jobs they do best.

'Tell me the worst,' I said. 'You mentioned this theater work might be a little bit dangerous. How?'

He cleared his throat, and something in my mind began to tighten. I thought, This is the old familiar Ted. He isn't going to tell the truth now, but a part of what he says will be true. I may be able to winnow out the truth from the falsehood if I listen close. Oddly, it didn't make me angry. This was Ted Nye, the bad mixed right in there with the good, as it is in all of us.

'This theater project is a big operation,' he said. 'Important. A lot may depend on it. We're having a – a little trouble in the place where you'll be going.'

'All right. Name the place.'

He hesitated. Then, almost wincingly, as if the word hurt him, he said, 'California.'

I said, 'All right, California it is.' Then I did a quick mental double-take and said, 'What? California!' For at the back of my mind a sudden door seemed to swing wide and then shut with a slam. Through it I had the briefest of glimpses of – something I couldn't remember. Something in a dream. A man named Comus stooping over my bed and telling me I was headed for California. How could I have known that, even in a dream? Or had it been a dream at all?

'What do you know about California?' Nye demanded suspiciously. I wasn't listening. This looked like a paradox and it needed figuring. Had someone really stooped whispering over my bed while I slept? Part of it made sense. But only part. The rest of his message, involving the death of Comus and the mysterious use of something called an antic – no, that was ridiculous. Had it really been *antic* he'd said? I murmured it aloud to myself, testing the sound. 'Antic,' I said. 'Antic.'

There was a furious swirl in the fog and Ted Nye was stooping over me, shaking me by both shoulders.

'What did you say? Answer me, Howard! What do you know about the Anti-Com?' His little eyes, hot and anxious, blazed at me.

I said, 'Let go. Stop it, Ted. I didn't say anything.'

He shook me again. 'I heard you. Tell me what you know!'

'I don't know anything.' I sat up and pushed him away. My heart was beginning to thud a little, because his excitement was infectious, but none of it made sense yet. 'What in the name of God,' I asked, 'is an Anti-Com?'

'You said it,' he accused me. 'You know.'

'I said *antic*. It doesn't mean anything. It's just part of a crazy dream I had. You reminded me of it. What are you talking about, Ted? What's wrong?'

Still searching my face anxiously, he sat down again on his slab, muttering mostly to himself as he gazed at me. 'You can't know. I remember now. You'd have spilled it under Pentothal if you knew anything.' But he shook his head doubtfully.

'Put me back under Pentothal if you doubt it,' I urged him. 'But you can't just drop this right here. What's the story?'

'I guess you'd better know,' Nye said heavily. 'I hope it isn't common knowledge. As near as Comus samplings can tell, we've kept it quiet so far, but—'

'Then you've kept it quiet. When a Comus sampling turns up false, they'll repeal the law of gravity. Even in my ivory tower I know that much.'

'Howard,' Nye said, leaning forward on his slab, 'in California the law of gravity has been repealed.'

I looked at him and waited. He licked his lips. 'This isn't to be repeated outside California,' he said. 'But you'll soon know anyhow. We've withdrawn Comus from California.'

I said quietly, 'My God.'

Then I got up on one elbow and stared at him. Then I sat clear up and put my bare feet on the floor, and we sat them knee to knee in our sheets, looking at each other across the steamy dimness like two ghosts on tombstones, trying to comprehend the end of the world.

'You really mean it!' I said.

If you were born, as I was, after 1960 you have, as I do, a strange sort of image in your mind. When you think of the United States you see it in the shape of Andrew Raleigh. You see the map and the nation standing up on two legs with the outlines of a man containing it, vast, diaphanous, towering, all the states in place, all the borders outlining the figure of Andrew Raleigh. It doesn't make sense and it doesn't have to. That's just the way you grow up thinking if you went to school with my generation.

And Raleigh and Comus mean the same thing. You can't imagine life without Comus. Comus is everybody. It's the newspapers, the schools, the entertainment. It's the communications-theory boys who quantify language, the public-relations people, the psychologists, the artists in all media who take the prescriptions the computers feed them and build sugar-coated truths that will cure any social bellyache before society knows it had one.

You can't get along without Comus. Life would be too unpredictable. Society would crumble like cheap cement. I looked at Ted Nye in the swirls of steam, and a sudden sense of awe came over me. Sure, he was a big shot, high up in the government, but then I used to be a big shot too. I took the man for granted in the old days.

But now the awareness of his tremendous responsibility suddenly hit me in the face, and it came to me with a shock that I was talking to the man who ran Comus. The man, in fact, who had organized Comus for nearly half its lifetime, the latter and expanding half, and who was therefore responsible for a lot more than half of its complexity and power over the lives and minds and future of the United States.

Nye was the man who bossed the god.

And Nye was the man with the fox gnawing at his vitals. Maybe the fox was California. I had a sudden, idiotic cartoon vision of a long, narrow fox with a bend at one end, shaped like the state, ahead up near Eureka and a tail at San Diego, and little scuttling legs on the other side, gnawing away at a cartoon of Nye at the solar plexus of the nation, where all the nerve nets join. No wonder the man was jumpy.

'What's wrong with California?' I demanded, hearing disbelief and perhaps a little hysteria in my voice.

'Shut up,' Nye said. 'I don't want the whole country to get

hysterical just because California gets out of line temporarily. With any luck, we'll have the whole thing patched up in a month—'

'What's *wrong* with California?' I demanded again, louder in spite of myself. 'Out of line how? Patch up what?'

Nye got up, put his hand on my chest, and pushed me back into the slab. 'Lie down and shut up,' he said, wrapping his sheet tighter, as if the steaming-room were cold. He sat on the foot of my tombstone and scowled anxiously at me.

My mind was rushing out and around and back again in wild ellipses, like an excited pup. It had figurative ears laid back and streaming in the wind of its own speed. So California had got out of line. And Comus was taking steps. I was aware suddenly of that sneaking feeling of pleased excitement at bad news that most of us feel if the news doesn't hit us personally. Everybody at some time or other must have wondered just what would happen if Comus drew a blank someday.

'Now listen and keep quiet,' Ted Nye said. 'California is – well, hypersensitive right now. The story's too complex to explain, but we know what we're doing. Just say the state's a frustrated social area at this time. They – well, they react badly to Comus. Oh, food shipments go through, and utilities work, and all that. But anything obviously labeled Comus in the public mind is just not operating.'

'No Prowlers?' I asked incredulously.

'No Prowlers. No check stations. No Comus uniforms. Our boys have gone into plain clothes and we've withdrawn all but a minimum. We're giving California its head.'

I gazed up at him, wild suspicions circling in my mind. What wasn't he telling me?

'The Anti – what was it?' I said. 'Anti-Com? Anti-*Comus?* What about that, Ted?'

His face got darker. 'I don't know what about it. If I did, I wouldn't be – never mind. The thing is, there's a bunch of wild-eyed neurotics out there who want to overthrow the government. We stumbled across one of their big shots by accident, in a routine Prowler check, and he spilled enough to scare us – if it's true. *He* thinks they've got something doped out that can stop Comus cold.'

I laughed. Nye glared at me.

'Shut up. It isn't funny.'

'I didn't think it was. It's ridiculous, not funny.'

'I hope so. I don't see how they could do it. We can't figure out any way a thing as big and complex as Comus could possibly be licked by any means we know of.' He paused and rubbed his face with the old, anxious gesture. 'Of course, new things turn up all the time. We've got to believe there's an Anti-Com and we've got to believe it could work until we can prove otherwise. One good thing – it isn't finished yet. They're building parts for it at little separate workshops all over the state, assembling it as they go along in some central spot we haven't located – yet. With any kind of luck, we'll pick up a thread before it's ready to blow. We're trying.'

I said, 'On one man's say-so you've pulled Comus out of a whole area? I don't believe it.'

Nye shook his head irritably. 'Don't be a fool, Howard. We keep picking up word about the Anti-Com all over the area. We add a bit here and a bit there until a picture starts to shape. And besides—' Here he stopped and glared at me.

'Damn you, Howard, stop picking my brains.'

'Listen, Ted,' I said suddenly, 'if all this is true, then it isn't safe in California! I'm not going. I—'

'You're going.' His voice was grim. 'It's safe enough. And we need you.'

'But why?'

'We want to keep the patient happy. Light entertainment.'

'That's the phoniest story I ever heard. You know nobody out there gives a damn about stage performances. Who's going to watch a traveling theater perform when you've got movies in three dimensions and full-color, mass-tailored to the regional interests? We can't compete in the sticks and you know it.'

Ted sighed. 'You'll get your audiences. For one thing, they won't go into the Comus Centers any more, so they don't see movies. They won't watch the broadcast. They'll be starved for entertainment and you'll provide it. Arena performances right out in the middle of the street, so nobody will feel hemmed in. The living theater is an exotic to people like that. They'll come.'

'What kind of plays are we doing?'

'Just one. Very carefully written, too, by experts. *Crossroads*, it's called. A fine job of writing. Oh, it'll pull, all right. And don't underestimate your own drawing power, Howard. People haven't forgotten Howard Rohan.'

I said, 'Is that why you've been releasing our old films?'

He made a nervous grimace. 'I have a lot of reasons for everything I do. You know how your films were built. They happen to put over some ideas we need to circulate around the country right now. Loyalty to old friends. The value of tried and true experience. Stuff like that. In case of—' He glanced at me. 'Raleigh can't live forever. We expect trouble when he dies. That's what your job is, Howard. Helping block the trouble before it starts.'

'How?' I asked bluntly.

'Follow orders. Put on the play exactly as written. No revising. It's very simple.'

'Too simple. What's behind it, Ted?'

'Don't be too sharp, Howard. Just say I need a large-scale diversion in California. The people have to be distracted while some big things get done. Let me do the worrying, Howard.'

I said, 'You always liked grabbing tigers by the tail. But I'm not a tiger-grabber by choice. If California's that far gone toward real trouble, what am I getting into?'

'You want to back out, Howard?' he asked quietly.

For just an instant I remember very clearly the canary in its cage diving vigorously into its feathers for mites. A ghostly tremor of the old itching went over me. No, I couldn't go back into the magic room. It was no refuge now. I shook my head.

'Suppose there is a little trouble,' Nye said. 'Couldn't you handle it? Seems to me you had a reputation for an iron hand in the old days. That's another reason I wanted you for the job.'

I ran a palm over my head in a gesture I couldn't remember making since I hit the skids. It felt good. My hair was short again, cut to a whisper, a thin cap over my skull. For an instant I stood outside myself as I used to stand, seeing myself as a tool to use on the stage. I remembered how it felt to hold a whole play in my hand, all the people on stage and behind it, all the people in the audience. The whole world, I thought. Yes, I could handle trouble. I can do it again, if I have to.

Ted Nye was watching me. 'Well, that's that, then,' he said in a brisk voice. 'We'll fix you up with a troupe and get things rolling.'

'Who's available?' I asked. 'Do I hold readings?'

'There isn't time. I've got several troupes lined up and on the spot, or on their way. You'll have to take what's ready. Do you know anything about the Rosemeyer Players? Or the Circle Guild? Or the Swann Company?'

'Swann Company?' I echoed stupidly.

'Paul Swann and his players. You know them?'

'Swann?' I heard myself repeat, as if he hadn't spoken. And to myself I was saying, 'It has to be coincidence, it *has* to be. Because I never had prescient dreams before, but now it's happened again. The man in the dream did say Anti-Com, not antic. He was going to kill Comus with an Anti-Com. And he told me to collect swans . . .'

'Yes, I know the Swann Players,' I heard myself go on, fairly smoothly, considering how I felt. 'Give me the Swann people, Ted.' I was probably looking at him now, but all I could see were the letters of fire spiraling down into darkness while a voice told me the fate of the nation depended on me and a flock of swans. Pure coincidence. It had to be. I thought, Maybe I should tell Ted— But when I tried to my mind went blank. I couldn't even speak.

'All right, then,' Ted Nye said. He stood up and wrapped the toga tighter around him, looking like Caesar's ghost in the haze. 'I'll see what I can do. Get some rest now, Howard. You leave tomorrow, and remember; I'm depending on you.'

I said, 'Yes, I know,' in a disinterested voice, hardly hearing.

I was trying to read what those letters had said and feeling a strange, unwilling panic as I tried. The steam thickened and swirled. I heard Ted's bare feet thud on the floor, and then a door closed softly between us.

CHAPTER V

The wind blew through the redwoods, smelling of pine. I slid down farther in the jolting truck with every bump, until the back of my head rested on the upholstery and I was looking up at an angle through the redwoods at the sky. Under us I could feel the road climb, and a river somewhere beyond the trees made brawling noises.

All the way from the landing field I'd had that unreal feeling you get when you've come too far too fast. Part of me was still back in New York among the tall buildings, part of me jolted along the highway through the redwoods. Somewhere in between, the rest of me, maybe the essential part, felt drawn out thin and long like a thread between east and west, not sure yet which end of the line was the real Rohan. Maybe neither.

You could smell the difference in the air out here on the edge of the Pacific. Something was stirring. There was trouble in the wind. Old tags of history floated through my mind. No law west of the Pecos. No Comus west of Blythe ... It gave me a strangely naked feeling.

Under us the broad black highway twelve lanes wide swept in climbing curves, every lane veined with its faintly singing automatic drive line, living arteries pulsing with the lifeblood of Comus. That felt a little reassuring. The broad hand of Comus was still stretched out under us. But above us no red helicopters monitored the air, and I had not seen a single Prowler or a single red Comus coat anywhere since we landed. I kept giving my driver quick glances, wondering what he made of things. I didn't even know if he was Comus or civilian. And there wasn't any use of asking. I'd tried.

We whipped past a sign that said SAN ANDREAS 5 MILES. The driver switched off automatic and pulled over to the left, crossed the highway, and swung into a big paved clearing where half a dozen trucks were lined up like parked behemoths in front of a low concrete building. Luminous script on the front windows said *LUNCH COUNTER*, but the building was so big it was probably also a dormitory for the truckers. I saw one driver swabbing at the flank of his trailer where somebody had chalked the outlines of a human head very crudely, just an oval with dots for features. Around the head was a band with a padlock and the padlock was labeled Comus.

While I was thinking about that the man moved a little and I saw lower down on the trailer a chalked blue star with a red 93 inside it. It didn't mean anything as far as I could tell, but it looked subversive. The driver was wiping that off too, so it probably was. I wondered what would happen to anybody caught with red and blue chalk in his pocket, and with a little shock realized what the answer was. Nothing. There wasn't any Comus in California.

My driver nodded at me. 'This is it. Your outfit's back in there at the camp ground. Get your stuff.'

I lifted out the light travel case that held my belongings, all new. It didn't weigh much. I walked around the side of the building, seeing men at the lunch counter inside watch me warily. This must be one of the regular Comus-operated stations, I thought, that feeds and sleeps the drivers who spell each other around the clock and keep the supplies of the country rolling. Ted Nye hadn't cut off California's food or other necessities, then. Because he didn't dare? Because he was afraid of the men and women who were rushing that mysterious thing called an Anti-Com toward completion?

'He's stalling for time,' I told myself with sudden realization. He could crack down on the whole area any time he felt like it. I'd never heard before of a whole area in revolt, but I thought Comus could handle it if it had to. There must have been some good reason why it hadn't happened here. Ted Nye was waiting for something.

The death of Raleigh?

I walked past the back of the building with its line of laundry and big trash cans. The woods closed up to the edge of the pavement here, deep and quiet and incredibly high. A hillside sloped off toward the sound of water and a path led off among the wide-spaced trees, a little sign informing me half legibly that this was Public Camp Number Something. It was an old sign. I thought how strange it must have been a long time ago, people traveling just for the hell of it, in the days before the Five Days' War.

The silence was something I hadn't expected. It pressed the eardrums. I could almost feel it. Underfoot a thick cushioning of needles made a bouncy carpet, and with every breath I drew in deep the fragrance of pine. The enormous redwoods, too broad to seem like trees at all, went up and up until the sky stopped them. The quiet and the gloom were restful and a little oppressive.

I paused at the entrance of the camp to admire an enormous slab of redwood which some civic body must have set up a long while ago. It was a cross section mounted on edge, taller than I am. Metal labels nailed into the wood pointed out the growth ring the year Socrates died, the year Rome was founded, the year Columbus discovered America. This had been an old, old tree when it gave up its arboreal ghost. A special plate with red lettering pointed out the last ring of all, laid down the year Andrew Raleigh saved the nation.

And somebody had seen fit to thumbtack to the thick bark at the edge of the slab a little notice that said, 'Charlie Starr licked Comus at San Diego – 1993.' I stood there looking at it and wondering. This was something new. Back in '93 when Miranda and I were in full swing, what had we heard about a man named Starr and trouble in San Diego? Nothing at all. Suddenly I remembered that chalked star on the truck trailer with '93 scrawled inside it.

I shrugged. It was just barely possible, I told myself with

some irony, that things had happened in San Diego in '93 that Comus hadn't cared to publicize. Whatever it was, I felt excitement waking in me uncertainly. Even that long ago, then, trouble had been brewing out here. A little scuttling sound in the needles startled me and I looked down to see a chipmunk dart along the path, twitching his skimpy tail convulsively. I put San Diego neatly away in the back of my mind and followed the chipmunk down the path. Off among the trees somebody was laughing.

At the edge of the trees I stopped. This would make a good stage-set for some still unwritten play, I thought. Call it *Howard Rohan, His Fall and Rise*. Rohan stands at the edge of the clearing and gazes into his own future.

The firelight was the first thing you saw, flickering pale in the gloom and the quiet. It burned in a low stone stove with an iron plate for a cover. Beside the stove were two plank tables spotted with grease. Somebody a long time ago had made benches by splitting big redwood logs in half lengthwise and nailing one of the halves up vertically for a back rest. Beyond the benches three trucks stood, with SWANN COMPANY PLAYERS very ornate in luminous pink paint along the sides.

The trucks were good-sized but they looked small under the towering columns of the trees. The whole encampment looked small. There were six people in the camp, and they looked small too. They were talking and laughing a little among themselves, but even their voices sounded small, hushed and dwarfed by the enormous silence of the redwoods.

I stood there quietly, looking them over. I knew I was scared. I could feel the disquiet shiver in me because of all the times in the past that I'd tried a comeback and failed. But here it was, the raw material of my last chance, waiting to be shaped.

Six people. The six Swann Players the man in my dream had told me about – if that was what he told me. Maybe it's a far cry from collecting swans to joining the Swann Players. Maybe it isn't. I looked from face to face wondering which of them I'd come on the strength of a dream to see. But it had been only a dream, after all. The letters of fire circled

39

unreadably before me for an instant and then faded. Whatever that dream had tried to say to me would have to stay unsaid so far as I could tell. I drew a deep breath, ran my palm over my head with the old gesture, and braced myself. This wouldn't be easy. But if anybody got hurt this time it wasn't going to be Howard Rohan.

Six faces rose to look at me as I walked toward them over the dust and the pine needles. All expression faded from every one of them. They had been laughing a moment ago, but now nobody even smiled. They looked at me coldly and waited.

'Hello,' I said. There was a stony silence.

I said again, 'Hello.' Then I added, 'Oh, for God's sake. The name is Howard Rohan. Weren't you expecting me?'

Nobody spoke.

A man in a checkered shirt sitting on one of the benches laid down the screwdriver he'd been using to probe the innards of a flat sleep-teach box. The wooden handle of it thumped on the bench. He reached under his collar, scratched, gave me a quick, furtive grin, and went dead-pan again. I glanced around the circle. Nobody else flickered an eye. It was the freeze-out.

'I see you've heard of me,' I said.

Still silence. The whole clearing pulsed with it. Somewhere off stage the river made its brawling noises. A bird chirped, a pine cone fell with a soft, decisive thump. Nobody moved. They were a closed group, close-knit, shutting me out. For just an instant the only thing I felt was an intense and terrible loneliness. In the instant it seemed to me I smelled not woodsmoke and pine, but the exciting, musty, indescribable smell of the theater backstage, sweat and dust and old wood, make-up, tobacco smoke. I saw not this group alone, but every cast I'd ever worked with, and somewhere on the fringe of them, just out of sight, I had the strange impression that Miranda stood in the wings, one foot poised to step forward and join me.

The old feeling came over me again for a moment and I was glad to have it come. These aren't real people, they're clockwork figures among cardboard trees and nobody on earth is alive since Miranda died. So if they close up into a unit and shut me out, it doesn't matter. They're only clockwork. And like clockwork, I looked them over appraisingly.

My friend in the checkered shirt was now lighting his pipe. He didn't look like an actor, but he did remind me of something intensely familiar that I couldn't quite place. He was pushing sixty-five, I thought, and he looked broody, as if with any encouragement he might turn into a cracker-barrel philosopher.

At one of the grease-stained plank tables two other men sat over a spread of dog-eared cards. One of them was youngish, say thirty-five, which made him about five years younger than I am. He had a heavy, good-looking face and tan curls cut short. His eyes were too deep-set, and when he scowled, as he was scowling now, they seemed to sink back into their sockets until he looked like an ill-natured ape. The other man was soft and plump, with a respectable white thatch and a red nose.

Three women and a coffeepot made up the rest of the group. The old woman sat away from the rest, on a blanket spread out on the pine needles, giving most of her attention to a little box about a foot square, out of which a very small yammering rose, like distant mice staging an opera. The woman had white curls, wrinkles, and the mild, mad look of an aging Ophelia. The box had a glass front and was full of little brightly colored figures gesturing and singing in tiny voices to the music of some unseen orchestra that must have fitted into a matchbox. The strange feeling of smallness and magic persisted even after I'd recognized the thing as a cheap playbox for canned opera. I could see its cord tailing off and plugged into a socket set in the nearest tree, which had in itself a touch of the fantastic.

Nothing here in the clearing seemed quite real. I kept thinking if I turned my head fast enough I might catch a glimpse of Miranda moving always just beyond the periphery of vision. She was so much a part of the theater and my own past that my mind couldn't quite accept the idea of one without the other. That, at least, was how I rationalized it, until I got a clear look at the youngest of the three women in the troupe.

The middle-aged one obscured her. She was in the very act of pouring coffee into a cup held by the youngest when I stepped into the clearing, and the two of them paused in arrested motion, both faces turned to stare. The middle-aged woman had a plump, pretty, hourglass figure and a haggard face. Her blue eyes bulged a little and she had bright red hair combed slickly back to a knot high up on her head. It was not red like hair, but red like blood. Or Comus. The kind of color you get only after a plastic dip job, because only a plastic coating will take color like that. Under the coating the hair was probably mostly gray. Whoever she was, she looked tired and a little embittered, as if somehow she had never really expected age would catch up with her. I didn't care. I had my own problems.

Then she moved a little and the girl behind her looked me fully in the face, and for a moment time stood still.

Only for a moment. This was no miracle. The Swann Players were a second-rate troupe and you don't find Mirandas among the second-rate. But she looked so like Miranda that for one wild, ridiculous, joyful moment my mind against all reason said to me, 'She's come back – she's here – it was all a nightmare and I've woken up again . . .' Maybe in heaven, if there is a heaven, that moment will really come when we see the dead again face to face and for an instant believe and can't believe. But only then. Not now. Never here and now.

She was no Miranda. But she had a dim reflection of the luster that had made Miranda radiant, made her name so perfectly right for her that you really did think, oh, wonderful! when you first saw that lovely face. Something in this girl's poise, the way her body moved and her head sat on her pretty neck and the way she tilted it, was like Miranda. She had proportions like hers. And she wore her hair in the same halo of big loose curls that Miranda invented and every girl in the country copied three years ago. Miranda's hair was a very rich chestnut, and this girl's was bleached to a corn-silk pallor, but the likeness at first glance was too strong not to notice.

I felt like turning around and walking away.

42

I looked them all over, impassively, face by face. My mind said, 'Second-rate, second-rate.' And I thought, This isn't for me. I can't face it. I won't try. The state's in revolt, the troupe's scraped up from the barrel bottom, the play's untried. The audiences will be yokels. It isn't worth the effort. Because I was washed up and I knew it. And I couldn't stand the reminder of Miranda, and I knew how painful the living world can be. Better go back to being clockwork and live in a dead world. All I wanted now was a drink.

In front of them all, knowing what they knew about me, I set down my bag, got my bottle out, and drank one long, deep, satisfying draught. It burned my throat and started the little bright fire going inside me that I'd missed without quite knowing what was wrong. I was perfectly clear about what I meant to do. A man can take just so much.

I put the bottle back in the bag.

'Ladies and gentlemen,' I said distinctly, 'I see you've all heard of me. You don't like what you've heard. That's all right with me. I've never heard of you. I don't like this setup. There's a lot I'd rather be doing than coaching a broken-down carnival in a country on the edge of a revolution. But we haven't got much choice.' I picked up my bag. 'I'll be back with you in ten minutes,' I said. 'I want everybody ready to start work when I get here. All right. That's all.'

I turned and walked briskly off the way I'd come. Strangely, I felt a twinge of regret as I did it. The troupe in the clearing with the twilight gathering and the fire crackling shared their own kind of magic room, I thought. The tall, still trees, the smell of coffee, the small distant singing defined their circle, shutting me out. But the part of my life that touched the theater world was over and gone. And Miranda with it. And I wanted nothing to do with it any more.

(It wasn't entirely true. Miranda might be gone, but she was always with me. Everywhere. Waking and sleeping, wherever I went I never went alone.)

Out of sight of the camp I left the path and cut through ferny thickets toward the highway. The pine needles bounced so springily underfoot I had a false illusion of youth as I walked quietly away from the campfire and my own past. It was getting dark under the trees, but the road glimmered ahead of me and I scrambled toward it, slipping now and then on the needles. I remembered a slope north of the truck stop where the drivers would have to go slow. I could hitch a ride, or steal one. It didn't much matter. All I wanted was to hit the Canadian border before Comus caught up with me.

I came out on the highway and began trudging north. It was very still here. The wind in the sequoias made a lonesome sound, but a good one. Now and then a bird made faint chirping noises in the foliage, and the river ran over rapids somewhere down to the left. The camp and the troupe were part of a world that never existed. My own past, my own future. I never wanted to see the girl like Miranda again. I never would. The best I could hope for was to let the beautiful dreamer sleep on.

The road was wide and faintly visible in the last lingering light that still made the sky paler than the earth. The automatic drive lines glowed white in long, singing ribbons, humming their endless song about the power of Comus.

Because of the dimness at first I didn't see the man in the checkered shirt leaning against a tree at the edge of the highway between me and the road. He just leaned there, quite comfortable, arms crossed, and cradled over his left elbow a little blue pistol with a gold Comus ring around the muzzle. It was my broody friend the philosopher. He grinned at me in the dimness rather sadly. His voice was mild.

'You might have got halfway to Oregon at that,' he said. 'But you'd run into Comus sooner or later. Things are still going on just as usual in northern Oregon and all through Washington.'

I swallowed a couple of times and drew a deep breath. I kept my voice as casual as his.

'I thought you weren't an actor,' I said. It was perfectly simple to place him now. Comus cops have a sort of generic likeness. I've never known if it's acquired or inherent, screened out by the very fact that they qualify for Comus.

'Oh, I earn my way,' he said. 'I'm the sound-truck man, among other things.' I noticed that when he had to stop grinning to speak the polite melancholy settled back on his face. The smile never went deep or stayed long. 'There's one of us with every troupe on the road here,' he said. 'We keep order and – well, make sure of things. I'm sorry, Mr Rohan, but you'll have to go back.'

I looked at the gun and at him. Could I out-talk the man, I wondered, or out-dodge him in the twilight? He was much too old for active duty. They catch Comus cops early, train them hard, and retire them as soon as the reflexes start to slow. Maybe before the thinking processes really begin. I wondered why this one had been called back. Nye must really be scraping the bottom of the barrel. But the melancholy eyes above the gold-ringed muzzle were very steady. I could imagine the polite regret with which he'd pull the trigger. Meeting my gaze, he motioned with the gun. 'You first, Mr Rohan,' he said.

I shrugged. 'What's your name?'

'Guthrie. Tom Guthrie.'

'All right, Guthrie. I won't play games. You're too old to wear a uniform but I think you may still be faster than I am. Shall we go?'

He gestured again. 'You first.' Then his voice dropped slightly. 'Mr Nye tells me he had a talk with you.' He sounded as if Ted were just around the next tree. 'It would be better if the rest of the troupe didn't know any more about you or me than they have to.'

'Then put that gun away,' I said. 'I know when I'm licked. I'll stay put until I figure a better way out than walking off.'

'Mr Rohan. Wait. Look at me.'

I looked. The towering silence was like a solid wall around us.

'I'm getting old, Mr Rohan,' Guthrie said. 'They called a lot of us back because they needed us. I'm too slow for active duty, but I was trained in things a man never forgets, and I can do my job fine. You're not a very important part of it, but I'm going to keep you here and you aren't going to outguess me. Do you believe that?'

I waited a moment. Then I said, 'Yes, I believe it.'

'Good. Well, now. We're in dangerous territory. You don't like it. Maybe I don't either. But we do our job, both of us. That means you stay reasonably sober. It means whipping the troupe into shape no matter how tough they make it. When orders come in from headquarters we both abide by them. You're a part of Comus now whether you like it or not. We can work better if the troupe doesn't know I'm a cop. But we work together, easy or hard.'

I thought it over, feeling the turmoil swirl in my mind. Past failures, hopes and fears about the future. The beautiful dreamer stirring in her sleep. All right, so I had no choice. But we were headed south. The Mexican border is down there. I shrugged.

'Let's go,' I said.

CHAPTER VI

I walked into the firelit clearing and threw my bag down hard on the nearest bench. I was in a murderous mood. I looked with savage contempt around the campsite and then licked my lip, drew a deep breath, and whistled the raucous, two-toned whistle that calls the cast to order. Some directors use a tin whistle. Some yell. I whistle. Loud and peremptory.

Heads came up with a jerk. Everybody stared. The red-haired woman had been opening flat dinner cans at the farther table and setting them out to heat themselves up in a row on the planks. The girl was filling a bucket at a splashing tap, the corn-silk curls jumping as she snapped her head around to stare at me. At the nearer table the two men had been figuring something out on a sheet of paper, their heads close together. They looked up, startled. Only the old woman still sitting on her blanket never glanced up from the little singing box.

'All right,' I said in a loud, hectoring voice. 'On stage, every-body. Let's stop playing games.'

They all looked at me. Nobody spoke, but I saw the red-haired woman move a little so she could keep the corner of her eye on the heavy-faced man scowling up at me from his seat at the table. I saw how she kept her face turned so he was always just within the limits of her vision, and I got the feeling she always stood like this, holding him just in sight.

I took another deep breath and felt the shakiness in me deep down along with the anger. This was my raw material. Out of this and the script in my bag I had to build a play. Out of these scrapings from the barrel bottom, plus whatever was left in

47

me. And however little it was, I told myself savagely, it was still worth more than this whole troupe of has-beens would ever know. Has-beens, never-weres. Never-would-bes unless I could somehow take hold of them and force talent into them enough to get the show under way. If I had to do it, I told myself, by God, I'd do it in a way they'd never forget.

'You there!' I called, making my voice firm and loud. 'You, at the table. What's your name?' And I pointed at the youngish man. His brows met over his nose and he set his jaw and glared at me defiantly. I snapped my fingers. 'Sound off!'

Nobody stirred except the old woman, who now looked up and blinked mildly, trying to place me. I took three long forward steps, kicking up dust heavily with every footfall. I was rolling the muscles of my shoulders as I went, liking the feel of heavy power locked up inside me, liking the violent eagerness I could feel welling up. I hoped he would fight. I hoped for trouble. I felt suddenly very good, even the anger submerged. Now we'll fight. This is the easy way.

He stumbled his way out from behind the bench, still scowling. He was as tall as I was, not much younger, thick through the chest. But he'd never been a Cropper. He didn't know what I knew. He didn't expect anything new. I could have laughed, but I didn't.

It was perfectly clear from the look in his eyes and the way he shifted his feet exactly what he meant to do. I was there before him. I caught his first blow in the palm of my hand, contemptuously, not letting the impact even rock me. And while he was still off balance I gave him one hard, straight-armed shove that carried him over backward into the fire. It was too easy. I hoped savagely that he'd catch fire and burn – anything to break up the troupe and prospect of the work I had to do.

But he caught himself with one palm on the hot iron slab, snatched it off again, staggered against the smoky stones. I jumped to grab him by the shoulder and jerk him forward, off balance, before he could get set again. I held him up with one hand and cocked the other fist shoulder-high, waiting with fierce anticipation.

I saw the pain of his burned hand hit him hard. I saw the fight drain out of his face. The features went flabby and under my grip all the muscles in his body slackened.

In the same instant a woman's hoarse voice shrieked something wordless from beyond the stove. Instinct moved faster than reason and I ducked just in time. Straight over my head the heavy coffeepot went hurtling, trailing cord and plug and spilling boiling coffee as it flew. I heard it thud against a tree beyond me, but I hadn't time to look. For the red-haired woman herself came hurtling close behind the pot, her face convulsed and both hands raking at me.

I let the burned man go and swung to catch her. She smacked hard into me and I shut my arms around her to hold her safe. She gasped muffled, furious protest against my chest, struggling to get her hands free. I should have expected it, I knew. That look of tigress protection in her sidelong glance should have told me.

I looked up and saw Guthrie standing over the fallen coffeepot. I said, 'Here, catch!' and swung the raging woman at him. She went staggering and stumbling across the dust and Guthrie caught her neatly by the arms. The bright red hair loosened from its knot in her raging and swung Medusa-like over her convulsed face as she surged against Guthrie's grip and tried in vain to break free.

'Damn you, damn you, let me go!' she shrieked, writhing. 'I'll tear his face off! No drunken bum of a Cropper can come in here and—'

I bellowed, 'Shut up!' making my voice big enough to fill the whole clearing. It felt good to let all that volume out, stretching my chest to its depths and filling my throat with sound. 'Shut up and listen! All of you – listen!'

She looked stunned for a moment. Then she shrieked again. I roared her down without effort. I have a big voice. When I let it out no other voice I ever heard has a chance against it.

'Shut up and listen! Shut it off, damn you! Let me talk!'

She blinked. Guthrie gave her a gentle shake, and she caught her breath and hesitated. I glanced around the group.

For a moment it had been touch and go whether the whole cast jumped me. For that moment I hoped they would. But now I had the stage, and I let the savage contempt in my voice sound clear, talking fast before the woman began screaming again.

'Now's your chance,' I told them, looking coldly from face to face. 'Make up your minds. I don't like you. I don't want to work with you. I like to pick my casts, and I wouldn't have picked you. But I promised to do this job and I'm going to if I can. You'll never have a chance like this again. I can't make you work with me. But if you do, you'll jump when I crack the whip. I'll drive you like slaves. And you'll learn more in a week from me than you'll ever learn the rest of your stupid lives. Now make up your minds. Now! Don't keep me waiting. Yes or no? You!' And I shot my arms out again and leveled my finger at the man with the burned hand.

He was nursing his wrist painfully and the heavy, good-looking face was pale with shock. He licked his lips, glanced at the red-haired woman, and said uncertainly, 'I – I don't know, Rohan. It's not that simple. Let's take a vote.' And he glanced around the group.

I saw the red-haired woman catch her breath, and I said quickly, 'All right, you – this man's hand needs bandaging. Can you do it? You through screaming yet?'

She shook impatiently against Guthrie's grip. 'All right, Guthrie. Let go, let go!'

I nodded at him. She brushed herself down with quick, angry gestures, pushed the crimson hair back, and gave me one glance of hatred before she turned and ran for one of the trucks. She was back in seconds with a first-aid box, and from then on she was too busy with the burned hand to make herself much of a menace to me, though I kept a careful eye on her.

'I want names first,' I said. 'You!' and I pointed to the white-haired man who had stumbled to his feet on the other side of the table when all the trouble began. He still stood there, watching alertly. Now he said in a mildly surprised voice, 'Why, you know me, Mr Rohan. Henken. Pod Henken. And there's Eileen. Eileen, you remember Howard Rohan?'

The aged Ophelia patted her little opera box which had been singing quietly away to itself through all the tumult. 'Oh yes,' she murmured to nobody in particular. 'Oh, I remember Rohan...'

Guthrie said briskly, 'My name's Guthrie, Mr Rohan.'

I nodded at him and he added, waving at the red-haired woman working over my victim, 'Polly and Roy Copley.' The woman shot me a glance of venom, and the man returned my nod wanly.

That left the girl. I didn't want to know her name. All I could think about just now was the taste of whiskey and how much I wanted it. The excitement was dying down inside me.

I heard a clear, low voice from across the fire say, 'My name is Cressy Kellogg, Mr Rohan,' and I gave her one disinterested look and nodded. She couldn't help the way she looked. Not much, anyhow. The poor man's Miranda, I thought with anguish and contempt.

We stood there in silence for about as long as it takes to draw two breaths and let them out again, all of us gazing warily at each other. The end of a round had come. Not the end of a battle. They'd started the fight. I'd picked it up. They had good reason, I suppose, not to like me. Maybe to resent being saddled with me. My reputation wasn't very good among theatrical circles any more. But I was still, in my worst slump, so much better than they would ever be at their very best...

I can't make them like me, I thought angrily. But I can make them hate me. And I will.

'All right, cast,' I said, making my voice firm. 'About this play—'

Polly Copley lifted her disordered red head from the bandage she was sealing around Roy Copley's wrist. Were they husband and wife? She looked the older by a good ten years. 'Forget the play, Rohan,' she said. Her voice was hoarse and strong, a good carrying voice. The angry blue eyes bulged at

me. 'We aren't giving a play. The Swann Players are disband-
ing.'

I had my mouth open to bully her before the sense of what
she'd said fully reached me. It took the wind out of my sails a
little. I'd expected almost any complication but this. Looking
from face to face, seeing the same expression of agreement on
them all, I thought I knew what the trouble was. They were
scared. There was no Comus west of Blythe, the state was running wild around us for all I knew. I could hardly blame them.
But I made my voice confident.

'What's the matter with you people? Just because there's
been a little trouble in California—'

'Little trouble, hell,' Polly said. 'I don't know what you
mean by a little trouble, mister. Maybe you haven't heard what
happened to Paul Swann. He went down into San Andreas to
make arrangements for our first play and he came back in an
ambulance. I never saw a man beat up so bad. I never want to
again.' She struck the bright red hair out of her eyes angrily.
'I don't care if they beat you, Rohan. I hope they do. But they
aren't going to beat up Roy. Or me. Or anybody with the sense
God gave him.'

Pod Henken's voice chimed in with a slight quaver in it.
'That's the truth, Mr Rohan. Paul sure took a beating.'

I looked at Guthrie, who shrugged and averted his eyes
somewhat guiltily. He might have told me, I thought. But I
said with confidence, 'You let me worry about that.'

'You better start worrying then,' Polly said.

I squared my shoulders. They were all watching me. I said
in a flat, firm voice, 'We open in San Andreas on Saturday. I'll
set it up tomorrow and I won't come back on a stretcher. You
can leave that to me.'

The smell of coffee woke me and I lay there awhile perfectly
blank, wondering where I was. I knew Miranda had been
beside me up to the moment I opened my eyes. She always
was. But I myself might be in an agri-camp in Illinois, or a
hotel room in New York, with Nye's boys waiting outside the

door. The world eddied around me, unstable as jelly. Then it made up its mind and solidified down into a long dormitory truck with neatly made-up bunks on both sides and a shaft of morning sun coming through the door. The smell of redwoods and woodsmoke and coffee came with it.

A subdued murmur came from under my pillow. I reached in to shut off the sleep-teach box which had been reading *Crossroads* to me all night long. Last night Pod and Roy Copley and Guthrie had slept in here with me. I'd waked up alive, so evidently nobody held a serious grudge in spite of yesterday. Nobody except, perhaps, myself.

I fumbled into my clothes and went outside. There was no reason on God's earth why I should go into San Andreas and get myself beaten to a pulp this morning. I'd talked confidently last night because I'd taken on a role I couldn't put off without looking silly. But some changes were going to be made in the part from here on in.

Sunlight fell in unashamed grandeur in vast, slanting rays across the breakfast table, where my six colleagues sat over nearly empty plates. 'Good morning,' I said. Six pairs of eyes regarded me coldly. I went past them without a pause and carried my towel and shaving materials into the small square building set among redwood columns at the far side of the clearing. It was dingy concrete and it housed showers, toilets, laundry tubs. I went into the half marked MEN in the funny, old-fashioned block letters of the 1950s, trying as I shaved to imagine myself back in those untroubled times before the Five Days' War.

When I went back the six plates had been cleared from the table, but somebody had laid out and opened a single breakfast-plate can and the steam was beginning to rise as its self-heating unit went into operation. Cressy Kellogg poured coffee into a cup and set it by my plate. I didn't look at her. I felt good and terrible in layers. My outside couldn't help reacting to the cool morning air, unbelievably fresh. But under my skin the familiar crawling sensation was at work. I needed more alcohol than I'd allowed myself yet. Inside that layer of misery

53

was an irrational good feeling about the future. Dangerous, challenging, uncertain. I didn't even know what I was going to do. But it felt mysteriously good just the same.

Last of all, right down the middle of my awareness, ran a familiar core of pain and the fear of pain, the thought of the beautiful dreamer who would never wake again and never leave me.

I spread out a script of *Crossroads* on the table and looked through it as I ate. The chances were I'd never direct the thing, or act in it, but the sleep-taught lines were in my brain and I was curious about how it looked on paper. In spite of myself I'd begun to group my own speeches in my mind, block out the scenes tentatively, think over how I'd handle the part. If I handled it at all.

The play looked innocent enough. No obvious propaganda, though it had to be there, because Comus never does things without a purpose. It seems there were a boy and a girl (Cressy and Roy, that would be) who meet at a street crossing in a small town. There's an amorous female Comus officer who makes passes at the boy. It was a good touch. Comus is always handled with kid gloves in all official entertainment. This had the spontaneous look of non-partisanship.

Then there's an old couple who quarrel a lot but turn on anyone who comes between them. And a dashing older man (Rohan himself) who tries to break up the boy-girl affair. It was a part with many possibilities, that one. The whole play was good. A simple story about one evening in the lives of the six and how they solve each other's problems and their own in about an hour's playing time. Very skillfully done, and sure fire for comedy and drama.

I sat there visualizing the groupings of the actors on a circle stage, setting up pictures in my mind, wondering in spite of myself how this cast had conceived their own parts. That's always interesting. I was curious. No two people ever see the same part in the same way. It was very satisfying to feel my mind take hold again as if it had never let go.

Satisfying – and frightening.

Polly's forthright voice, quite near, made me jump.

'Rohan, I've got something to say to you.' I looked up. Her stiffly coated hair was smooth this morning, each strand glistening separately in the slanting light that fell through the trees. She looked as haggard as if she hadn't slept at all. Maybe she hadn't. 'We've been talking things over,' she told me. 'We don't want to disband unless we have to. We need the work. We're even willing to work with you as long as you treat us right. But I warn you, one more blowup like yesterday and—' Her face suffused and the veins stood out in her neck.

'All right,' I said. 'You treat me right and I'll treat you right. I'm not an easy man to work with. I warn *you*. I won't pull any punches in rehearsals.'

She nodded jerkily. 'We don't expect you to. We just wanted you to know that if you can set things up in San Andreas and guarantee we don't get mobbed we'll start rehearsing right away. We won't disband.'

I said, 'Good enough,' and turned a page of the script to show the interview was over. She flushed a little again and turned sharply, almost bumping into Guthrie, who was coming up to the table, buttoning his checkered shirt.

'When you're ready, Mr Rohan,' he said, 'I'll drive you into San Andreas.'

I didn't answer. I was watching something across the clearing. Cressy and Roy Copley were standing together in one of the solemn shafts of light, layers of woodsmoke floating mistily around them like incense in a cathedral. She was holding his bandaged hand with exaggerated sympathy, and the way they were looking at each other made me glance quickly to see if Polly had noticed. Guthrie said, 'How about it, Mr Rohan?'

I shrugged. Polly's troubles were her own business.

'Let's go,' I said.

CHAPTER VII

'Stop here a minute,' I said. Guthrie switched off the motor and the humming silence of the mountains settled all around us. Warm sunshine, bright, sparkling air, a breeze breathing with the smell of pine. Before us the highway stalked on long concrete legs across the valley where San Andreas lay. Two turnoffs led down into town, one to fetch and one to carry. At the foot of the Entrance Only turnoff the red Comus check station glowed like an enormous oval blood-drop, looking strange without the Raleigh banner lifting in the wind from its flagstaff.

San Andreas lay winking up at us among its trees. You could locate the center of town by the shaft of the Raleigh monument, white and tall against blue sky. Southward the valley widened into checkerboard fields, with trucks and men already creeping slowly along the rows. For an instant I was down there with them with an aching back, harvesting and hating it.

'I know what you're thinking,' Guthrie told me. 'Go on. Say it.'

I shook my head. 'I don't know enough yet to say anything. Yesterday you strong-armed me back into camp, but you didn't say a word about what happened to Paul Swann. What else are you covering up? Just how bad are things in California?'

Guthrie slated me one of his melancholy looks.

'That depends. Some of the state's quiet. Some of it – isn't. This town isn't. Maybe that's why we have to open here. I don't know.'

'You don't know much. What's this tour about, anyhow?'

'We put on plays where we're told to. If I knew any more than that I couldn't tell you. You ought to realize that.'

'Now look, Guthrie.' I turned in the seat to meet his eye directly. 'You can strong-arm me just so far. Next time I may say shoot and be damned. I'm no good to anybody if I'm dead. Right now I'm pretty near the point where I just get out of this truck and walk off.'

'So you walk off,' Guthrie said quietly. 'Then what? You can't stay out of sight forever. Either Comus picks you up or the rebels do. And they're tough boys. Even if they took you in, we're going to pacify the state within a few weeks. The rebels are headed for jail or the gas chamber. That puts Comus back in control, and Mr Nye tells me he holds a Cropper contract for you.' He nodded toward the toiling figures in the field below. 'Your choice is between that down there or jail with the rebels – or else going on with this job for Comus.'

I thought it over. 'Okay. You've said your piece. Maybe you gave Paul Swann the same pitch. That didn't stop his getting beat up. From here on in whatever I do, I do on my own. Your holding a gun on me doesn't mean a damned thing. If I'm going to do this job I've got to do it my way, and that means I'm boss of the company. You're under my orders on company business. Now suppose you tell me all you know about the rebellion in California. Everything. Whatever you hold back handicaps me and the job.'

Guthrie scratched his cheek with his pipestem. After a moment he said slowly, 'Well, I guess that's fair enough. I'll tell you as much as I know.' He meditated. 'Back in '93,' he said after another pause, 'a guy named Charlie Starr touched off the San Diego Massacre. That was what got things started. I don't know much about Starr. Comus got things under control again and I believe Starr was killed. But his followers took to the hills and Comus never did root them all out. They seem to have set up what they call Freedom Committees that cover the whole area. About a year ago as near as we can figure one of the rebel groups doped out a gimmick that *might* cause trouble—' Here he paused and looked at me cautiously.

'The Anti-Com?' I asked.

'So you know about that.'

'Nye told me. Not much.'

'We don't know much. We just know it gave the rebels so much confidence we've got to take it seriously. When Comus first got wind of it they clamped down hard on California, trying to find the thing before it got big enough to hurt us. And that's when the whole area blew sky-high.' He shook his head thoughtfully. 'You know how the social controls usually work?'

I nodded. I knew it well. I thought of it happening in California in an area already on the brink of explosion. Normally Prowlers like big red blood-drops patrol the roads twenty-four hours a day. At random, at any time, one of them may draw up to your door. Somebody in a well-tailored red uniform invites you politely inside. Nobody refuses. Why refuse? It's just an opinion poll to find out what you want so Comus can get it for you. You sit down in the big chair with the elaborate armrests and you react to key words thrown at you, and the polygraph records everything.

Out of a hundred people sampled at random probably ninety will have similar reactions. Comus feeds the records into headquarters to the constantly thoughtful calculators. They brood electronically over your pulse and respiration. They consider the psychological and sociological meaning of a sweating palm in South Dakota, a rapid heartbeat in Georgia. Out of the hundred sampled, ten who vary from the average reactions are a safe percentage. But if twenty vary, that's too many. And Comus knows before you do that discontent is stirring subliminally in your area.

Say the curve on the graph has risen steadily for two months and Georgia is observed to feel unrest. Isolate Georgia. Communications feed Georgia a different fare. News releases tell about happenings that aren't seen elsewhere in the nation. Movie films are slanted just a little differently. Even the food isn't quite the same. Biochemistry can change the functioning of mind and body to a lower level of efficiency. And Georgia becomes a closed system. Georgia can be manipulated.

Any organism can probably work out its problems if you let it alone. So don't let it alone. The more choices it has to make, the more disruption it feels. Multiply its choices. Keep it stirred up. Destroy Georgia's confidence. Make Georgia realize it depends on Comus for survival. Reaction time slows, efficiency drops, the slowly forming new groups of potential rebels dissolve under the stress. And when the danger has passed, integrate Georgia again with the nation. That's the practical way to hold the union together. It's always worked – until now.

And now? I looked out over the peaceful valley. Probably I knew more than most people did about how the social controls really work. But enough people in California apparently knew it too. Enough to set off an explosion when Comus began seining for sedition in this area.

'What happened?' I asked.

'All hell popped. We got a lot of resistance even in the cities, but the back country was where the rebels were strongest. We were up against open rebellion there. This a big area. Comus is spread fairly thin in the nation, as you probably know. Short of pulling troops out of other areas to blanket California, we couldn't do much. And there were—' Guthrie paused. 'There were reasons why we didn't do that,' he said. A flash of wild wonder went through my mind. Were there rebellions elsewhere too?

'As I understand it,' Guthrie went on, 'there was quite an uproar in the House about all this. The California Governor and Mr Raleigh got together, and I know Mr Nye put up a big argument for martial law. But the upshot was we withdrew Comus entirely. Raleigh's argument was that when people found out what life without Comus was like they'd come to their senses. He's old, Mr Rohan. He doesn't like trouble. He doesn't want to think he's saddled the country with a dictatorship. He said withdraw.'

'And Nye?' I asked.

Guthrie shrugged. 'He had to agree, of course. I think he was willing to partly because of the Anti-Com. Too much pressure on the rebels and they'd move heaven and earth to get their weapon finished fast. Too fast for us to stop them. As it is, what Mr Nye probably hopes for is just status quo – while we search the area for whatever we can find. It's a race between Comus and the Anti-Com now. Whether the rebels finish first or Comus finds the hidden factory before they touch off – whatever it is they've got.'

'And Raleigh,' I said slowly, 'is a sick man. He can't live long. When he dies...'

I let it fade. Guthrie nodded. Nobody knew what would happen when Raleigh died. An era would end. The world would change. History was moving toward a turn as we sat here wondering.

After a little pause Guthrie said, 'This town here is one of the trouble spots. We think it's headquarters for a whole group of Freedom Committees. Last week we pulled a flash raid. We dropped a quick helicopter-squad and tried to flood the central part of the town with sleep gas. It didn't come off the way it was planned and the town fought back. Now the whole countryside is in a turmoil.'

'In other words,' I said, 'if they find out we're Comus, we're done for.'

Guthrie bit his pipestem. 'About six months ago when the trouble was really bad,' he said, 'whole Comus units would just disappear when a raid failed and the people struck back. That's one reason Raleigh insisted on pulling Comus out of the area. Now – well, these are just people, Mr Rohan. Not wild-eyed revolutionaries. They don't kill for fun. At least, not the normal people. They don't even kill in anger, except by accident, or under direct attack. If they aren't pushed they won't hit back too hard. But I'll admit I'd hate to have it known we're connected with Comus.'

'What happened to Paul Swann?' I asked.

'He ran into a bunch of drunks, according to what I heard.' Guthrie grinned wryly. 'I had an informant in San Andreas, up to yesterday.' He nodded toward a thin upward waver of smoke rising above the trees on the north edge of the town. 'That was his house. They rode my man out of town on a rail. I guess he was lucky at that.'

I swallowed hard. 'And this is the town,' I said, 'where I'm supposed to put on a Comus show.' Guthrie sucked noisily on his pipe and gazed at me. 'I guess I'll go back to the Croppers,' I said.

He grinned. 'You mean that?'

I didn't know if I meant it or not. I looked down the valley at the toiling shapes in the field. I could feel a familiar aching in the muscles as I watched. A tremor of the ghostly itching ran over me again. I felt a sudden, scalding hatred of Ted Nye breaching the walls of my refuge and forcing me willy-nilly into a spot like this. And then through the remembered aching, and the ghostly itch, and the anger against Nye, a little flicker like summer lightning twitched in the background of my mind. The memory of fiery letters spelling out a message in a dream.

I didn't know what they said. But deep in my mind a small voice made sounds of reassurance. 'There is more here than you know,' the voice said rather smugly. 'Things may be better than you think. Go on, take the chance. Go ahead.'

I looked down at San Andreas, bright and peaceful-looking in the morning sun. I was scared. My throat felt dry and my hands felt wet and my heart was pumping too fast.

'Well, Mr Rohan?' Guthrie asked.

I shrugged. 'Let's go,' I said.

CHAPTER VIII

The Comus Check station at the foot of the road stood red and empty, with broken panes. No signal flashed, no red-coated figure stepped to the door. Somebody had scrawled the padlocked-head drawing in chalk across its side. As we rolled by, a breath of wind lifted a long, ragged blue streamer tied to the broken flagstaff. It turned lazily in the air and dropped again. Blue for revolution, I thought. This cell of Comus was dead. It gave me a strangely empty feeling in the pit of the stomach. All I'd heard until now was abstract compared to this sharp impact of reality, this sight of the empty station.

About a hundred feet farther on the wild mustard growing high and yellow by the road parted and two men jumped to their feet and shouted at us. Guthrie's foot touched the accelerator and the car gave a brief, abortive jump forward. Then we both saw the double-barreled shotgun in the first man's hand, the over-under barrels looking up at us like eyes turned sidewise. Guthrie stopped.

'Where you going?' asked the man with the gun. He was young and thin-faced.

The answer seemed self-evident, but Guthrie told him.

'What's your business?'

Guthrie looked at me. He waited.

'We're putting on a traveling show,' I said. 'I want a permit.'

The man with the shotgun gave me a long, cool look. 'The last guy tried that got the hell kicked out of him. You take my advice, you'll go right back where you came from. Town's kind of jumpy these days.'

'We've got to eat,' I said. 'I'll take my chances. Who do I see about a permit?'

The cool look moved to Guthrie and then back to me. 'We got a duly elected mayor and town council,' he told us. 'Certified legal by Comus.' He leaned over and spat carefully into the dust.

I said, 'Sure. And who issues permits?'

He shrugged. 'Mister, I wouldn't know.' His gaze shifted to the truck. 'What's inside?'

'Look and see,' I suggested. We were driving the sound truck, and I hadn't seen inside myself. Guthrie sat there placidly, not seeming worried. The man with the gun grunted to his companion, who stepped to the back. I heard the door open, felt the floor give a little as he stepped inside. After a while he came out and muttered to our friend with the gun.

I had been noticing idly how the lines of their weather-beaten faces looked incised, as if by stage make-up. I supposed I was studying them unconsciously for pointers as to how I'd play a rebel if I ever had such a role, how I'd speak and stand and look. Now it hit me with a sudden shock what had happened to their faces. This was more than ordinary dirt. They had been heavily blacked, and the blacking rubbed off casually. So they must have been among the fighters when the Comus detail swooped down. Or later, in troubles I didn't know about. The blacked face is a good and quick disguise. It hit me suddenly that these were really rebels, fighters against Comus. I thought of them as men from another world.

'Okay,' the man with the gun said, stepping back. 'Go on if you want to. You don't mind getting beat up, go on.'

San Andreas didn't look so peaceful close up. A lot of shop windows were broken, and everywhere in the center of town the street and walls were tinged with the faint purplish stain that sleep-gas spray leaves on all it touches. The fresh white marks of bullets scored the store fronts, and every window around the square had big blue swags of bunting conspicuous in it. Over all these evidences of strife the Raleigh Monument lifted the big white shaft and the big white marble-jawed head of the President serenely aloft. Raleigh was looking east above the rooftops, seeing nothing.

We pulled up in front of the Irish Rose Bar and Grill, and Guthrie sat there looking at me. I gazed at the street, the people, my own face in the rearview mirror. Would anybody here recognize Howard Rohan? I was scared. But I had to do something. I wondered what Paul Swann had done at this point, how he had felt.

A man with a bar towel around his waist was sweeping out the Irish Rose. The double doors were propped back with bricks, and a chair sat in the opening to indicate no admission. The man doused the sidewalk with water from a bucket and swept the water into the street. The air smelled pleasantly of wet concrete and stale beer, a smell I have always rather liked. The sweeper gave us an unfriendly look. He was fat, and he wore a four-cornered canvas cap with LOS ANGELES WORLD'S FAIR on it, and stuck in the brim a paper triangle with a blue star on it, and inside the star a scribbled red '93'. Charlie Starr. The San Diego Massacre.

I stole a side glance at Guthrie, wondering how all this made him feel. For me, seeing these evidences of rebellion, smelling the bright, cool air of the mountain valley, feeling the strange stirring in the air that I couldn't define, I felt like a man wakening out of a very long, very confused dream. Scared, uncertain, but mysteriously fresh and good.

I called to the bartender, 'Morning. Nice day.'

He looked sour and said nothing. I said, 'Which way is the Mayor's office?' He swept a wave of a dirty water at me and answered grudgingly, 'Across the square.'

I nodded to Guthrie, and we rolled forward, watching the store fronts for a sign that might say 'Mayor's Office.' Behind us a slow, piercing whistle began to shrill out a tune. I placed it after a moment – 'Yankee Doodle,' but with a difference. Not quite the same song. It quickened and rose as we moved along. People on the street glanced toward the source of the sound

64

and then looked quickly around, many of them straight at us. I didn't like it much.

A two-story white building came into view with CITY HALL across its façade. Guthrie parked. 'You'd better stay with the truck,' I said. 'I'll be back – I hope.'

A small boy sitting on the curb got up as I passed and sauntered after me, taking up the whistle. The City Hall had a small lobby that opened into a flowery patio in back. The Mayor's office was up a flight of narrow stairs. I started up. The small group followed me as far as the lobby, mysteriously augmented by two or three other small boys, all whistling. I ignored them. When I was halfway up the stairs a shrill soprano voice in the lobby began to sing the words that went with 'Yankee Doodle'.

'Charlie Starr took off his badge
In Nineteen Ninety-three.
He blew old Comus off the map
And set Diego free...'

His badge? I wondered. What badge? Well, the song wasn't very accurate. Old Comus was far from blowed off the map and San Diego was as much, or as little, enslaved as ever. Still, the song made its point.

The Mayor's office had two benches and a counter, behind which an old man shuffled papers disinterestedly.

'I want an entertainment permit,' I told him. 'Who do I see?'

He shook his head. 'Can't help you, son. Guess there just isn't anybody you could rightly see on Mondays.'

'Today's Tuesday,' I pointed out.

'Is it?' He shook his head again. 'Well, Tuesday's a bad day for permits too. Sorry, son.' He looked me in the eye and said no more. He just waited.

I stood there a minute, opening and shutting my hands on the counter. I felt the muscles tighten all up my arms and little explosions of violence kept starting and then drying out in my mind. I wanted to hit something, batter somebody, work off a mounting feeling of hot frustration. But there wasn't anyone to hit. It wouldn't even be a satisfaction to hit the old man. After the minute was over I turned and went out fast, shutting the door very quietly behind me.

The little boys were still in the lobby, looking up at me round-eyed as I came down the stairs. But they were perfectly silent now. I thought to myself, Something's coming. Something's going to pop. The silence was a scared anticipation. And when they saw me the boy nearest the door jumped for the sidewalk and began waving with excited beckoning gestures to somebody out of sight. I heard running feet on the pavement and saw the jostling shadows of men coming fast.

I drew a deep, happy breath and rolled my shoulder muscles experimentally, loosening up my arms, making sure my shirt didn't bind me anywhere. I felt good. I felt wonderful. I felt like laughing. I swung my arm at the little staring boys, 'Outside, kids, outside!' I said harshly. They jumped and then scattered like quail, erupting out the door in a sudden flurry of small forms just as the first of the oncoming men reached it. There was brief, noisy confusion on the sidewalk. And then the men came in.

Three or four men. Most of them ragged and unwashed. The lobby filled up with the smell of sweat and whiskey. This early in the morning? Then I remembered the bartender and knew what had happened as clearly as if I'd been on the spot. The recruiting of the strong-arm squad from the town's down-and-outs, the serving out all round of a few stiff shots to get the mood going. And I knew just what had happened to Paul Swann. But this time they had another man. I was no Paul Swann.

They came at me head on, businesslike and in silence. Outside I heard Guthrie yell and there was a noise of scuffling and a boom of blows on metal, as if something were happening to the truck. I paid no attention. I was busy. I could tell by their grinning faces they thought this would be easy. I knew what was coming, and it came. But not just what they expected.

The wave broke over me all at once, the whole group of them jostling to get at me in the narrow lobby. I got the first

66

one with a chopping blow from the side of my hand across his forearm, and I felt the bone fracture under the chop. Somebody hit me across the head and everything went starry and blurred, and after that for a while I only know that for a long time I hit and was hit, stumbling and grunting in the narrow room. I remember little things, the jolt of someone's chin against the heel of my hand, and the feel as his head snapped back. The feel of my shoe scraping heavily down someone's shin and the crackle of the small bones of his foot under the stamping finish. The springing give of muscle and bone over the solar plexus when I drove my fist in hard. I was fighting to cripple, as Croppers fight. And I'd learned the hard way. I knew how.

It seemed to go on a long while, and for no time at all. There was a point where I realized the walls no longer shut us in and there was grass underfoot. We had somehow surged out into the little patio and the morning sun bathed us with serene indifference as we fought. Once I caught a dizzy glimpse of Andrew Raleigh's white marble face above the rooftops, also serenely indifferent, gazing east into the sun.

Once I found myself face down among flowers, their petals sweet and moist against my cheek. And once, on my hands and knees and tasting blood in my mouth, I saw three ants in an infinitesimal huddle, antennae lying across each other's shoulders, heads together, conferring about some important deal on the microscopic level while the battle raged over their unheeding heads. Then a drop of blood fell from my nose onto the pavement, and when I saw them last they were probing it cautiously with interested antennae.

At some point soon after this, when I was on my feet again and grappling with a grunting, unwashed opponent, I kicked his feet from under him and we thudded heavily to the ground, him underneath. I remember telling myself I had to disable him fast, before somebody else came at me from above. And then, wonderingly, holding the stunned man down with both hands, I looked up and saw the little patio almost empty. One man lay silent on his face among the flowers. Another one in the doorway was doubled up and retching, out of the fight. Nobody else was here. I'd won.

I looked down at the man I was kneeling on. His eyelids fluttered. He was coming to. I slapped him sharply across the face. His eyes snapped open.

'Who hired you?' I demanded. 'Who's the boss here?'

He rolled his head from side to side, setting his jaw. I slapped him again. 'Answer me, damn you. Who's the boss?' Still he shook his head. This time I lifted him a little and cracked his head against the ground. I did it twice, savagely, enjoying it, letting him see I did.

After a while he told me.

I made him say it twice, because I couldn't believe what happened in my head when he spoke the name. A perfectly normal name. Harris. A man named Harris. But when he said the word, it wasn't his voice only that I heard. Like an echo behind it I heard another voice too.

I was asleep and dreaming in the hotel bedroom in New York, and the man named Comus was shaking me and telling me urgently about California, swans, antics, and to be sure and find – an heiress?

Oh no. It was Harris, not heiress. I could remember that now. One of the shutter windows in my mind opened just wide enough to let the memory through. Not until now, of course. Not until I'd found out the hard way. Harris, I thought. Harris?

I got up slowly. My man lay still, watching apprehensively. I kicked him in the side once, not hard but hard enough, and went out walking heavily and feeling my face to find out if I'd be disfigured enough to keep me off the stage. I cared with only half my mind. The other half turned slowly over and over in long, confused ellipses, wonderingly.

The truck still sat at the curb. Inside it Guthrie lay forward motionless over the wheel. There was nobody in sight on the street for a block in either direction, though window shades quivered slightly in upper windows as I came out. I got into the truck and shook Guthrie. He said something unintelligible in a thick voice. I shook him again. This time he opened his eyes and looked at me blankly. Then he sat back, put a hand to his jaw, winced, gazed at me with dawning recognition, and finally grinned his sad, wry grin.

'You all right?' I asked. He tried his jaw gingerly.

'I guess so. All they did was slug me. How about you?'

'I'm okay.' I said it abstractly. After a moment I added, 'Look, I think I've got a lead. You just sit here a minute. I'm going to make a call.' I was out of the truck while he was still in the middle of a protest.

There was a little drugstore next to the City Hall. I let the screen door slam open with a crash against the wall. There were no customers inside, and a man behind a counter vanished through a rear door before I got more than a glimpse of him. I grinned to myself, lopsidedly because it hurt. Let them be scared, I thought.

I leaned over the soda fountain and held my handkerchief under the water faucet. Using the mirror behind the bar, I wiped off the dust and blood. I had a scraped area along the jaw and I'd probably develop a black eye by evening. My nose had begun to swell, but it wasn't bad yet and I thought it wasn't broken. I didn't look too menacing for the TV screen.

So I slid into a booth, dropped my coin, and when the operator came on in the flyspecked screen I gave her my best smile. 'I need a little help,' I said. 'There's a man named Harris I want to talk to. Would you know the one I mean?'

She looked at me searchingly. Maybe she knew my face. Maybe she already knew about the battle of City Hall too. If she did, she must realize what I was asking.

A fly, trapped in the hot booth with me, lit on the screen and walked across the operator's face. We flapped at it simultaneously, and then both grinned. 'I'll see what I can do,' she said. 'Wait a minute.'

The screen flickered and went blank. Then an advertising card listing specials on sale at Andy's Hardware Store shimmered at me. It had just faded into an announcement of a rummage sale at the Patriots' Daughters Hall when a gong rang, a metallic voice said, 'This is one-way visual only,' and out of the blank screen a man's voice, rather high and impatient, said, 'Yes?'

'I have a message for Mr Harris,' I said.

'Harris speaking. What is it?'

I looked at the blank screen in silence. What could I say? We have a mutual friend named Comus, who lives in dreamland? I felt his unseen eyes moving over my face and my skin tickled as if the fly were walking on me. It felt strange to stand almost face to face like this with somebody who had taken the definitive step. The enemy. He sounded like an ordinary man. But behind him loomed all the shadowy structure of the fighters against Comus, the men and women who had taken their lives in their hands. They might be wrong, but they were impressive.

I said, 'I just had a little argument with some friends of yours. Maybe *you* can tell me what a man has to do to get a work permit in San Andreas.'

Silence. Then, 'How did you get my name?'

'I persuaded one of your boys,' I said. 'He didn't persuade easy.' There was silence again. Suddenly Harris laughed.

'All right. I'm sure he didn't. Well. So you want an entertainment permit.'

I blinked at the screen. 'I haven't mentioned entertainment yet.'

Harris laughed again. 'You don't need to. We've been watching you. We wondered if you'd make it. The man before you didn't. I'm glad to hear from you – Rohan. That's the name, isn't it? We can use people like you.'

'Hold on,' I said. 'All I want is to put on one show in San Andreas.'

Harris chuckled. 'Sure. And you need a permit. Well, we'll discuss the price. Can't expect something for nothing, you know. Wait a minute, Rohan. I'll be back.'

I waited. I looked at the swimming surface of the screen until specks floated before my eyes. I admired the dim outline of my own head in reflection. After a while I opened the door a crack and tried to chase the fly out. It wouldn't go. When the screen spoke it startled me.

'Rohan? Can you be at the back door of the Medical Building in fifteen minutes?'

I said with some bitterness, 'I could if it were up to me. There's been a little trouble in San Andreas this morning. Maybe you heard.'

He chuckled with some complacence. I decided I didn't like the man. I also thought he'd sound less complacent after he'd seen his goon squad again. He said, 'That was by way of being a test, you know. Don't worry. This time you won't have any trouble. The Medical Building is right across the square. And come alone, Rohan.' He paused. Then when I didn't speak he said casually, 'You'll be there?' It was hardly a question.

I thought, This is a threshold. Once I cross it I'm asking for more trouble than I've had yet. Do I want to go on? Paul Swann didn't make the grade. Do I want to? But I knew I didn't have any choice, now. Little by little, drawn on by threats, circumstance, and the tenuous memory of a dream, I'd entered too far to back out.

'Oh yes,' I said to the blank screen. 'I'll be there.'

CHAPTER IX

I watched the back of the sound truck diminishing down the street, going in and out of the oak tree shadows and in and out of the bright morning sun. Guthrie seemed to be driving all right. He said he felt okay. He said he would be back for me at noon. He said he didn't approve of anything I was doing. I hadn't expected him to. It took a good deal of argument to persuade him to leave at all. But I was in a trap, and we both knew it. A trap the size of California, sure, but still a trap. I couldn't get out. There was no way to go but forward.

On the way to the Medical Building I had two minor surprises. One was a bulletin board in front of the San Andreas Hotel. It startled me to see how wide open the town really was. Between a notice of a cattle sale and a nursery school ad was a hand-lettered card signed by the Freedom Committee urging everyone to contribute what food, ammunition, and first aid supplies could be spared to the Coldspring Guerrillas. An ominous footnote added, 'Looting in the northeast broke out again last week. Our men are fighting for all of us. What can you spare?'

And there was an acerbic notice from a Major Andreas (a pseudonym, no doubt) ordering all local guerrillas to keep their weapons strictly out of sight until the CORRECT signal sounded. Somebody had scribbled under this the terse comment that 'Maj. A. is a dam fool'.

I was smiling to myself about this one as I crossed the square, and saw my second surprise in the distance. Pedestrians were still scarce in my immediate area, but the streets were fairly busy. And among the heads I caught a glimpse of familiar corn-silk curls bobbing along beside a Stetson hat, the Stetson bent attentively. I couldn't be positive, but I felt pretty sure it was Cressy. The chance seemed remote that two women in the San Andreas area would have hit on just that pale yellow tone and just that bouncing halo of loose curls. I made a mental note to ask questions later. Cressy had no business in San Andreas.

The flat white back of the Medical Building was locked. I tapped politely. After a minute a lock clicked and Harris's high, impatient voice said, 'Come in, come in,' as if I'd kept him waiting.

I went. I went about three steps into darkness and then stood still, blinking, as the door shut behind me. Harris said out of the dark, 'I'll have to blindfold you for a while, Rohan. Sorry. Here.' A hand invisibly touched my cheek, pressing something sticky and cool across my eyes. Firm fingers sealed it into place. 'All right,' Harris said. 'Come along.'

Guided by a hand on my arm, I went forward, stumbling. A door creaked noisily and Harris said, 'In here. This is an elevator. Brace yourself.' The floor rose under me. Air sighed heavily in the shaft and the floor stopped rising with such suddenness I staggered. The door creaked open again. 'Come along,' Harris said.

There were several people in the room. I could hear chairs creak and sense the tempo of varied breathing. Somebody coughed and somebody else cleared his throat. I felt their eyes on me. I smelled disinfectant, tobacco, clean linen freshly ironed, and just a suggestion of some flower scent floating over all the other odors.

Harris said, 'Put your hand out. Here's a chair. Sit down if you want to. We have a few questions to ask.'

I kicked the chair a little and then sank into it. My bruises had begun to hurt, and it felt good to sit down. It was strange to be sitting here in total darkness, feeling the eyes of the Freedom Committee on me. Because that, of course, was what they must be. And even the melodrama seemed justified, under the circumstances.

Harris said, 'First I want to say we're glad to have you here, Rohan. We hoped Swann would make it, but he didn't have what it takes. You came through the fight and you found out whom to contact. So we know how tough you are, and how resourceful. We need somebody like you, with a Comus road permit and a reason for traveling. We hope you'll work with us. If you don't' – he paused – 'you won't work at all. Comus still rules the roads, but the Freedom Committees are in nearly full control everywhere else. If you don't co-operate you haven't got a chance of staging your show anywhere in California.'

'What's your proposition?' I asked cautiously.

'Are you a Comus man?' Harris asked bluntly. 'Or will you work with us?'

I hesitated only a moment. 'I'll do what I have to do to get the show lined up.'

'Are you willing to co-operate with the Freedom Committee? Think it over, Rohan. It could mean trouble for you if we lose out to Comus when the showdown comes.'

'Depends on what you want me to do.'

'A few small jobs. We aren't sure yet ourselves.' His voice sounded cagey. I wished I could see his face. 'Somebody with the freedom of the highways might be very useful to us. Before I go into details, we'll expect you to answer some questions about yourself fully and frankly—' He hesitated.

I said, 'Nothing wrong with that.'

'—in a lie-detector jacket?' Harris finished.

I swallowed hard. This is it, I thought. I walked into it. I can't back out now. But I can't go ahead. And I remembered how the Comus units that dropped down for raids in these mountain areas sometimes disappeared completely, swallowed up and buried. If I said yes I'd have to speak the truth, and the truth could mean destruction for us all. But if I said no I'd be admitting the worst too. Either way they had me.

The room was quite silent, waiting.

'Why not?' I said.

A little sigh went through the darkness. Chairs creaked from three sides and footsteps sounded briskly on the floor. They knew what they were going to do now.

'All right,' a new voice said. It was contralto, warm and confident. A woman? I thought so, but I couldn't be quite sure yet. 'Stand up, Rohan. Take your shirt off, please. Good. Now put out your arms—'

I felt the smooth, cold, gloved sleeves of the lie-detector jacket slide up my arms until the mittens at the end stopped them. I felt the little pads and studs against my palms, the thick collar of the thing snug under my ears where the arteries pulse. Someone drew the chestband tight. I'd seen this done in the movies often enough. I could picture the complicated dials somewhere near me, needles quivering to record all the inward processes by which sweat and blood pressure speak louder than words.

A breeze blew cool across my cheek. A window must have been opened. Something clicked and a steady humming began somewhere nearby.

'Your name, please.' It *was* a woman's voice.

'Howard Rohan.'

'Your age?'

'Thirty-five.' Several voices laughed simultaneously. 'All right,' I said. 'Forty.'

'Do you know the name of this town?' I did. I told her the date and the day of the week. They ran me through a list of the usual neutral questions that establish a base to go by. Then—

'You have a valid Comus road-travel permit?'

'I have.'

'But you yourself have no other connection with Comus. Is that right?'

I waited for a fraction of a moment. There wasn't going to be any out. I had no choice. I'd never had any choice, I realized, since the Cropper bus stopped at the check station and a man in a red coat called, 'Howard Rohan.' Everything

75

that had happened was moving me straight along toward this. Maybe everything that had happened since I was born.

'No,' I said. 'That's wrong. I was hired for this job by Theodore Nye. Comus picked the cast and wrote the play and set the itinerary.' It gave me savage pleasure to pile evidence on top of evidence. 'There's a Comus plain-clothes man working the sound truck for our troupe. He's in direct touch with Nye, for all I know. And you understand as much of this setup as I do.'

I sat in dead silence. The room was perfectly still around me. Not a chair creaked. Not a person seemed to breathe. I had a bitter taste in my mouth and the world had gone brassy again around me, the people clockwork, all sound meaningless, all motion without purpose. I didn't care what happened to me now. I didn't care what happened to Guthrie or the troupe. They could push me so far and then no farther. I sat passive, waiting.

The contralto voice spoke in silence, quite steady. 'Why are you here in California, Rohan? What was Nye's purpose in staging this tour?'

There was a humming in my ears that might have been the lie box and might have been my own blood beating dizzily. I don't know what I'd expected. To be shot right now? To be ridden out of town on a rail, like Guthrie's stool pigeon? Almost anything except this calm acceptance.

'Is that all you've got to say?' I heard myself demand. 'Aren't you going to—'

'Answer the question, Rohan,' the calm contralto said.

'Repeat the question then.'

She did. 'Nye's purpose?' I echoed. 'I don't know. Believe me, I don't.' Then I laughed a little, because whatever else went wrong, at least they had to believe me now. That gentle humming at my elbow bore witness to the truth. 'Nye said the theaters were a diversion, part of a larger plan. That's all I know.'

'Did he mention the Anti-Com?'

'Yes. Not in connection with the troupe.'

'What did he tell you about it?'

I thought. The invisible people around me waited in silence. 'Some kind of mechanism,' I said. 'Big enough to wreck Comus – maybe. I don't believe that. It's being assembled fast but it isn't ready yet, and Ted Nye—' I hesitated, but I was hooked up to the lie box and you have to know more than I did to beat that. 'He's feeling the pressure. The way it looks to me, if the President dies before it's finished, Nye wins. If he doesn't maybe you rebels win. I don't know. It gets vague around that point. That's as far as I can take you.'

Silence. Then the steady contralto saying, 'Will you work with us and keep quiet about what you know?'

I answered her slowly and carefully, making sure I meant what I said, testing each word before I spoke it. The hum of the lie box must confirm all I said. 'Yes, I'll work with you. As long as it doesn't interfere with my real job, I will. But I'm not a spy and I won't play spy. I'm just an actor. I won't – oh, gallop around on white horses yelling the British are coming. I won't take long chances. But I'll keep my mouth shut as long as you help me do my job. I haven't any choice about that. Just don't ask too much of me. Don't push me too far.'

They sat there thinking it over, maybe watching the needles quiver. Then Harris spoke. 'Fair enough, Rohan,' he said. 'Now—'

The contralto voice broke in. 'I think,' it said, 'that we might take the mask off him now.'

There was flurry of voices starting to protest. The contralto was firm. 'I think he should see our faces. He should know we trust him.' There was a short silence in which I thought I sensed unspoken messages flashing from eye to eye around the room. Then a cool hand touched my cheek and peeled the blindfold pad away. When I breathed, I breathed the smell of disinfectants and flowers. When I opened my eyes, I looked into a woman's face bent over me, her black eyes intent on mine.

She wore a doctor's white coat, buttoned smooth over smooth, full breasts and tight to a narrow waist. She had a tanned face with good planes to it, and her black hair was slick to her head and drawn back in a coronet of braids so tight it seemed to pull her face smooth at the sides and made her black eyes tilt.

She had sounded calm and controlled. But the black eyes watching me managed to suggest that all this might become very exciting. I looked away. I didn't want to respond to feeling any more. I was already repressing all response to Cressy Kellogg and I pushed all reaction to this woman away too. I had troubles enough as it was.

Harris had a round face, round eyeglasses, and a receding hairline. There was a man beside him with aquiline features and a ragged brown sweater. Two more members with no notable features made up the Freedom Committee. I gazed at them with disappointment. I don't know what I'd expected. Bearded anarchists? Lean Leatherstockings with flintlock rifles? Still, I don't look too much like a rebel myself either, and from then on, I supposed, I was as revolutionary as any of them. Or was I? I didn't know.

I looked down at the transparent jacket, seeing my own cuts and bruises on the bare skin under it. I was a little surprised at how many there were. I looked at the table beside me with its bank of dials and quivering needles. Something about them touched a chord of memory, and I looked at the woman again, a twinge of recognition stirring.

'Who are you?' I asked.

'This is Dr Elaine Thomas,' Harris told me. 'You know me. The others—' He told me their names too, and I forgot them at once. I was still looking at the girl. Faintly, faintly, I seemed to see letters of fire circling in an abyss.

'I know somebody who looks a lot like you,' I said. 'A doctor with the psycho-screening division of Comus in New York. He put me through the mill a couple of days ago – I think. Any relation?'

The girl flashed me a quick, dark, troubled look.

'My brother,' she said briefly. There was an awkward little silence in the room, as if I'd said something gauche. The girl went on quickly, as if she wanted to change the subject. 'We want you to know you can trust us. You know our names and faces now. You *could* turn us in.'

I nodded. 'I won't. Not now, anyhow. What is it you people want me to do?'

Harris cleared his throat. 'We'll find you a job or two just to see how you work out. For a starter, do you know how to drive a hedgehopper?'

'Yes,' I said. 'But—'

'We'll arrange for you to steal one from the next 'hopper patrol,' Harris said calmly. 'After you've stolen Comus property we'll feel we can trust you further.'

I drew a deep breath and watched it register on a dial. 'Is that all?'

'Oh no,' Harris said quickly. 'That's just your insurance.'

'But I get my entertainment permit?'

Harris nodded, looking at me speculatively. He said in a matter-of-fact voice, 'Of course we realized there had to be something ulterior about this theater tour of yours. We thought from the start it was some kind of Comus device. What we have to find out is just what it is and how it works. For instance, does it strike you as normal to have a sound truck as big as the one you've got to stage a show on the road?'

I thought it over. 'Well, no, it doesn't. Maybe not.'

'Have you ever looked inside it?'

'No,' I said.

The man in the brown sweater said, 'I'd like to have a look myself. Unless it's something pretty subtle or new, I can probably spot something. We'll have to think of something before you put your show on.' He met my eye, frowned a little, and added, 'You hedged when we asked you a question a while back, Rohan. Before you get out of the jacket, can you promise you won't work against us or give away anything we've said? No hedging. Yes or no?'

I gave him scowl for scowl. 'How do I know what's going to happen after this tour?' I asked. 'What do I do if a Prowler picks me up and asks me questions under another lie-box jacket? Remember, none of this is my idea. You people gave me a rough time. I didn't like it. Your goals aren't my goals. You want me to say I'll die a martyr's death for you?'

He searched my face with a steady gaze. In a gentle voice he said, 'Men do give their word, Rohan. Even if they don't always agree with the cause, they might value the keeping of the word. Some men.'

'Not me,' I said.

He looked at the jumping dials. 'All we want,' he said, 'is free elections back again. Our own choice of our own government. Does that sound worth having?'

I shrugged under the cold, smooth jacket. 'You're a Jeffersonian. Advanced thinkers go along with Hamilton where I come from. He's just as good an American and a lot more realistic. He believed in a lifetime President and Congress, just like what we've got now. I'm not sure I care much for representative government, mister. Under any rule the guy who has what it takes rises to the top. The rest – well, they won't amount to much under any system. That's the way I feel about it, so now you know.' I looked at the steady needles. 'You wanted the truth. That's it. You know what I can and can't do for you. I'd lie if I could. I've got to make a success of my job. Until it's done I'm your man. After that I'm my own man again.'

Nobody spoke for a while. Then Harris said briskly, 'Well, you steal the 'hopper for us and we'll know we can trust you. Up to a point, anyhow. We'll get word to you. Meanwhile you can go ahead with your show.'

I looked from face to face. 'I will. I don't understand just what's going on here. I know there's more in it than meets the eye. A lot's going on that – just eludes me. Anybody want to say anything?' I let my gaze travel from face to face. No answers showed anywhere. I sighed. 'Okay. This is Tuesday. We open here in town, at the corner of Main Street and the square, on Saturday night. Now let me out of this straitjacket, will you? I've got a lot of work to do between now and Saturday.'

CHAPTER X

I sat on the rail beside the broad black highway watching the trucks go by and waiting for Guthrie. Between trucks it was very still up here. The wind had a bland, sweet fragrance and the day balanced straight overhead in a flawless sky, just on the turn, not quite ready yet to wing over toward afternoon. High up in it a white gull wheeled, and I remembered with a little surprise that the ocean lay deep blue, deep-breathing, just beyond the mountains.

I chewed a yellow wild mustard head, liking the pungent burning taste, and wondered what was going to become of Howard Rohan. I thought of the young doctor's bright, expectant gaze and the way her body curved from rich fullness down to a narrow waist. I thought of Cressy. Imperceptibly in the last half hour the world had turned real around me again. The sunlight was luminous, not brass. I and the day and world were all alive. That oppression of the spirit had only drawn back to wait. It would come again. And now that my mind wasn't focused hard on any one thing, the desire for alcohol floated to the top, a physical need and a longing for the spiritual solace that only indifference can give. But for now the world was real and I was more than sorry.

And what about Howard Rohan? What about the dream that could hardly have been a dream? And the rebels – what was I going to do about them? I could play along. Maybe I would report to Ted Nye when I'd found out enough. Something told me I'd better not notify him until I did have information to balance against what I'd spilled. There was a chalk line to walk and I'd better not fall off on either side. Had I wrecked the whole theater project in California by talking too much? I doubted it. Nobody had been very much surprised at my big news. I thought about that, getting nowhere.

I thought about Comus, vast and rigid, humming at my feet in singing power lines that knit the nation tight. How curious to know that all around me in the mountains, maybe watching me now from the high wild mustard, were people who had taken up arms for the first time in almost a whole generation. People who had to stand ready at a moment's notice to grab their guns, black their faces, and stand up to whatever might happen. It seemed wild and unreal and in a way romantic, like a movie. Life isn't like that here under Comus. People die of old age or accident or disease. Not in battle.

It gave me a shaken feeling inside. And yet – I liked it. I felt fresh and alert in a new way. The world had clearer colors and sweeter smells and purer sounds than before. The smell of trouble in the air made everything tense, and I found myself liking the newness of it.

I wondered – oh, the hell with wondering. *Stop thinking, Rohan.* I looked up into the dizzy depths of the sky. My mind took two or three random swings and then circled back, as always, to Miranda. The restless ghost that would never leave me because somehow, somehow, it was my fault she died. Because of what I'd done or hadn't done and would never know. I thought large, formless thoughts. *Miranda, wherever you are... If you are...*

The big emptiness and the sweet bland wind and the memory of Miranda. My mind balanced away up over me with the balancing afternoon and the gull that could see the ocean from where it floated. Lazily through my thoughts went plans about the play. Rehearsals. The deep silence of the redwoods. Cressy Kellogg's face. Now and then a truck went by with a boom. Sometimes the drivers waved at me. Sometimes I waved back.

Guthrie was late. It seemed there'd been some excitement at camp. One of the gigantic transport trucks with a load of lettuce had turned over and caught fire on the road just above the grove. The troupe had had to swarm up and help pull the driver out before the thing exploded. Big excitement.

'Maybe we'll get some local publicity out of it,' I said, settling myself into the seat, favoring my bruised side. The doctor had sprayed me with germicide and given me some pills to deaden the ache, but I still knew I'd been in a fight.

'We're set to open in San Andreas on Saturday,' I told Guthrie. He gave me a sharp look.

'So. How'd you work that?'

'Fast talk to the right people. Your boy Swann just didn't have the right approach.'

'Mr Nye may want a report on how you did it,' Guthrie said. Rather belatedly he added, 'Good work, Mr Rohan.'

I nodded at him. 'One thing,' I said. 'I thought I saw that girl Cressy in town today. What do you know about her?'

'Why?'

'No reason. I just wonder why she wanders around town when she's supposed to be in camp working on her part.'

Guthrie looked at me, started to speak, stopped himself. Finally he said in a rather strained voice, 'She's a nice girl, Mr Rohan. A very nice girl. We all like her.'

'Glad to hear it,' I said. 'But—'

'If she was in town she had good reasons,' Guthrie told me, still stiffly. 'She's a very nice girl. I hope you won't—' He stopped. I looked at him and laughed.

'Nice girls are perfectly safe around Rohan,' I said. 'What's the matter, you think I take *droit du seigneur* over my troupes?'

'What?' he asked.

I laughed again, flushed a little and looked straight ahead. 'She's a very nice girl,' he repeated stubbornly, as if I'd doubted it.

The wrecked behemoth lay across two lanes of the highway just above camp, still smoking. Lettuces paved the road and two smaller trucks were loading up with salvage. The men working them looked grim. I wanted to ask if this had been sabotage by the rebels, but nobody seemed very talkative and it didn't seem to matter much anyhow.

Roy Copley was hunched over his script spread out on one of the tables. He looked up and scowled, ostentatiously nursing his bandaged hand. I scowled back. I didn't like him much, but he was a good choice for the juvenile lead. He had the kind of good looks that keep the illusion of youth for a long time. Maybe he had that kind of personality, too. An essential boyishness in his face and his motions made you feel he'd never quite accepted the responsibility of growing up.

Polly bent her glistening red head over a salvage lettuce she was washing under the faucet. She shook the water off in a shining shower, not much caring if some of it fell on me. She looked haggard under the greenish light under the trees. It occurred to me that Roy might not actually be as much younger than his wife as I'd thought. She could have aged more than he. She had those kind of features. For an actress this is a serious problem. I could see why she seemed to be in a temper most of the time. I didn't have to like her, but I thought I could understand her. Partly, anyhow.

'You look terrible,' she told me with satisfaction.

'I feel fine,' I said. 'Everything's set in San Andreas. We open Saturday.'

'How do we know?' She sounded quarrelsome. 'You don't look so good to me.'

'What would I gain by lying, for God's sake?' I asked. 'We've got about three weeks' work to do in three days, so I want to start rehearsals in about half an hour. Where's Cressy?'

Polly gestured toward the river. 'Swimming.'

Guthrie watched me with some anxiety as I walked across the clearing toward the river path, but he didn't say anything. I started downhill, my jaw set and my mind set with it. I'd changed a good deal since yesterday. Since this morning. I couldn't have said how I'd changed, but the difference was there inside. I wanted to test my own reactions. I wanted to look straight at Cressy. I wanted to talk to her. Maybe I was beginning to feel that it was possible to exorcise ghosts.

I found I was whistling between my teeth as I went down the steep path that doubled back and forth on itself on the way to the river. *'Now may all clouds of ... sorrow depart ... Beautiful dreamer, wake unto me.'*

The neat, cleft tracks of deer marked the powdered dust, and a chipmunk whisking across the path paused for a moment to defy me at one bend, sitting upright and chirring at me, his shoulders heaving convulsively at every chirr. Like a rebel defying Comus, I thought. Or maybe not. That depended on the Anti-Com, whatever it was worth.

I heard water splashing and saw through trees the level surface of a pool where the river widened. I called, 'Cressy?' and heard her voice saying, 'Here I am,' with that hollowness voices have sounding over water. I walked out from the trees over the pebbly verge. The broad brown pool was green in the shadows, with ripples running nervously all over its surface. Cressy stood – or was she sitting? – up to her shoulders in the water. Her shining hair was knotted on top of her head and she seemed to have no body beneath the surface, only the reflection of the same head and shoulders upside down in the pool, like a playing-card queen.

I made myself look directly at her. Miranda's pale copy, I thought. Living flesh and living bone, a girl with her own life to get through, her own problems to solve. Nothing to do with me. Just raw material I had to weld into the cast and use to make a play from. I could look at her and not feel much hurt. She wasn't even so very like Miranda, when you come right down to it.

'What were you doing in town today?' I asked her flatly.

She started to say, 'Isn't that my business?'

'Damn it, answer me!' I said. 'Why were you there?'

She flushed a little and moved uneasily in the water, the ripples she made breaking up the inverted reflections. With some dignity she said, 'This job means a lot to me, Mr Rohan. It does to all of us. We don't want to get lynched, but we don't want to give up the tour either, unless we have to. I've got – well, acquainted with a few people since we got here. I wanted to do some checking up on my own.'

'You thought I couldn't handle things?'

'Paul Swann muffed it,' she said. 'How did I know?'

'Why didn't you get a permit for the troupe yourself?' I asked. 'You don't seem to have any trouble in San Andreas. I thought you were all so scared you wanted to disband. It doesn't add up.'

She shrugged in the water, making her reflection shudder. 'Politics,' she said. 'Rebel politics – that's where the trouble is. I hear you found that out this morning. I hear you worked it out fine. I'm not asking any questions. I just know it was a problem for you and the local big shots, not me. I had that made perfectly clear.'

'By whom?'

She gave me a fleeting smile. 'Some of my local friends. I get around. I've had a couple of dates with a Comus trucker up at the restaurant. I went to a dance with a rancher from San Andreas, the same one who bought me lunch today. Oh, I hear most of the talk that's going around. As long as I'm with the local boys I'm safe enough. But getting up on the stage without a permit would be something else again. Sure we were scared. We had a right to be.'

'Are you scared now?'

'I hear you got to the right people. It's okay now.'

'You might tell Polly,' I said. 'She's not so sure.'

'Polly,' she said delicately, pursing her lips.

That reminded me. I kicked a pebble into the water and scowled. 'I don't want any trouble in this cast. Suppose you stay away from Roy Copley. Understand?'

She gave me a flat-eyed look. 'I mean it,' I said. 'You could be a trouble center in this troupe, and I don't want trouble. I don't want Polly throwing boiling coffee in your face someday when she catches you with Roy. You've even got Guthrie worried for fear I'll make a pass at you. I don't want him missing his cues because he's trying to save you from corruption. You stick to your farmers and truck drivers and we'll all get along fine.'

She met my eye with a sudden, dimpling flicker of humor that vanished almost instantly, like a breeze running over water. 'We'll get along. We're pretty good, really. We may surprise you.'

I gave her a measuring look. 'What's your background?' I asked. 'Where are you from?'

'Chicago Area. I've done a lot of stock playing and that's about it. Maybe you know. It's hard to get past a certain point. What I really want is a work card for Hollywood. Without one I haven't a chance to get very far. I've made two big plays for a card. No luck so far.' She smiled at me. 'When Comus offered this part I held out for a Hollywood card and they promised me one. If we finish this run.'

'We'll finish it,' I said automatically. She gave me the bright, compliant glance of the opportunist. I could almost see the thought go through her head that I had been a big name once and might easily be again. She'd be happy to play along with me about as far as I cared to go if she could think there was much in it for her. I know that 'I want to be a star' look pretty well. I looked at her meditatively. 'Cressy, I want to ask you a question. Have you got a bathing suit on?'

She met my eyes gravely. A ripple of the quick, shadowy amusement crossed her face fleetingly. She shook her head.

I nodded. 'That's what I thought.' I stood there looking down at her face and the smooth wet shoulders and their reflections on the water. The murmuring silences of the redwoods and the river closed us in together. Half my mind felt as buoyant as a balloon as I stood there in the stillness looking down. But the other half of my mind was not my own. And as long as I lay down every night and woke every morning with Miranda still beside me, how could I let myself think of Cressy or anyone at all?

After a long pause Cressy said, 'Well?'

I shook my head. 'We start rehearsals in about twenty minutes. There's a lot of work to do. You'd better come up as quickly as you can. We'll be waiting for you.' And I turned away.

CHAPTER XI

The sun slanted at an angle between the trees as we laid out our stage among the redwoods. In the dusty carpet of pine needles we paced off a city street. Guthrie measured the shape and length of the bleachers our audience would sit in. They closed off opposite ends of the stage. The other two sides would be the business buildings that lined the street. We scratched out the pavement areas and stuck dead branches upright to mark doors and windows. And that was our stage.

I would have liked a leisurely reading rehearsal, with all of us sitting around discussing the play, working out characterizations, getting acquainted. I would have liked a lot of things, including more time. Even though all of us had sleep-learned our lines, the hardest part of the job was still to do, and we had a fantastically short time to do it in.

The cast didn't like me. It didn't matter much. I made myself ignore everything in the world outside the job at hand. I ignored the time pressure, and how much I wanted a drink, and what I had or hadn't let myself in for with the rebels. Nothing mattered now except getting on with the play.

We walked through it fast once, blocking in the action and getting a general idea of the stage business each of the actors had worked out for his own part. We found out where these conflicted. We found out how terrible things looked. They always do, at first. We ran into each other at entrances, exits, and crossing. We found we didn't have either time or space to make the proper crosses and still get the lines said. We discovered long dead stretches that looked hopeless to fill up with any sort of stage business. At one point we all piled up together in one corner of the stage, everybody having to be on the same spot at the same time to make any sense of the scene. It didn't look as if anybody on God's earth could make a play out of this script and this cast.

Working on an arena stage like this, with the audience on two sides, made it a lot harder than it really needed to be, on top of everything else. On a normal stage you start all your crosses with the upstage foot to keep your body turned toward the audience, but when there are people on two sides, how are you going to work out your movements to face both ways? All you can do is keep moving. When we had floundered through the last scene I said dispiritedly, 'All right, take ten,' and walked over to Guthrie, sucking his pipe beside the fire.

'Is there any good reason,' I asked, 'why we can't hire a hall and put this thing on the easy way? None of us knows enough about circle staging to keep from falling over our own feet. Even if we had time enough for rehearsals, we'd still—'

'Sorry, Mr Rohan. Orders are orders.'

'Where are you going to get the bleachers?'

Guthrie nodded toward his truck. 'In there. I've got light-weight risers and benches enough to seat more than we'll probably draw.'

'In there?' It was incredulous. 'I don't believe it.'

'Come and see.' I think he was proud of the packing Comus had done for us. He got up a little stiffly (I remembered with some guilt that he'd taken a licking himself in San Andreas today) and threw open the back door of the sound truck.

It was like looking into the belly of the whale. So many visceral-looking coils and compact masses of cables. So many folded steel beams and benches all cramped tight into fetal positions like the unborn young of the truck. There was a clear space about three feet wide and less than six feet high running down the middle of the visceral cavity, with a panel board and a bench along one side of it, and at the end a blind television screen with very technical-looking controls all around it. It occurred to me that I could probably talk to Ted Nye any time I wanted simply by stepping into the truck and turning the right knobs.

It also occurred to me that if there was any covert purpose behind our tour of California some of the answers to what it was probably lay right under my nose here, if I had the training to see them, which I hadn't. Anybody who stood where I stood now and leaned forward like this – I leaned, and something caught in the door hinge tickled my cheek. I brushed at it absently, and found I had a strand of raveling brown wool between my fingers. Guthrie gave me a sharp glance over his shoulder.

'What's that?'

'Nothing,' I said. 'A pine needle. Could you get New York on that television set?'

But I didn't listen to his answer. I'd covered up the ravel of brown wool without conscious thought, instinct moving faster than reason. But reason caught up fast. I'd seen brown wool today – where? A sweater with a torn place at the cuff. On one of the men at the Medical Building, leaning over the lie box while my truths and falsehoods flowed out on the moving tape. The man who had spoken of word-keeping and Jeffersonian political philosophy. So maybe somebody *had* leaned here and looked, and probably seen and understood a lot more than I did. When? After my interview, while I sat waiting by the highway with the afternoon turning slowly overhead.

Suddenly I knew why that truck of lettuce had overturned and caught fire just when and where it did. I saw the whole thing taking place a long way off, puppet-sized, planned and executed to get Guthrie away from his sound truck just long enough for an expert to probe its secrets. They were fast, these rebels. Fast and flexible in their thinking.

I could be wrong, of course. It was a lot to build on one ravel of brown wool. But I knew I wasn't wrong. And I knew that they knew now whatever there was to be learned about the belly of the metal whale. Maybe, in their own good time, they'd let me in on the secret.

'So you see, Mr Rohan,' Guthrie was saying, 'there's a

complete setup here. And we have good raisons for everything we do this trip.'

I said, 'All right. We do it the hard way.' And turned back to the camp.

I whistled for attention and gathered the cast together around the fire. 'We'll talk about the play a little bit,' I said. 'Then we'll break for supper. And from then on in until we fall flat we'll rehearse. Okay? Sit down, then; and get comfortable. Now—'

I told them what I thought about the play. What we were trying to get at in it, how it seemed to me the moods built and changed, where the main conflict points were and how we built up to them. I asked for comments and got them. We talked over the characters and how they fitted the theme and how they lined up against each other. I complimented them on their interpretations, and meant it. They were all good, competent actors with enough experience behind them to make me hope we might really work this thing out by Saturday after all.

We seemed to me in pretty smooth accord when we broke up for supper. But the minute the meeting ended the freeze-out set in again. The cast went to its meal around the cook-stove, working together to get it ready, turning collective backs on me. All of them. I walked up to the restaurant and ate in morose solitude, thinking about the play and making notes.

When we assembled again the darkness had come on and the fire was sending up its streamers of red and gold sparks. The air smelled exhilaratingly of woodsmoke and pine. In the underlighting of the fire, the redwoods leaned together overhead, their enormous floating continents of foliage swaying silently. At the very top of the well a few stars burned. One of them winked red and blue and white in rapid, endless succession. I could see a strip of the Milky Way, which I had almost forgotten was up there in the sky. I looked at the winking star. Red, white, blue. The rebels' star, I thought. And then, with a silent laugh, Charlie Starr.

Guthrie had strung one glaring incandescent lantern on a

rope above the stage. We went to work in a tent of white light whose edges swayed soundlessly around us when the wind blew.

We walked through the play once fast, script in hand. Everybody but me knew his speeches by now, and I was learning rapidly. On this it didn't matter. Each of us read his first few words and then gabbled a quick blah-blah-blah until the last few, speaking only the cue words clearly. It was still rough, but already it began to take shape. We didn't fall over each other quite so much and we began to grasp the necessities of playing to two audiences at once. Possibilities opened up we hadn't thought of at first. It went pretty well, considering.

We took another break. The rebels' star had slid perceptibly down the sky and my scrapes and bruises were stiffening in the chilly air. I borrowed a sweater from Guthrie and whistled up the cast.

'All right, now let's take it through from the start. On stage for Eleven – Eileen, Pod. Ready?'

Eleven means Act One, Scene One. Eileen Henken put down her coffee cup and trotted briskly to her station between two upright twigs in the door of what would, we hope, be a hotel when we got to San Andreas. Pod shuffled calmly after her and sat down on what would be a curb, going through the motions of a whittler without a knife or wood.

'Dad!' Eileen called loud and clear. 'Dad, you hear me? With all these people in town tonight, seems like you'd find something better to do than sit here whittling.'

'Now, Mother' – Pod whittled imperturbably – 'you'd holler a lot louder if I was in—' He glanced at me.

'It's the Irish Rose in San Andreas,' I supplied.

'If I was in the Irish Rose tonight,' he went on, and then waited, making elaborate play out of holding up his unseen knife and thumbing the blade to fill in the pause for laughter that was sure to follow a local reference.

And so it went.

It was a good play for its purpose, which seemed as nearly as I could judge to be simply pure entertainment plus extreme realism and immediacy. It all took place within the most rigid

92

set of unities I ever saw worked out. (And that made me think a little of Comus, rigid and functional.) All the action happened right out there in the street at the heart of any town. It happened within a few hours of one evening, and it referred freely to local places, current politics, the troubles of the time. But it wasn't about politics at all. At least, not on the surface.

I'd be willing to bet a lot of the less sophisticated people in the audience went home afterward convinced all this had actually happened just as it seemed to. That some local girl they didn't quite recognize had really made a date to meet a city slicker (me) and got into serious disagreements with her local lover and her grandparents about it. Polly as a farcical Comus cop had a song toward the end of the play, and right afterward Roy and I put on a fight. And it all worked out to a happy ending in about an hour's playing time.

The lines were fast and packed, and though for convenience the play had been broken down into acts and scenes, it had to be played with no real breaks at all, like an Elizabethan play. We had no curtains, of course, and we couldn't darken the stage, so it had to be that way. But the playwright had taken advantage of the handicap and made it into a virtue. The thing was going to put over a very strong effect of happening spontaneously before your eyes. If we got it into shape in time, of course.

You learn a lot about people after you've been through a play with them a time or two. I'd thought rather enviously when I first saw them what a compact in-group this seemed. I should have known better. There's no such thing as a theatrical troupe without conflicts.

I hadn't realized, for instance, how heavily Roy Copley depended on his wife until I put him through his first scenes. He had a lot of boyish charm and he projected the impact of it quite well, but what it sprang from was the freshness and ease of man who has never had to make a decision in his life. Polly carried his burdens for him, and the result was the curious effect of a man not quite present before us. He was quick enough, he gave his part a good, well-thought-out

93

interpretation, picked up his cues promptly. But I never had the feeling Roy Copley was there before me.

Eileen Henken was surprising. Strong and hostile tensions centered around her all the time she was on stage with anyone else. I found out why right away. She was the most expert scene stealer I ever saw. She didn't give a damn about the rest of the cast, the play, anything I said to her. All she wanted was to be the center of attention on stage. Off it she was as sweet and mild an old lady as you could hope to find, on stage a demon.

She knew every trick in the book, and believe me, it's hard to upstage another actor when the audience is on two sides of you at once. The actor you maneuver with his back to the audience on one side will be facing them on the other. But I knew that five minutes after the play started Eileen would know instinctively where the dead areas in the audience were and get her rivals facing that way with a minimum of effort.

She knew how to throw unexpected changes in stress into her lines so the other player's answers would sound flat. She knew how to start a speech on a key just high enough to force the other actor to flat his voice into a squawk if he tried to top her. Twice she stole the key word out of somebody else's line and left him dangling. The first time I thought it was an accident. There was a scene in which Roy played up to Polly in the hope of rousing the ingénue's jealousy. Eileen was supposed to ask him if he liked his coffee hot, and he, with a roll of the eye at Polly's Comus coat, answered, '*Red-hot.*' It was amusing the way he did it and would certainly draw a laugh from most audiences. But Eileen Henken asked innocently, 'How do you like your coffee – red-hot?' And Roy stood there without an answer.

If I thought it was an accident, Polly didn't. She was sewing a button on the red coat as she sat beside me, and when Roy's voice failed to come in on the right beat she looked up sharply, realized what had happened, and jumped to her feet, shouting, 'Damn you, Eileen Henken, if you pull that once more I'll – I'll kick your playbox in!'

Eileen apologized, very mild and sweet. Polly sat down again and stabbed the button's eye ferociously. 'Just watch it,' she muttered. 'I warned you.'

Guthrie held the prompt book for us, and he seemed to be paying abnormally close attention to the timing of some of the lines, entering the exact second of a speech every time we went through the scene. I thought of asking him why, then thought again. I knew it wouldn't get me anywhere. So far we hadn't openly clashed. Ostensibly he was a sort of second-class citizen of the troupe, deliberately making and keeping himself that way. If he defied me, people would start to wonder.

I watched Cressy make delicate byplay with a redwood, gazing up at it reproachfully and saying, 'I wasn't out of your sight ten minutes, and now you start yelling as if you owned me.' She paused as if listening to what she had just said, then backtracked and began again. 'I wasn't out of your sight *ten minutes*—' After that she tried, 'I wasn't out of your *sight* ten minutes—' Then she gave the redwood a little stroke, shoulder-high, very delicately and placatingly, and looked down at her own thrust-out toe as if she felt suddenly shy.

She was good. She had subtlety and imagination, and that inner authority over a scene that only good actors have. I felt suddenly that I wanted to see her make her entrance into a scene perfectly paced for her, and I yelled at Roy to pick up his cues faster. He said, 'All right, let's go back to "Have you seen Susan anywhere, I can't find her." ' I said okay, and everybody on stage paused for a moment, looked a little unfocused as they cast themselves back in time about a minute and a half, and then began the scene from 'Have you seen Susan'.

It was a pleasure to watch her go on.

But watching carried me back. I thought of the stage of the Raleigh Theater at a point in rehearsals like this, everybody working hard against time. I wondered who was directing there now. Whoever it was, I knew what he'd be seeing. The actors going doggedly through their lines while the stage sets went up around them, the sound of sawing and hammering sometimes drowning out the speeches. Nobody paying any attention to any job but his own. Maybe the lights being tested, so the stage was flooded with warm sunshine and darkened with dramatic suddenness as if some tremendous event were about to happen. Out of the darkness the voice of the actors would be going imperturbably on. That sense of complex forces working all together – the electricians and carpenters, the stage manager, the set and costume designers, the elaborate production schedules set up – I wondered why I didn't miss them more.

And then I thought, This is how it all started, a long time ago, little groups of people rehearsing simple plays outdoors, under the trees. Time had set the stage for us, reared the redwoods, ignited the stars. There was a lot to be said, I thought, for preparing a play in a forest clearing, with a lantern's glare hollowing out a stage for us under the redwoods. If you could forget about the unknown elements outside, a countryside seething on the very brink of explosion.

The part of my mind that had been left on guard, watching the stage, rang an alarm bell. I looked. Cressy and Roy stood facing each other, staring expectantly, mouths slightly open, not speaking. As I watched they both began to giggle foolishly, leaning their foreheads together. Somebody had forgotten his lines. Probably Roy. I knew it a moment later when Cressy said, 'You aren't fooling *me* a minute—' in an undertone full of laughter.

'You aren't fooling *me* a minute, Susan Jones,' Roy picked it up. And I saw suddenly what should have been obvious from the start. I saw at least a part of what was the matter with him. I saw it in the way he looked at her, the way his hand hesitated before it received hers, the way his mind went blank when she came on stage.

If it was news to me, it was an old story to his wife.

'Just keep your mouth shut, Cressy,' Polly said in a weary voice. 'Don't prompt him. He knows his lines, if you'll give him half a chance.'

'Mr Rohan,' Guthrie said behind me, 'could you spare a few minutes?'

I turned around and he nodded toward the sound truck. Mystified, I got up. The voices on stage dropped as I whistled sharply. 'Go back to Cressy's entrance and run through it again,' I said. 'I'll be back in a minute. Keep it moving.'

Guthrie opened the truck door just far enough for one man to slip in. 'Somebody wants to see you,' he said mysteriously. 'Go on in.'

The inside of the truck looked a lot bigger now. That was because a door seemed to have opened at the far end, and beyond it was a familiar room with moving murals on the walls. Ted Nye looked up from his desk and smiled at me. Above him in the round cage the round yellow canary sat asleep, its naked eyelids folded shut and bulging.

'Hello, Howard,' Nye said casually. 'How's it going?'

I gave myself a quick, violent shake, trying to pull the universe into shape around me. Just in time I stopped myself from saying to the TV screen, 'How did *you* get here?'

He laughed at the look on my face. Then he took a closer look and said, 'What's happened to you, Howard? Somebody drag you through a knothole?'

'Very funny,' I told him. 'It should happen to you sometime. Why didn't you tell me I was walking into a revolution?'

'Oh, it isn't that bad,' he said comfortably. 'I hear you're doing a fine job. How does it feel to be back in harness?'

It seemed to me he was watching me very closely. I said, 'Good. I like it. Why?'

He looked a little offended. 'No reason. I'm just about to knock off. Thought I'd check up on you first. I'm just wondering if you could step up your schedule a little bit. Put on two shows a day, maybe.'

I said 'Well, I – sure, I suppose we could. We open Saturday. I might—'

'That's another thing.' He bit his thumbnail, a familiar gesture that had always meant he was under more tension than he cared to have you know. 'Could you step up the time a little, too? Open on Friday, say?'

I started to explode.

'All right, all right!' He made soothing motions with both hands. 'Try for Friday, Howard. It's important. I've got my reasons. Later on I'll tell you all about it.' He sighed, and his narrow shoulders sagged. He looked like death, I thought. More like death than Raleigh himself, perhaps, who must be very near to it now, or this hurry-up interview wouldn't be happening.

I said with resignation, 'Oh, sure, we'll open right now if you say so. Who needs rehearsals?'

'It means a lot to me, Howard,' he said, watching me anxiously. 'If anybody can do it, you can. I know that.'

I said, 'I'll try.'

'Howard—' He hesitated. 'Is everything all right?'

A sudden alarm bell began clanging noisily in my mind. I thought, He's heard about what happened today. He's got pipelines to the Freedom Committee, or maybe the Committee itself was only a test to see if I'd – but, no, that was too complicated to follow up. I thought, He didn't take five minutes out of a busy day spent running the United States just to ask how I feel. Or did he? I looked at the sad little wizened face and thought, Maybe he's a lonelier little guy than I ever realized. After all, we've been friends for a good many years now, nearly half our lives.

There wasn't time to think things out and draw conclusions. I had to turn everything over to instinct. Instinct kept my face perfectly straight as I said, 'Thanks, Ted, everything's fine.'

He searched my eyes with his. Then he wiped his hand across his face like a man in the last stage of exhaustion. 'Well, do your best, Howard. I'll see you again in a day or two. Good luck.'

'Okay,' I said. 'Good night, Ted.'

The door into New York shrank to a shining sliver and vibrated into nothing. Nye and his office and his slumbering canary shot backward into space three thousand miles and I almost felt the twang as the thread snapped that had linked us together.

Then for a long moment I sat there and shook. Had I made the worst mistake of my life in not telling him everything? Or had I done the smartest possible thing? Or did it make any difference at all?

After a while I got up wearily and went out into the lantern-lit room under the redwoods and the play that meant so much to so many people, though I didn't know how or why.

We rehearsed until midnight. About one o'clock we fell into our bunks, dead-tired but too keyed-up to sleep at first. Outside the vast quiet of the night lay ready to receive us, but it was hard to slip the bonds and glide out into that dreaming oblivion. Pod Henken and Roy talked quietly now and then, and I heard voices sounding desultorily from the women's truck, but Guthrie and I lay silent, thinking our private thoughts. I wondered about his. An old Comus man, slowed by the inevitable creep of calcium in the joints, the inevitable thickening of the arteries – what would he think about in a country rioting with guerrilla war?

After a while I got out my bottle and took several noisy, defiant swigs, not offering any around the bunks. I wondered if Guthrie was thinking of Cressy. The very nice girl. I had seen him watch her under his grizzled brows as he bent over the prompt book. I hadn't figured him out yet. Anyhow, I knew Roy would be thinking of her. And Rohan?

No, I thought of Nye instead, lying uneasily on the far side of the big upward curve of the continent. I thought of Raleigh, lying in some impressive bed and hardly breathing. I thought of how much depended on just when the life flickering in him finally blew out. And for a moment it seemed to me that in the dark around us as we lay on the verge of sleep I could feel the whole state humming with secret motion. Like some gigantic living body striving to assemble inside itself the mechanism of the Anti-Com, rushing the separate parts as they were completed toward some private center deep inside itself, knitting them barely into a whole that might or might not reach viability in time.

I began to feel drowsy. A truck went by on the highway with a noise like thunder, or artillery in the distance. It didn't annoy

99

me. It was Comus, and a sound of reassurance in the night. I thought of Cressy lying warm in her bunk, the lashes gentle on her cheeks.

I thought of Miranda and then took another drink and stopped thinking at all.

CHAPTER XII

Morning breakfast at the truckers' restaurant, since nobody invited me to join the yawning little group around the cook fire. I didn't care. It was good to walk into that warm, smoky little segment of Comus again, feeling security fold around me, knowing that, no matter what rioting swept the state outside, in here Comus ruled calm and strong.

And there had been rioting. The truck drivers were getting to know my face by now and the talk flowed a little more freely when I was there. I heard about a raid on Carson City in which a rebel leader had been seized and the rebels fired the town to drive the Comus forces off. What else besides their captured leader they had been trying to protect by such drastic action was speculated on at great length.

Somebody down the counter from me, hunched over bacon and eggs, said he heard the reb forces weren't eating so good to the northeast of here, and a grimy-faced driver with a bandaged jaw said, 'Looters are out again in Paradise Valley. They scare even the rebs.'

I remembered the notice I'd seen posted in San Andreas on the subject. It scared me, too. And if any of my troupe got wind of it, I probably wouldn't have any troupe left.

When I got back to the campsite Roy was walking up and down the clearing muttering his lines now loudly and now in a hissing whisper, and Polly, hanging a skillet on a nail in the camp table, straightened to look at me challengingly.

'I hear there are looters out,' she said. 'Really bad ones,

deserters from both sides. Maybe we ought to call the whole thing off.'

'You can hear anything,' I said. 'We'll start with Thirteen then, and let's pick up our cues tighter right from the start. There's been a slight change. We open on Friday night, not Saturday. All right, cast on stage.'

And in the slanting morning light, in the deep silence of the trees, we pantomimed a city square again and endlessly went over the little episode that had never really happened, but would happen over and over again. Roy and I practiced our fist-fight scene in slow motion, rehearsing the action like a ballet, until it began to look spontaneous. If he was reminded of our clash on first meeting, he didn't show it. His early hostility was gone now and he had retreated to his own little detached existence peopled only by himself and perhaps Cressy, and perhaps a lot of beautiful, impossible dreams. Having spent a good deal of time in a private room of my own, I ought to be the last to object.

In the noon break Guthrie, after spending a good deal of time in his electronic cubbyhole with the door shut, came out and silently moved each of the trucks up to the paved area back of the restaurant, parking them close together. When Pod Henken asked why, he said there was news on the air of a rainstorm moving in from the Pacific and he didn't trust this unpaved ground if it got wet. Polly asked if it wouldn't be noisy up there, and Guthrie said no, the drivers had to sleep too, and I said by then we'd all be too tired to care.

We worked hard all that day and far into the evening. By now any newness had worn off and the job was sheer drudgery, rehearsing and rehearsing every motion and inflection until it becomes first stiff, then mechanical, and finally acquires that strange spontaneity that looks as if no one on earth has ever made quite this gesture or spoken this phrase before.

The personalities of the characters in the play were emerging too, and a new set of qualities began to superimpose themselves over the cast, so that I came to feel Susan Jones was someone I knew better than I knew Cressy Kellogg. And I myself was somebody else entirely, a man who had never worked in an agri-team or seen his name on Broadway or even heard the name of Miranda. A tenuous city square took shape around us, blotting out the redwood holes. Time became a fluid and a solid, something we could stop or run backward at will, and the lines of the play were the only words man had ever spoken on earth. Even when we weren't rehearsing I found myself listening critically to Polly saying, 'Pass the coffee,' or Guthrie asking after a missing hammer, wanting to try a different emphasis and wondering just where this fitted into the play.

Toward evening we were all automatons, moving stiffly through terribly familiar actions, following grooves our rehearsed crossings had worn in the pine needles and feeling grooves in our minds. Coldly, hating each other, we embraced, shook hands, exchanged light banter. Without feeling, we cursed each other, and wearily Roy and I balanced through the motions of our fight, too tired even for enmity.

We had a little brush with Guthrie over the fight. I had to get my hand raised, palm out, at the level of my chin just in time for Roy's fist to smack loudly into it. Timed right, it looks and sounds exactly like a crack on the jaw. But we had trouble with the timing. One way to handle this is to set up a count.

'We can give you a line like, "Why you—"' I said to Roy. 'That gives us a count of three, and right after the "you" my hand will be ready.'

We tried it and it worked fine. But then Guthrie looked out of his truck like a cuckoo popping from a clock on the very stroke of something new.

'Sorry, Mr Rohan,' he said, 'that throws my timing off. The orders are no changes in the script. No changes at all.'

So we cut it out again.

It was a very long day. By eleven nothing I heard or did made any sense to me, and the cast was staggering when they walked. The play looked hopelessly bad and we were all depressed and irritable. I called a halt in a hoarse voice and we moved away from the grooved stage, nobody looking at anybody else.

At this point Guthrie surprised us by bringing out a bottle of scotch and a set of folding cups and pouring drinks all round. When he came to me the bottle ran dry and he got out a fresh one. He poured his own last of all and we drank numbly, and numbly separated and dropped into our bunks.

I noticed only dimly that Guthrie wasn't in his. The trucks going by on the highway made booming noises in the night, crickets sang shrilly in the silences between, and the world faded out around me in a welter of over-rehearsed lines and motions. I ceased to exist.

CHAPTER XIII

Somebody was pulling cautiously at my foot. I woke with great reluctance. Blue moonlight, artificial as a stage set, fell through the open door upon Guthrie's face bending over me. He made shushing motions with one hand and beckoning ones with the other. I rolled over and groaned. He pulled my foot again. Too tired to be curious, I doubled up and got stiffly out of the bunk. The truck swayed under me but neither Pod nor Roy stirred. Wondering dimly what now, I stumbled out.

As my feet hit the ground, Guthrie smacked something hard, cold, and heavy into my hands. I looked down stupidly. It was a gun, ring-mouthed and dangerous-looking.

'A scatter-gun,' Guthrie said in a low voice. 'Ever use one?'

'Only impracticals, on the stage,' I said. 'What's going on?'

'Raiders,' he told me tersely. 'Maybe. If we're lucky they'll miss us. Even if they don't, maybe the cast will sleep through it. I gave them something in that scotch that ought to help. These scatter-guns are quiet. And you can't miss.'

I looked around, bewildered, not yet sure I was really awake. The station lay dark and still in the moonlight, but I saw now that a rough circle of trucks had been drawn up around it, nose to tail, like the covered wagon circles you see in films about the old West. Inside lay the station, several hedgehoppers quivering on bent legs, and our three valuable theater trucks with the sleeping cast oblivious inside. I heard footsteps grate on concrete, and two or three dark figures went by walking heavily, moonlight glinting on the long scatter-guns in their hands.

'Listen,' Guthrie said. I listened. Far off to the south a fusillade of distant firecrackers seemed to be going off. It burst out twice, and then was silent. 'A farmhouse, probably,' Guthrie said. 'This is a big gang, scattered out, working south. They won't attack fortified places, but I'd hate to be caught on a farm tonight.'

'How do you know about it?' I asked stupidly, hefting the shotgun and wondering if I could handle it. My heart had begun to pump and I knew I was scared.

'We've been getting reports since last night,' Guthrie said. 'We hoped they'd miss us, but a truck came in about ten minutes ago that saw some of them slipping through the woods this way. The main thing is not to make too much noise when we tackle them, or we'll have the whole gang down on us. Come on.'

'Where?' I followed him through the serene blue moonlight. 'What are we going to do?'

'Join the line-up. And pray' – he laughed in a low voice – 'that the cast doesn't find out. One look at these guys and you couldn't keep 'em in California if you chained 'em up.' There was an undernote of exhilaration in him, and I thought, This is what it must have been like when he was new in Comus and things happened fast. I wondered if he remembered tonight that he was past sixty.

A steel behemoth loomed up before us bathed in bland moonlight. Guthrie said, 'In here,' and we slipped between two trucks and saw the hillside slope away before us down toward the unseen river, shadows lying black and still and the moonlight slanting like smoke between the trees.

A big man in a cap and leather jacket crunched across the concrete behind us and paused to give us a measuring glance and say heavily, 'All set? Keep it quiet if you can. If we're lucky they won't even spot us. But if you do fire, don't miss. We don't want a lot of yelling and rifle shots.'

'Don't worry,' Guthrie said. The man grunted and moved off.

I looked out over the moonlight slope and felt the gun shake in my hands. I was scared, yes, but filled up with anticipation, the sense of something new and important happening for the first time in history. To me, anyhow. I told myself I would probably fire a gun at a man and kill him in the next few minutes. I didn't believe it, but my hands were cold and unsteady on the gun, and my hands felt convinced. They were ready, any time.

I'd seen the result when make-up men reproduce (just for a quick-flash at the audience, not too gruesome) what these scatter-guns can do. I didn't exactly believe that, either, and yet I had no reason to doubt it.

Nothing seemed real. It was a stage-set. The silence, the little patch of stars bleached by the strong moonlight, the muffled sounds of men around me, somebody coughing and smothering it, somebody clinking his gun against a truck and swearing – none of it was real. I heard a cricket's strong, measured spurts of sound and wondered what more I would hear out there. How would we know when they came?

And who were they? Followers of Charlie Starr? Men working on the same side I worked on? I wondered which side I really belonged with. Neither, maybe. Except that if Ted Nye loses I lose, so I guess I'm for Comus in the long run. A sudden sense of the vast power of Comus swept over me there in the dark, its immeasurable nerve nets and muscles and steel bones knitting the continent together. And I knew that no matter what I did or didn't do nothing could hurt Comus. Nothing could burst the net.

I was glad, and a little sorry.

Guthrie said, 'Listen. Hear that?'

A dry stick had snapped somewhere downhill in the dark beneath the trees. Another a little to the right. Two or three more to the left. A good many men were coming uphill toward us through the redwoods, spread far out, walking slowly. We were very silent now. Nobody coughed or stirred. We were a single encircling fortress of tensity and waiting, every sense strained toward the oncoming men. At that moment I had no awareness of myself as a separate thing at all. I was fully a part of Comus and the defenders of the station, and the fortress of tension we created around us in the night, a closed circle domed over with listening and watching.

Guthrie's voice was a breath in my ear. 'Down there – see?'

I couldn't see. Only a shadow that moved fast behind the trees and was gone. Then off to the left a hiss and a sighing cough burst out, and I saw a flash of bluish light and a man under the trees fell backward and thudded to the ground without a single sound except the sound of falling. The hiss and the cough was a scatter-gun in operation. I was abstractly surprised at how silent they were. They only cough and spit blue fire politely – and mince to shreds any surface they strike.

I found my own gun at my shoulder and my cold finger on the trigger. But I didn't see anything to shoot at. I had an instant's vision of Harris's round, balding face, the man in the torn brown sweater. Rebels, sure. But did I really want to mince them with a scatter-gun? Could I?

Somebody down the slope called a hoarse, low question. Somebody else answered uncertainly. Then a man broke cover and started up the hill, and Guthrie's gun beside me sighed and flashed blue fire, and the man's shout was cut off and smashed backward in his throat as he fell.

A rifle cracked among the trees and I heard something whine nasally past and strike fire upon the side of the truck next to me. The sound was like a truck backfiring down by the river and a bullet smacked loud on the resonant steel.

Instantly all along the row of trucks the hissing cough and the fans of blue flame sprang out as if the trucks were one long, segmented dragon wheezing and spitting fire. Guthrie glanced at me irritably, saying, 'Go on, shoot, shoot! Wipe them out fast! Sweep the hillside!'

I saw dark shapes drop and lie jerking a little on the slope. I saw the flash of gunfire down there and heard bullets whine. I wondered with some abstract chamber of the mind whether our troupe was still asleep back there, drugged with weariness and dope, thinking the rifle shots were trucks on the highway, perhaps, and the distant shouts truckers going off duty. Or were they awake and cowering?

The whole arc of the dragon was hissing now, spitting blue flame from every joint. And still I could not fire.

I could not take sides.

Beside me I heard Guthrie give a sudden grunt. I had never heard quite that sound before, but I knew what it meant. Maybe some ancestral memory from the great wars of the last century. I knew. I whipped around toward him and saw his face for a moment drained and stark in the blue moonlight. The blood began to seep through the checkered shirt high on the shoulder and he sighed a little and said, looking down, 'Not bad – I think. Too high.' Then he glanced up and his face convulsed suddenly and he said, 'Rohan – shoot, shoot! Over there!'

I spun back to look. There were three men running up the slope toward us, crouching, clear as day in the bright moonlight. The foremost was looking me right in the face and everything inside me seemed to turn over in one quick heave of horror and revulsion.

There was so much about him to take in with one glance. I can see him now in every detail, and I think I always will. But it takes the mind a little while to sort out what the eye sees. I only knew then that a shock of hatred and revolt went curling outward from the pit of my stomach, a shock as strong as sudden pain even before I understood what it was I saw.

He wore a red Comus coat perfectly fitted and tailored to his body, but open down the front over a bare, shaggy chest and stained with grease and dirt. He looked thick because of all the things he was carrying. Two dead and headless chickens hung by their feet from his belt, blood streaking down his pale gray trouser legs from the bloodstained necks. On the other side of his belt there swung by its silver chain a woman's evening bag flashing with brilliants. He had two necklaces around his neck over the stained Comus coat and the tatters of the open shirt beneath it. One was a string of pearls. The other—

I wondered why anybody would trouble to string dried apricots like that, but even as the wonder formed I knew they weren't apricots. Apricots don't bleed. So I knew what they had to be. It's strange how much like dried apricot halves human ears can look, strung like trophies into a necklace. A great many human ears. The white shirt was dark in the moonlight where the necklace crossed it.

I can still see his face, if I let myself. But there was nothing human about it. Not in the eyes, or anywhere behind the thick, intent features. I squeezed the trigger of my scatter-gun at last, with perfect confidence, knowing how badly this needed doing.

It gave me a savage pleasure to hear him grunt as the charge struck him. I felt the jolt of the gun against my shoulder, heard its cough, swung it left to catch the man beside the one who was just now falling. The blue flash illumined him briefly and I saw he too wore a necklace over a blue stained shirt with a fragment of white paper pinned to it. A travesty of Charlie Starr's insignia. Or maybe no travesty. There were renegades from both sides here.

The thoughts flashed through my head like the blue flash of the scatter-gun as I pulled the trigger twice and the last of the three men thudded backward to the moonlit ground, puffing up dust from the pine needles when he hit them.

I remember almost nothing about what came after that. But I know the whole episode took place in a shorter time than I'd ever have believed possible, except that time itself extends under pressures like this. It ran its course and ended in less than a quarter of an hour from the first shot to the last, and for the most part it had happened as silently as a dream. And now everything was as still as death itself out there in the woods. The looters had filtered on past. The raid was over. But far off and muffled by the mountains I heard another distant outburst of rifle fire as I went heavily back to the station to turn in my gun.

Passing our parked caravan, I paused to put my head in at the door, incredulous that they could have slept through it, even under drugs. Blankets rustled as I looked in and Pod Henken's voice asked thickly if anything was wrong. I said in a soothing voice that nothing was, and heard him settle back. Roy didn't stir. I paused to look at the two trucks in the moonlight for a moment, feeling a fleeting and foolish paternal warmth for the troupe over whose slumbers I had just stood guard.

Guthrie sat at the counter in the station, elbows on the table, rolling a water glass between his hands with an inch of scotch in the bottom of it. The station was still dark except for the little blue flame under the coffee urn and I could see him only dimly. He looked pale even in this light, and his face had a drawn look, as if gravity were somehow pulling a little more strongly on him than it had ten minutes earlier. He turned painfully toward me, moving his bandaged shoulder no more than he had to.

'How do you feel?' I asked.

'Not bad.' He drank a single swallow of whiskey and shut his eyes as it ran down his throat. 'No harm done. Lost a little blood is all. Nobody has to know about it if we keep our mouths shut.'

I sat down beside him and reached, uninvited, for the bottle on the counter. My shakes had come back strongly and the scotch helped only partially. 'Who were they?' I asked. 'Out there – the looters. Are they rebels?'

Guthrie shook his head. 'Renegades, mostly, from both sides. Deserters from Comus. Jail-breakers. Gangs as big as this one get out of control for the locals.'

'Can't Comus—'

'Comus doesn't want to. Use your head. These people wanted to run things their own way – let 'em.'

'What about us, though?' I asked. 'How about tomorrow? Is the campsite safe any more?' I turned my head to listen and thought I heard the distant firing again, perhaps around some other isolated farmhouse that hadn't been warned in time. 'If I'd known things could get this bad – I don't know. I can make my own choice, but how much of a right have I got to choose for the others? For Cressy, say. Or the old people.'

I saw the trouble on his face. He was staring down into the amber deeps of his glass as if it were some unfathomable well with wisdom, maybe, at the bottom. He said, 'Cressy,' in a meditative voice, his eyes looking sad and hooded.

I prodded him gently. 'Cressy?'

He blew out his breath, winching as the shoulder muscles under the bandage moved. The breath smelled of scotch so heavily I wondered how full the water glass had been to start with.

'Rohan,' he said suddenly, turning to meet my eyes, 'you answer me something. You killed a man tonight. Probably your first. How do you feel about that?'

I shut my eyes briefly and tested myself, a sort of careful prodding for sensitive areas in the mind. 'I don't know. Not yet. Yes, he was the first. I shot two more later, and I may have hit more than that. I didn't regard them as men, but that's quibbling. Maybe it'll hit me with a real jolt tomorrow, when I've quieted down. Why?'

'It's always a jolt,' he said. 'I've done it many times, in line of duty, just as you did tonight. I never get used to it. But it's part of my job.' He lowered his voice, looking into the empty glass and not at me. 'Parts of my job I don't like. Maybe it was a mistake to try to come back after all these years. When you're young you never doubt yourself. You never wonder if you're justified. But as a man gets older he learns to doubt. Whether he can do a thing – whether he should.'

He rubbed a hand across his eyes, hesitated, and then said, 'You and I have a lot in common, Mr Rohan. We've both been away from our jobs too long. We've both had to come back into a real world that's a pretty merciless place sometimes. And we have one more thing in common.' He gave me a quick glance. 'I've been drinking,' he said, 'or I probably wouldn't be talking like this. The fact is I lost my wife too, about a year ago. We'd been married thirty years.'

I don't know whether he really paused or whether in my mind a moment of complete silence fell.

'You asked about Cressy,' he said. 'Maybe you wonder why I think about her more than you'd expect from a man my age. I'm not making a fool of myself. It's just – she puts me so much in mind of my wife when I first met her. I don't know if she's told you anything about herself, Mr Rohan. She's had a hard row to hoe. I admire the girl. She's like Bess in more than looks. If we'd ever had a daughter . . .' He let his voice die. Then he set down his empty glass carefully.

'You asked me a tough question, Mr Rohan. How much of a right have you and I got to make a choice for the rest of the troupe when their safety's at stake this way? I know how you feel. I know how they feel, too. I've got a lot of sympathy for the old people, and Polly and Roy have a big problem, and Cressy— Well, I can only tell you the answer I'm making.' He swung round on the stool and looked me right in the eye.

'We're going on with our job until we finish,' he said in a firm voice. 'That's what we're going to do.'

CHAPTER XIV

The birds sang, the chipmunks darted, the morning sunlight moved warm and red up the gigantic trunks of the trees. Sempervirens is their name – the ever living redwoods. They'd seen a lot in the past couple of thousand years. They'd seen plenty last night. They would stand here to see much, much more. Last night was nothing. It hadn't happened.

When I came down to the fire after breakfast the clearing had bloomed with enormous yellow and blue flowers as large as washtubs, hanging from a rope stretched between trees. Polly, stooping over the water bucket, shook moisture from the crisp, belling skirts of a pink circlet and barked with sudden laughter at my expression.

'We open tomorrow, don't we? I thought you'd want dress rehearsals today.' She upended a three-foot tube and shook the last crumpled circle of ruffles out, soused it in the bucket. She looked tired. The prominent blue eyes were a little bloodshot and the lines in her face seemed deeper this morning than usual.

What had happened last night had been, in a way, reorienting to me. I'd forgotten the play. I'd forgotten the rebels and my promises. I'd forgotten Nye and whatever it was that lay behind his call to me that night. Everything except the things that happened in the moonlight beyond my gun muzzle had receded and shifted focus in some indefinable way. Seeing Polly still tired from yesterday's rehearsals, seeing the costumes lined up for today's, bridged the gap abruptly and I found myself back with a jolt in my everyday existence. It was an uncomfortable feeling.

'Rohan,' Polly said suddenly, 'I want to talk to you. Carry this bucket over to the washhouse for me, will you? I want a little privacy.'

The needles bounced resiliently under our feet. I glanced around the clearing as we went, looking for traces of what had happened here last night. Nothing showed. If men had fallen in the clearing, other men had dragged them away.

Polly said her abrupt voice, but quietly, 'Rohan, something happened last night. What was it?'

I gave her an uneasy look, quickly averted. 'I don't know what you mean.'

'Don't give me that. I want to know. There was trouble on the road, wasn't there? Shooting?'

'Maybe you had a nightmare,' I said. 'It's noisy on the highway, sure. Trucks backfiring sound like shooting sometimes.'

'I heard yelling,' Polly insisted, but she looked puzzled. 'We slept like the dead, but I know I heard men yelling and gunfire somewhere, not very far off.'

'Did you get up to see?'

'No, I didn't. I was too groggy. By the time I decided I'd better it had stopped. But I know something happened, Rohan. There's a – I don't know what. A feeling in the air this morning. Things are going on around here I don't like. I have a right to know what they are.'

'Why do you think I know any more than you do?' I asked.

She searched my face with large, anxious eyes under the brassy hair. Uneasiness, weariness, long-term unhappiness were in them. You couldn't know her even as long as I had without realizing here was a woman who had carried a heavy load a long, long way. She said in a low voice:

'Roy and I need this job, Rohan. We get a good big bonus if we carry it through. Can't you understand? I have to make the decision for us both and I haven't got enough facts to go on. I've *got* to find out if the danger's bigger than the bonus.

Look at me, Rohan. What happened last night? I think you know. Tell me.'

I didn't want to look at her. Ever since I left Ted Nye in New York my confusion had been deepening, until by now my motives were more mixed than Polly's. Far more mixed.

It had looked so simple in New York. Come out to California and do the job. Come back to life, in a sense, back to the life I'd abandoned when Miranda abandoned the world and me. Guthrie and I together were staging comebacks into life. But I hadn't thought it would be so difficult. Did it make sense to lie to Polly and say there was no danger? Did it make sense to stay on myself, knowing what I knew?

'Roy depends on me, Rohan,' Polly said a little diffidently. 'We've got to have that money. I don't want to back out now. But if there's really big trouble going on, if we're in real danger, I've got to know. Tell me the truth, Rohan. Where do we stand?'

I couldn't answer her. I couldn't tell the truth. I had too much at stake myself. I knew that now, if I hadn't known it before. The risks I had taken, the beating, the exhaustion, the dangers past and the dangers still to come, even the betrayal of Ted Nye for his own good and mine, even the risk that he knew about it – all this was nothing if I could earn the reward I wanted. Last night, looking at the sleeping caravans in the moonlight, I had felt a sense of foolish warmth and responsibility for these people. I felt it still, but not enough to give up the goal I was working for.

All I could do was look at Polly with sympathy and resolution, and lie to her.

'As far as I know,' I said, 'there's no danger. Does that answer your question?'

The prominent blue eyes searched mine again. Without speaking she shook her head a little and turned away. I went after her in silence. Guthrie looked out of his truck and gave me a casual salute with his good arm. He looked tough and placid, an old man who wasn't old at all, an old man who would take a lot of killing when the time came.

I saw Cressy combing her hair before a mirror hung on the side of a redwood, fastening an earring in her ear. I thought of the men with the trophy necklaces last night. Men who fought on both sides, I told myself, whichever side suited them best for the moment.

Men like me.

Thursday went by like a nightmare. We still didn't know our lines too well when we had to speak them in action. Scenes that should have been swift and biting drew out into lethargy. Scenes that should have built to a climax limped and went flat. I was beginning to get the kind of grouping I wanted, so the stage at any given moment would present a balanced picture, and a certain rhythm of motion was developing. But it was all very slack still. Time after time we kicked over the grooves we had worn in the pine needles and went through the scenes without these obvious guides, and time after time we forgot them and fouled up our crosses and groupings. Unless we could chalk the street when we gave our play, it didn't seem we'd get through the performances.

When I was off stage myself I could yell at the cast for errors and see for myself when things went wrong. But on stage, as part of the play, I made the same mistakes they did. And yet, in a way, it was good to have these problems. Here at least was a job I knew how to do. And the more I concentrated, the farther into forgetfulness I could push those other problems, the ones that had no answers.

We worked all day and stumbled into bed at midnight, too dazed to think or feel. The trucks were still parked by the station and I suppose a guard was posted that night against any return of the looters, but I knew nothing about anything from the moment I hit the bunk.

Friday was just like Thursday, except it had more despair in it. We opened tonight, and it didn't look to any of us as if we could possibly do it. The play seemed a lot worse than it had the day we started. That's normal, of course, but rehearsing only three days isn't, and maybe this time the play would turn out just as bad as we expected.

At three o'clock we had gone through one last complete dress rehearsal without interruption from me. When they finished I ran over my list of errors. Pod Henken never got off stage fast enough. Roy kept forgetting he was working on an arena stage and didn't complete his turns so he faced all parts of the audience successively. Cressy was still shaky in too many of her lines. Mrs Henken had perfected some absolutely fool-proof way of stealing attention during a love scene toward the end, but she just looked smug and innocent when I complained and I didn't know how she was working it so I couldn't tell her not to.

I said gloomily, 'Well, that's about it. We open tonight ready or not. Take the rest of the afternoon off and relax if you can. We want to hit town about eight, so we'd better leave here by seven at the latest. Guthrie, what about you?'

He said he'd leave at six and would Roy come along to help him set up the stands. Roy nodded and the cast moved dispirit-edly off the stage. A sudden thought struck me and I called after them, 'And nobody go out of sight of camp. Nobody. Understand?'

Polly swung round and asked defiantly why not. I started to yell at her. But something stopped the yell in my throat. It wasn't that I'd lied to her and couldn't explain now there was still danger in the woods for all I knew. No, it was what I saw in her face, and the sudden feeling of compassion that came up in me. I knew the weariness she sagged under. We all did. But the uncertainty and the fear she labored under were uniquely her own. Not only fear of the unstable world we lived in, but fear of the future, of time, of Cressy or the next version of Cressy, or maybe the version after that. I saw her own awareness of herself, with time moving up on her until she could play only character roles while Roy went on forever the young lover win-ning the ingénue at the play's end. I couldn't yell at her. But neither could I show compassion.

'Just do as you're told,' I said brusquely. 'Now beat it, all of you, and lie down or rest or something. I want a fresh cast tonight.'

She turned away, too tired to argue, but resenting me and showing it. She hadn't accepted me as a person. None of them had. I was a good director and they knew it. They worked hard, took criticism cheerfully. And individually they seemed willing enough to confide in me, up to a point. But as a group – no. I was still the outsider. They scattered around the clearing, leaving me alone.

At three-thirty a flock of hedgehoppers came buzzing along the highway, heaving and bouncing on their grasshopper legs, their antennae whipping the air. They swarmed in to roost in the parking area around the station. Plain-clothes Comus men (there's no mistaking them) went in and apparently had a conference somewhere out of sight. I wondered if Comus had decided to take a hand after all in cross-country running down of the renegades.

A little after four I glanced up from the script I was studying and saw a fat man in brown denims standing among the trees that edged the path to the highway. He blended with the brown trees and the brown carpet of needles so well I almost didn't see him. When he caught my eye he lifted a finger beckoningly and then moved in silence up the path and out of sight.

I looked around the clearing. The Henkens lay on blankets under the trees, their playbox singing tiny tunes between them. Polly and Roy had disappeared into one of the trucks, and Cressy was talking to Guthrie on the steps on the sound truck. Nobody seemed to have noticed the fat man but me.

I got up and strolled along the path. The man was waiting for me on the far side of one of the big sequoias with a fire-eaten chamber hollowed out of its heart.

'Harris sent me,' the fat man said. 'Got a job for you.'

'What now?' I asked. 'I haven't very much time. We open tonight in San Andreas.'

'Not unless you do the job for us, you don't.'

'Damn Harris,' I said with sudden anger. 'He told me—'

'He said *maybe* you could open before you helped us. No yes or no. Maybe.'

'Listen,' I said wearily. 'I've worked like a dog for three days rehearsing. I was up night before last fighting off looters with strings of human ears around their necks. Tonight I've got a play opening and I not only act but direct. There's a limit to what flesh and blood can do. You go tell Harris—'

'You want me to tell him you aren't putting on the show?' He had little reddish-brown eyes in a heavy face and I think he rather liked pushing me around.

'After all,' he said, 'now we know what the show's really on the road for, there's some of us feel more like stringing up the bunch of you than playing along.'

'We know that, do we?' I asked, trying to guess whether this was bluff or not, excitement stirring in me in case it wasn't.

'We do. You don't. Yet.' He grinned broadly. 'Tell you what, Rohan. You do the job and maybe Harris will tell you why you're really here.' He was tantalizing me, and the reddish eyes watched for a response.

I sighed. 'What's the job?' I wasn't giving him any satisfaction.

He leaned forward and lowered his voice. 'Seems like the organization could use an extra 'hopper now. You're going to pick one up for us, Harris tells me.'

I said, 'All right.' I was feeling resigned by now. 'I just walk up and drive off with the first one I see, right?'

He grinned. 'You got a Comus cop in your outfit. When does he leave camp tonight for town?'

'About an hour or so before we do.'

'All right. You name the time. When you say so, there'll be a commotion up at the truck station. After that it's up to you.'

'And if I get it?'

'You'd better get it. Cut through the woods toward town. You know the farmlands down at the foot of the valley? There's a brown barn farthest of all down toward the bottom. Door's unlocked. Leave the 'hopper there. We'll pick it up in the morning. Okay?'

I nodded. 'Oh, sure,' I said.

'What time you want the trouble to start?'

I thought it over. 'Six-thirty.'

'All right. Remember – no 'hopper, no play. I'll see you later.'
And he went off up the path swaggering a little, cigarette smoke
pluming back over his shoulder.

CHAPTER XV

Guthrie and Roy loaded up the sound truck at six. Just before they left I beckoned Guthrie aside. 'After the other night,' I said, 'I don't feel so good going outside the camp unarmed. I want a gun.'

He gave me a speculative look, nodded, and went over to the truck. Coming back with his hand out, he laid into mine a small, snub-nosed automatic, cool and heavy in my palm. I slid it into my coat pocket, the weight dragging it down a little on that side. I liked the feel of it.

Ten minutes after the truck had vanished up the trail I said to the nervously silent group waiting on the benches, 'I've got some business to attend to. If I'm not back by seven, go on without me. I'll meet you in town.'

They nodded without interest, too wrapped up in their opening-night jitters to care whether they ever saw me again.

I strolled up to the station trying to look casual, trying to control my quickened breathing. I didn't know what the penalties would be for stealing a 'hopper, but the state the country was in now the chances were they'd shoot first and ask questions afterward. I wasn't sure I was going to do it even now. All I intended to commit myself to was looking things over, evaluating my chances.

There were about twenty hedgehoppers in the parking area. I stood on the edge a minute, then pulled a handkerchief from my pocket, dropped a half dollar noisily, and watched it roll. Hunting it among the 'hoppers, I went on stooping and peering until I had located two vehicles with keys left in the ignition.

Then I went inside the restaurant for a beer I didn't want. I kept an eye on my watch, and five minutes before the critical moment I went out again, strolling slowly, lit a cigarette, looked up at the treetops leaning together away up over head. I walked around the side of the station toward the laundry lines in the rear where sheets and towels fluttered in the breeze. I stopped in an angle of the building to shake a rock out of my shoe, taking my time about it.

The commotion, when it came, was terrific. I hadn't known just what to expect, and the noise of the explosion on the far side of the station rocked the ground and me. I heard glass breaking. There was a moment of stunned silence. Cautiously I put my head around the corner. A truck which had just pulled off the highway was heaving on its big tires, reverberating thunderously and belching fire through its ruptured sides. Then the silence broke, and the yells and the thud of running feet began.

Stooping low, I made straight for the nearer of the two 'hoppers I'd spotted. I slid into the low bucket seat and felt the springy cradle of the machine throb to life as I switched on the motor. It seemed no different from any other car, except for that queasy bouncing. I backed it out and ran it recklessly down the slope toward the river, trusting to the laundry lines to screen me and to providence in case I was overestimating how steep a hill a 'hopper can take and stay upright.

I wasn't. I realized halfway down the slope that I was crossing the battleground of two nights past. About here, on this quickly passing spot, I had killed three men and their blood must still be a little moist deep down under the layers of fallen needles. Then the terrifying speed of my rush downhill blotted out all other thought. I crossed the rocks and the river in a bouncing burst of spray, and sheer velocity carried me up the opposite bank. River water ran down the glass shell in streams as I went bucketing along through the trees, steering the responsive little car frantically to cut around thickets and weave figure eights among the sequoias. Ferns streamed against the glass in strong green currents and parted to let me out again. I was going too fast and I knew it, but a sort of panic was on me now and I couldn't stop.

Suppose somebody at the station had seen me go? Were they after me now? I hunched low over the wheel, expecting the thin scream of a bullet from behind. And the renegade gangs – they'd prowled the woods here only a little while ago. Did stragglers still linger? My ears stung at the bases as if the knife were already shearing them off my head.

Once I frightened a little herd of deer and saw them start to go bounding off, heads turned sidewise to look at me out of big startled eyes, but I was gone before they were and the trees seemed to move in behind me to shut us off from each other. And once – I think – I passed two dead men lying face down among the ferns. Maybe they were casualties from the fighting. Maybe they were sleeping woods prowlers, except they didn't stir when I went by. Maybe they were only shadows or hallucinations that whipped past too quickly to focus on. I'll never know now.

About halfway in my trip the voice box on the panel before me coughed and spoke, and the sound of a human voice pulled me out of the panic a little. I think it was real panic in the original sense of the word, the woods terror the Greeks named after Pan. I didn't like the way the trees closed in behind me or the sense of *not* being alone. Hearing another man's voice broke up the terror for me and the trees stopped closing in.

The voice box said thinly that a hedgehopper had been stolen from Station 12-101 and traced across the river. It seemed to be heading for San Andreas and would all hands please be on the lookout. I had more to worry about now, but I felt much less frightened. My heart had slowed down almost to normal by the time the fields I was heading for came into sight between the trees, and if there were pursuers behind me they had lost the trail.

The voice box kept up its thin complaint about having been stolen as I bounced across another little stream and burst through a screen of tall weeds into the lower San Andreas valley.

Up out of the grass ten feet away rose a man's head and the

two steel-rimmed eyes of a shotgun looking straight into mine. I drew my nervous car up trembling in the grass.

'Harris sent me,' I said quickly. 'I'm looking for a brown barn.'

The man looked me over, listened, waited a minute or two and, evidently deciding I wasn't the vanguard of an invasion, waved me on.

'Your barn's down that way about half a mile. Get going – I'll kick over your tracks.' He grinned as the voice box announced all over again that it had been stolen. I left him industriously erasing tire marks and drove off down a sandy lane between high walls of corn. It was quiet here except for the soft throb of the motor and the complaints from the voice box. Twilight was deepening and a few stars had begun to wink uncertainly overhead.

The barn loomed up dark in the failing light. I got out and opened one of the big double doors. The warm, dusty smell of alfalfa breathed out in my face as I ran the nervous little 'hopper in.

Then, because it was very quiet in this cathedral-shaped place, I shut the door, got back into the 'hopper, and gave myself one cigarette's worth of rest and stillness, switching on the 'hopper's single headlight so I could see where I was. Dust shimmered and sank in the beam. The gray-green alfalfa was packed deep in the mow, and all around ranged empty stalls which had once, by the ghost of a rich, strong smell, held cows. On the wall hung a cracked leather collar which a horse must have worn a long time ago. There was a yellowed remnant of a poster nailed to the wall and I looked at it idly and wondered what was going to happen next.

The moment I sat still and let my mind go fallow the questions I hadn't yet had time for came clamoring into it. 'Now we know what the show's really on the road for . . .' I remembered the thread of brown wool caught on the hinge of the sound-truck door. 'There's some of us feel more like stringing up the bunch of you than playing along.' I remembered Ted Nye's voice cutting across the fat man's voice in my mind like words spoken in an echo chamber. 'Just say I need a large-scale diversion in California . . . People have to be distracted while something else – something big – gets done.'

One thing was sure. We were part of Comus still. And the presence of an elaborate sound truck with a play that didn't need much in the way of lighting and sound effects added up to something pretty obvious. It hadn't taken the man in the brown sweater long to find out what he came for – it couldn't have, for he hadn't much time. And now the rebels knew, and maybe I would know, too, when I saw Harris next.

The question – what do I do then?

Warn Guthrie that our little traveling trap, or whatever it turned out to be, is discovered? Warn Ted? Time enough to decide that after I knew what I'd been lured into.

A sudden and overpowering desire for alcohol made my throat constrict for a moment. The problems were coming at me too fast. I needed a refuge from reality. I hadn't bargained for anything as hard as this when I let myself be roused back into life. I thought maybe if I could get into town fast enough there might be time for a quick drink or two before the show.

I patted the nervous 'hopper's flank, switched off the voice box in mid-complaint, killed the motor, dropped the key in my pocket to clink against the automatic.

'Good night,' I said. 'Take it easy.' And I left it there alone with the ghosts of the horses and cows.

The evening crowds in San Andreas were bigger than I'd expected for a Friday night. The lights were bright, many of the stores were open, women in bright print dresses and men in denims and wide hats moved up and down the street noisily. I didn't like the feel of the crowd somehow. There was an undercurrent of tension, almost hysteria, in the pitch of the voices and the quick, nervous motions of the people. I wasn't surprised, considering what San Andreas had been through lately, but I didn't like it.

I still wanted the drink, but now I was afraid to take it. Yet, anyhow. I hadn't counted on a crowd with a temper like this. To find the troupe all I had to do was follow along with the majority, and the current carried me right up to the bright new glint of steel bleachers looming over the heads of the crowd. Guthrie had set the things up across a street just this side of the square, and Raleigh's stern marble face gazed resolutely out into the night above us. The monument shaft wasn't floodlit any more, but you could see the pale, noble jaw swimming above the roofs in dramatic shadows.

The bleachers faced each other across an expanse of street that was going to be our stage. Left and right were the store fronts that were part of our scenery. I noticed with admiration how Guthrie had strung his lights overhead to shine into the eyes of anybody who tried to watch from upper windows and outsmart the paying customers.

The sound truck was parked behind one set of stands and I saw Guthrie had left a narrow space between the seats through which he could watch the stage from the back door of the truck. The two other vehicles stood at the curb, and from certain nervous pitchings of the truck bodies I inferred the cast was inside now, dressing and making up, worrying as everyone worries on an opening night. I had to dress and make up myself, but I wanted to check with Guthrie first.

I found him under the bleachers, peering up and testing supports. He looked worried, and he had plenty to worry about. The crowd around him was full of noisy young fellows, most of them wearing paper triangles with the red 93 scrawled inside the blue star. We seemed to have more than our share of the young and reckless around us, yelling and laughing, shoving each other and catcalling for Guthrie. He was ignoring them, but his jaw was set and his face red. I noticed he kept his shoulder immobile, but other than that he seemed surprisingly spry for a man who had been through all he had.

He looked glad to see me. 'You're late,' he said. 'I thought you had the town set up for us. What do you think now?'

As he spoke a little knot of overgrown adolescents burst out of the crowd to hurl themselves shouting against the supports of the bleachers. The whole row of seats staggered and the metal sang on a complaining note.

Guthrie said angrily. 'This has been going on ever since I set the thing up. It's getting worse. What do we do now?'

I started to say something, but a hollow, booming sound like a sheet of tin shaken drowned out my voice. There was an outburst of yells and heavy laughter. The crowd parted and a little mob of men who looked like Croppers came laughing and staggering up the street carrying huge slabs of something bright crimson and very thin. It reverberated when they shook it. The red was Comus color. (A quick, involuntary thought flashed through my mind. What's bright crimson and thunders when you strike it, but it's thin enough to put your fist through when you see it disassembled? A riddle. And the answer?)

I knew what the red stuff was. Sheets of molded plastic ripped off the side of the Comus check station near the highway. One of the Croppers stooped over, yelled with drunken laughter, and sailed the big sheet toward us level with the street. It smashed into the steel legs of the bleachers and splintered with a booming crash, fragments flying into the crowd. People screamed and laughed protestingly.

Guthrie looked at me.

'Wait a minute,' I said. I glanced around the bright, crowded street behind us. As I'd expected, I saw one face I knew. I sauntered softly across to the sidewalk and stood at the corner of a grocery for a minute or two surveying the crowd. Then I turned left and went down the alley between stores. Looking back, I saw after a moment a dark figure shutting out the light, coming after me.

'Harris?' I asked quietly.

'Hello, Rohan,' he said.

'What's going on here?' I demanded, hearing my voice rise a little.

'Nothing yet,' Harris said placidly. 'We just want to make sure you kept your end of the deal. Got what we sent you for?'

'I got it. Didn't your boy with the shotgun report in?'

'Not yet. Want to prove you delivered the goods?'

'How the hell can I? I haven't got it in my pocket.'

'Haven't you?'

'If you want the key you can say so,' I told him irritably, plunging my hand in my pocket. 'Is that it? Here.'

He accepted it, nodding. 'Good enough. I'll have the thing picked up sometime tomorrow. All right then, give me ten minutes and you can start your show.'

'Wait a minute,' I said. 'I hear you've got some news for me about the reason we're here.'

He hesitated, but only briefly. 'We think we know. I guess you have a right to. You're working with us. Seems you've got a kind of portable mine detector in that truck of yours. Only it isn't looking for mines.'

'What is it looking for then?'

He didn't answer me directly. 'Comus has a lot of probing apparatus set up around the country. This gadget probes too. But it's sensitive, very sensitive. It's looking for a special kind of radiation, and there's only one kind of radiation Comus could be hunting in California.'

It didn't take long to think that one over. The Anti-Com would be what Comus was worrying about. So we were traveling with an Anti-Com detector. If Harris was right. If the man in the brown sweater had known enough to dope it all out from the one quick glance which was all he might have had time for. It occurred to me to wonder if Ted Nye might have thought of some such search as this and planted a red herring device to cover the real facts. But there's such a thing as being *too* devious. I only nodded.

'You don't seem very much worried,' I said. 'You going to call off our tour?'

'Not yet. Not for a lot of reasons.'

'Why are you telling me this?' I asked suddenly.

He laughed.

'Maybe I just want to see what you'll do,' he said with an ambiguous look at me. 'Never mind, Rohan. We know what we're doing. Now why don't you get back to the square and start your show? I'll be in the front row, so make it good.'

Rather hollowly I said, 'I'll make it good, all right. Let's go.'

CHAPTER XVI

The Croppers and the adolescents must have been Harris's to a man, because the crowd quieted down right away. But I kept my eye on the Croppers. I knew what it's like to work the way they do, all day every day, and nothing to look forward to but sleep and more work tomorrow. You need excitement. You welcome trouble. A revolution would be a godsend to men like this. And I thought some of these particular boys weren't far from moving over to the renegade bands like the necklace men of two nights ago.

We got a pretty good crowd. The bleachers were almost full by the time Guthrie, who was taking admission money, decided that was it and signaled me to open the show.

My face felt stiff under the make-up. My hands and feet were cold. I noticed this only abstractly at first, because my mind was so full of what Harris had been saying, and I had to make sure the Henkens were ready to go and the rest of the cast standing by. There was something wrong with me, but until the Henkens were on stage I didn't have time to wonder what.

Both of them seemed terrifyingly composed for an opening night. Rosy-cheeked with make-up, wrinkles penciled in black, they squeezed calmly past between the end of the bleachers and the buildings. Eileen moved into a store-front doorway. Pod strolled forward in his dusty brown denims, hat on the back of his head, looking like one of the audience strayed on stage, waiting for the show to start. He pulled up the knees of his trousers and sat down on the curb, grunting a little as old bones complained. He took out his pocket-knife, pulled a block of white wood from his pocket, and began to whittle, holding the work up now and then to squint at it. Gradually the crowd fell silent, not sure quite what was happening.

Eileen's voice from the door made everybody start just slightly. It was a firm, full voice under perfect control. 'Dad!' she called. 'Dad, you hear me? With all these people in town tonight, seems like you'd find something better to do than sit here whittling.'

'Now, Mother.' Pod didn't even look up. 'You'd holler a lot louder if I was in the Irish Rose tonight.'

A wave of gratified laughter swept the stands. Pod thumbed the knife blade complacently, waiting out his laugh. The show was under way.

I breathed a deep sigh of relief and had time to think about the next thing – myself. It was startling to find my heart thundering, my lips stiff, my hands icy and shaking. Curiously, though my mind had been too busy with other things, my body remembered. This was stage fright. A bad attack of it, maybe the worst I've ever had. And everybody has stage fright who ever stepped on a stage. I shut my cold hands hard to keep them steady and looked around at the others.

Cressy in a bell-shaped dress of clear yellow stood with bent head, lips moving, eyes fixed on nothing, drawing her own private world about her to shut out all distraction, making herself over into the Susan Jones who would step out into the lights in forty seconds from now. Polly stood with her hand over her eyes, her moving lips visible under it, forgetting even Roy. And Roy was pacing up and down with short, quick steps, muttering, very pale under his make-up. He had a dot of carmine at the inside corner of each eye and it gave him a strange, lustrous look seen this close.

I looked at them once and then looked away, my mind blank to their troubles, blank to the revolution still in progress around us, blank to the danger that might yet be waiting us from the crowd. Totally blank. I had no idea what my first line was or where I came in. And it didn't matter, because even if I could remember, my lips were too stiff to speak and my knees too shaky to carry me.

'And even if all this weren't true,' I told myself, 'still, we haven't rehearsed enough. We can't put the play on. We'll be booed off the stage. We're six fools for even trying.'

Dimly I watched Cressy take a deep breath, smooth down her skirts, listen intently to the voices from the stage. She counted five with careful beats of an uplifted finger, and on the fifth squeezed past the end of the steel stands and moved composedly out into the lights. I heard her voice saying words that had no meaning to me.

Polly was joggling my arm. 'You're on! Wake up, Rohan, you're on!'

For an instant the continent wheeled under me again and this was New York and the Raleigh Theater, and I was standing in the familiar wings again hearing these familiar words. But the last time I had heard them were through a swimming haze of alcohol, and the words bubbled incoherently in my mind. The memory was so vivid I felt for one instant a deep wave of intoxication from liquor I had not drunk. I thought, *I can't do it, I can't. I've failed too often and I'll fail this time, too.*

But Polly's hands whirled me around and faced me toward the entry. I moved forward on stiff, uncertain legs.

The lights were dazzling. I could feel their heat on the top of my head beating hard. I saw swimming seas of faces on all sides – *all!* Knowing it would be this way was one thing; stepping out between them was something else again, something shattering. Always before I had stood surrounded by the stage itself, the audience invisible beyond the fourth wall. Always before the illusion of the play had closed me in. But here we had no stage, no set, no walls. Nothing but the bare street open all around and lined with watching people. It was like stepping out into life itself when I had lived for so long in a world of shadows. For a moment the sheer weight of the gazing eyes upon me was paralyzing.

Then Cressy swung her yellow skirts toward me, put her

head on one side a little, looked up and said, 'I didn't think you'd come. I really didn't.'

My ice-cold hand rose entirely of itself and knuckled her gently under the chin. I saw her start very slightly at the coldness of it and then smile. I heard my own voice speak...

And then the miracle took over. The familiar miracle I had almost forgotten the feel of, it had been so long. I heard my voice speak out, full and confident and richer than it had ever sounded before on stage. (Maybe because I had changed a lot in the last few days, more perhaps than I knew.) I heard the words as if I had never heard them before, fresh, spontaneous, shaping themselves in my mind and mouth out of a surge of deeply felt emotion, because this yellow-haired girl in the yellow dress was not Cressy, but Susan Jones. A very young, fresh, lovely Susan whose youth might be a touchstone to renew my own if I could win her. And I had to win her.

I wasn't myself any more. I was a jaded city exile making a casual pass at a country girl. But the part had more implicit in it than that, and the part created itself. I wasn't in a play any more. I was the part I played, the man who makes the casual pass and finds himself trapped in it, helpless against his own passionate need for the fountain of youth the girl becomes for him. Knowing he can't have her, but knowing he has to try. I felt the deep and anguished longing as if it were my own. The words I spoke were the words I had rehearsed, every step and gesture was on cue – but a new power flowed into the part that carried along with it not only me but the whole cast, the whole play.

I rewrote the play without changing a line or a motion. It was still a comedy, but now it had depth and emotion and something to say about the universal verities of life that was a little sad and a little foolish, and very moving for everyone who watched.

I knew these things about it later. At the time I knew nothing except that I had to pour forth all the power that was in me to win the girl called Susan and renew my youth at the fountain of her freshness. And the power in me was infinite. The play structured and glowed into life around me. I could feel the outpouring emotion that flowed in upon us from the audience so that it seemed not even to breathe except as we breathed. The whole cast was swept up in it along with me, and new meanings seemed to bloom into life in every line. I couldn't have brought it off without them, but I think the onward sweep of the feeling I was creating was so strong none of them could have bucked the tide even if he'd wanted to.

Crossroads wasn't a play about a young lovers' quarrel any more. It was about an aging sophisticate who sees too late what he wants and can never win. Maybe he never could have. Maybe if he got it he wouldn't want it. But while he wants it and tries to win it he goes through an intense emotional upheaval, and the audience goes right along with him.

We were nearly at the end before I came to myself a little, feeling something ahead in the play that wasn't right for the new *Crossroads* I was creating as we went. Polly's song and my fight with Roy. They were high points in the comedy at the end, but false, very false for the mood I wanted to leave with the audience.

I knew what I was going to do about it. I was the pivot of the play and there wasn't anything I couldn't do. The confidence that swelled in me was larger than myself, larger than the world. I felt the earth turning under me simply because I stood here balancing it under my feet as a logger rolls a log in midstream. I had created a magic world around us no wider than the magic room I used to spin to keep reality out. But now it enclosed infinity and the realities inside it were so intense they burned to the touch.

The moment for Polly's song came inexorably onward as we spoke our lines. But the song followed on a cue speech from me – and I didn't make it. Calmly and confidently I cut a dozen lines of dialogue and jumped the whole song sequence entirely. Then I threw very strongly at Polly a question from the next page of the script, a question she had to answer to lead up to my fight with Roy.

She picked it up magnificently, without a stumble, without

a blink. I felt only the briefest ripple go over the others on the stage as they made mental cuts in their own lines and very deftly moved left and right into the new groupings that went with the later dialogue I had jumped us all ahead to.

And I moved into the climax and my fight with Roy. But I played it without the fight. We followed the script exactly except that there were no blows exchanged. Not physically.

It was a very strange feeling, this living the events as if they were happening for the first time in the world, spontaneous and fresh, yet knowing as by prescience what the outcome had to be and reaching ahead through time to mold it to the shape I wanted.

The man I had become in the play was fighting a lost cause, and by now he knew it, and the audience knew it, and knew it was right that he should lose. But it wasn't right that the victorious lover should win by a knockout blow. The knockout was emotional, not physical.

There was a strange, strong quality to the scene because we never came to blows, a feel of subdued violence discharging itself on some emotional level in the minds of the audience itself, since it wasn't discharged on stage. I felt the anguish of the defeated lover more actual in my mind than I'd ever felt the bruises from the falls I took when we were rehearsing. It was intolerable to give up the youth and the fresh fountain of joy that the girl Susan had become to me. I felt the desolation and the despair . . .

And at the last moment I realized that the man I had made myself into would have one further feeling now. Being the man he was, he had to. He would begin to feel the first faint flickering of relief.

So I gave it to them that way at the end. Just a nuance, but they got it. A very slight jauntiness to the shoulders, a straightening of the back, and a shrugging off of a burden I hadn't really wanted – *maybe* I hadn't wanted it – after all.

The play ended to a dead, intense silence for a long moment, and then a solid avalanche of applause that made the bleachers rock and the windows rattle on both sides of the street.

The ovation lasted a good five minutes and could have gone on all night. After that we were nearly mobbed by dazed people frantic to touch us and rub off a little of the glamour onto their own hands.

When it was over and the stage nearly clear, I heard Guthrie's voice, sounding flat and grim from the back of the sound truck.

'Mr Rohan, will you step inside here a minute? I want to have a word with you . . .'

I've never seen a man so mad. For what must have been ten minutes I stood there and let him yell at me in a whisper, purple in the face from the strain of keeping his voice down.

I didn't hear a word he said.

Because Rohan was himself again. Better than himself – better than ever before. All I'd been through was worth it if it built to a feeling of confidence and triumph like this. Anything else I had to go through would be nothing if I could only win my way back to the place where I belonged. I kept seeing the Raleigh Theater shining out in its dark street, crowds streaming in under the marquee, and HOWARD ROHAN RETURNS in dazzling lights half the height of the building. Rohan had come to life. Rohan was on his way back to the top again, and nothing Guthrie could say or do penetrated the blaze in my mind.

I let Guthrie rage. I said yes and no and never again, not really hearing, until his color began to decrease and the veins in his forehead went back to normal. It didn't matter. I didn't even see him. The world was turning only because my feet stood on it, rolling it over, and nobody else existed except me.

CHAPTER XVII

A soft, strong wind had begun to blow by the time we got back to the redwood grove. Somehow we had got ourselves packed up and on the road back, Guthrie too angry to speak and the cast strangely silent too. I don't know what I'd expected of them. Not this. But it didn't matter. I hardly knew they were alive.

The air was full of rustling and the creaking of enormous boughs in the wind, so we all kept glancing up apprehensively at the floating continents of foliage. The whisper of needles against each other made a sound as continuous as the wind itself, filling our senses as the wind filled the grove. The stars were big and bright and burning.

The strong, warm wind was blowing through me, too. Blowing away the past, polishing every facet of the new Rohan until I glittered like a diamond. I was new and shiny. I was strong and free. I was *more* than I had ever been before. Even the bad years hadn't been wasted. I'd gone down fast after Miranda died, and the Cropper years were bad too, but even that had been worth living through if it helped add up to this.

And the bad times were over.

I said to Guthrie as he swung stiffly down off the sound truck, 'Come inside here. I want to talk to you.' And I nodded toward the back door that opened into the belly of the steel whale where the television apparatus was. He may have turned red again and started arguing. I didn't even notice.

I was a good many different Rohans that night, and one of them had been thinking, clear and sharp, on the trip back to the grove. Another had been just riding along breathing deep, watching the stars, feeling the warm, strong wind. And another was still back there on the stage with the audience fused into a single unit and breathing only when Rohan breathed.

But the thinking Rohan had worked out something important on the way. 'So I'm back again,' he said to himself. 'I'm good again, I'm better than I ever was before. I've got it all, flowing like a river, an endless stream of power that only needs channeling. So I've got to channel it. I've got to get back on stage. And I've wasted enough time. I want money enough to start where I left off. Plenty of money. But who's going to back me? I fell on my face too often. I had too many curtains rung down. I haven't any friends left and nobody's going to invest a dime in me unless I work my way up again the hard way. And I'm tired of the hard way.'

No, not a dime. So I could see in front of me the dime I couldn't expect, round and shiny, with Raleigh's rock jaw jutting in profile and the mushroom cloud behind his head to show what he fought and conquered a long time ago. And floating between me and Raleigh's silver profile I saw Ted Nye's little miserable face.

And I thought what a fool I'd been back there in New York taking on a job like this for peanuts. I could have held out for – well, how much? Enough to back me in a new show? Probably not. Anyhow, the moment for bargaining on the old basis was passed. But maybe there could be a new basis. That's what I needed now – a bargaining point. Something new and valuable worth money in New York.

The thinking Rohan had been shuffling things over, hunting for treasure. 'I'm here,' he told himself, 'here on the spot. An important spot. A place where things are happening.' (A spot, the part of the mind that slumbers suggested drowsily, where the most important things of all may be stirring under the surface of rebellion.) So much was going on. So much had happened already that might lead to so much more.

'I want to talk to Ted Nye,' I said confidently to Guthrie.

Take the argument as read.

He said he wouldn't do it. He said he couldn't even if he would. He said he hadn't the authority. And even after he'd started, grumbling and swearing at me, the men at the other end of the line didn't like the idea either. I sat on the step of the truck smoking and watching the blue mist go streaming away in the warm wind, listening to the trees heaving all around, knowing that everything was going to work out all right.

Nye came on, scowling, about fifteen minutes later. New York glittered – through the window behind him I could see a corner of Times Square, very small, all the lights close together, garishly colored, eclipsed every time he moved his head.

'Listen, Ted,' I began confidently, interrupting whatever it was he was saying. 'Things are happening out here even you don't know about. I'm on the spot. I know. I want to bargain with you, Ted. I put on the best performance of my life tonight and I'm on my way back to the top.'

He said, 'Howard, you're drunk,' and I said, 'Shut up and listen. If I'm drunk, it's not on alcohol. Ted, I want money. I want enough to finance a new play. I can earn it. A lot's going on out here.'

He said sharply, 'No. You talk like a fool, Howard. I've got trained men on the job out there. Don't meddle. You'll just foul things up.'

'Okay, I didn't tell you everything the other night,' I said. 'Things *have* happened. I wasn't sure how you'd take it and, anyhow, I didn't care then. Now I don't give a damn what you think. I'm going to work my way into the rebel organization out here and learn enough to earn my theater back again. How about it, Ted?'

He started to say no. Then he paused and his little anxious eyes tried to penetrate my thoughts. Finally he said in a tired voice, 'Go on, talk. I'm listening.'

A distant flicker of caution told me not to spill everything at once. Not now. Not entirely.

'When I got here I found things were even rougher than you'd said,' I told him. 'I had to take a beating to get to the top boys in San Andreas. You saw me afterward. You know. Well,

I didn't tell you who I saw. I didn't say the people who gave me the permit to play in San Andreas were the local Freedom Committee. In person.'

Nye leaned to peer at me searchingly, unveiling most of Times Square behind his left ear. New York glittered three thousand windy miles. 'Did you get names?' he asked. 'Could you identify—'

'The hell with names. I could identify them but I won't. They're small fry. I can use them to catch bigger fish. I want money, Ted. You give me an assignment and I'll guarantee to follow through. You want figures on ammunition caches? You want the names of top men here? You want to know what the Anti-Com is? Just say the word and I'll dig up the answers. For a price.'

'You're dreaming, Howard.' He sounded tired. 'You mean they trust you? You just walked in and picked up your permit, for nothing. No lie-box check? I don't believe it.'

I looked him straight in the eye. 'They haven't got a lie-box. Not here, anyhow. And they trust me just about as far as I trust you. But I earned my permit. I did a little job for them. I stole a hedgehopper and delivered it to the local Committee. So now I'm a rebel. How do you like it?'

He showed his teeth at me. 'Damn you, Howard, I warned you! I don't want to interfere with the local authorities. You stick your neck out too far and you get your head chopped off. What did they want with a 'hopper?'

'They didn't say. I could find out. And let me do the worrying about my neck, will you?'

'I'll worry about it until your tour's finished. I need you to run the troupe, not play spy. Wait a minute, I want to think.' He rubbed his forehead wearily and his sigh was gusty over all the windy, night-time miles. I wondered how Raleigh was doing in his ornate bed somewhere in this same enormous night. Dying? Dead? (My mind worked out a sudden, senseless little rhyme. Ted – dead. Nye – die.)

'All right,' he said. So you stole a 'hopper. Is it still in reach? Could you get to it without anybody knowing?'

'I think so.'

'All right. I'll tell Guthrie to give you a tracer box. I want it slapped on the 'hopper underneath someplace where it won't show. Then we can pick up its signals and find out where it's going. After that you go to bed. Forget about spying. I've got trained men on the job. I don't need amateurs.'

'What's in this for me so far?' I asked.

He sighed. 'Oh, an extra hundred.'

I drew a breath through my teeth and told him what I thought of him. He laughed. The transmission wavered briefly and so did his face, like a reflection in water. He shook his head and his left ear eclipsed Times Square. 'Relax and do as you're told,' he said. 'Now send Guthrie in. He knows his job. You do as he says. Good night, Howard. Take it easy, and for God's sake stop trying to be a hero and just follow orders.'

'Sure,' I said. 'Sure I will. Good night, Ted.'

I stood looking at the truck that held my bunk, feeling the warm wind streaming around me, knowing I couldn't sleep yet. I'd drawn too deep, maybe, on the hidden wellsprings inside myself. Tonight the need the actor in the play had felt for the girl Susan Jones was still alive in me. I looked up at the stars and knew my own need. Rohan's need, for a girl like Cressy Kellogg. It was a strange feeling, clean and fresh and new, as if all my old troubles had washed away in the bath of lights and applause tonight.

After a while I turned my back on the trucks and went slowly across the clearing in the moonlight. The camp was quiet. The cast had gone silently to bed, ignoring me, and I was alone in the world, filled with happiness and confidence and this new, warm need. The moonlight slanted in long beams among the trees, touching everything with a blue unreality like moonlight on a stage. Or maybe intensely real, distilled to the clarity only the stage can give. The ferns were silvery against the rich, dark trees, and a sense of secret awareness filled the whole grove. The trees, the ferns, every living thing was alive tonight, and knew it. Even the air had a life of its own. Even I myself ...

I lit a cigarette and watched the pale blue smoke go streaming away in the wind and wondered if Cressy was asleep. I wondered if I could wake her if she was without wakening everybody else. And if she'd come out to me even if I could. Still thinking about it, I followed my blowing smoke slowly up the path toward the fire-eaten redwood, walking like a man in a dream through bars of blue light and bars of rich, windy darkness.

There was somebody leaning against the tree. I saw another streamer of blue smoke blowing and I heard stiff skirts rustle. Then a circle of pale ruffles like spun sugar moved into the light, and I knew I wasn't the only one who had recognized a need in the play tonight. I hadn't played alone. Cressy had been a part of the story too, and a responding part.

She leaned there looking up at me without surprise, not saying anything. I didn't speak either. The play had spoken for us. In somebody else's words we'd already said to each other tonight everything that needed to be said. I ground out my cigarette carefully upon the inward curve of the big tree's burned-out heart, killing the live coal upon the dead one. I took the cigarette from Cressy's fingers and ground it carefully upon the same burned side of the ever living tree.

She turned to me before my arms came up to take her, and the skirts like spun sugar rustled noisily, for one last moment making a barrier between us, before I felt her knees and thighs mold themselves against mine out of the resisting fabric. She was warm and alive in my arms, letting her head lean back against my hand so her eyes met mine and her smiling mouth stopped smiling and waited for my kiss.

It was all here for the asking. Everything I'd lost in the play and surrendered with such passionate need and such painful loss. But something was making trouble in my mind... I let my hand move down her back, shaping the essential Cressy firm and real under the springing skirts. But something was wrong.

Somewhere in my mind a door closed, firm and slow.

The fresh newness dissolved in me and for an instant the old and terrible feeling came back. I held a clockwork girl in my arms and the moonlight was brassy. A voice in my mind said, 'No, no, this isn't the way you go. This isn't for you. Not yet. Not now.' And then the uncontrollable memory of the dream seemed to glance at me like lightning and recede again before I could know its face. I saw a bright dazzle receding downward too fast to read, too dazzling to ignore. The words of fire I wanted to know and must not. Yet. And I opened my arms and let Cressy go.

There wasn't a thing to say.

I stood looking at her bewildered face a moment or two before I shook my head and let my arms drop, made a gesture of negation and helplessness, and walked slowly back through a night gone murky to the caravan and my bunk again.

I lay on the bunk for a long time, looking out at the stars, hearing the wind sough, soft and vast, through the swaying heights above me. I was at first too puzzled and disturbed to sleep.

One thing seemed certain. That dream I thought I had dreamed in the New York bedroom hadn't been a thing that happened in sleep. It had to be real. In a haze of alcohol and drugs I must have perceived dizzily a real man who whispered real words in my ear, the haze distorting everything that happened. Who it was, and why, still swam in the mists of hallucination. But he had told me things I couldn't have dreamed. He had—

I blinked at the stars. He *had* sent me here, to this troupe, this grove, this one itinerary among all the paths I might have chosen. This one place. Why? What had he told me that I must not remember? I beat my knuckles against my temple trying to jolt an answer out. But you can't get answers that way.

This much, at least, seemed sure – he had planted some compulsion in my mind that was guiding me – somewhere. Not against my will exactly. But against my knowledge. When I took a wrong turning the old, dead numbness came back as it had come tonight. And when I took a right turning ... I remembered the flooding happiness on stage tonight and the very memory of it lit the fire anew. It was all there. It would

143

come again. Suddenly I felt very tired, very relaxed, very confident. No matter what happened, I knew I could handle it as long as I followed the course my instinct told me.

The sky was powdered to pale silver with the infinite multitudes of the stars receding into infinite smallness. The dot of the rebels' star, Charlie Starr's light, winked red, white, and blue over and over among the tops of the ever living trees. The wind blew and the world turned and I sank into oblivion.

CHAPTER XVIII

A voice under my pillow spoke firm and brisk. It was my own voice. 'Get up, Rohan. Time to get up. Rohan!' I struggled painfully out of sleep so deep I wasn't quite sure who I was. When I could, I reached under the pillow and shut off the sleep teacher I'd set last night in lieu of an alarm clock. The dark was thin outside, just grading over toward dawn. In the bunks around me the motionless lumps that were Pod Henken, Roy, and Guthrie lay heavily. The wind had blown itself out, the stars shone pale above the still sequoias, and far off on the highway a truck went by with a muted roar that sounded obscurely comforting in the deathly chill of dawn.

I went quietly about my business, nobody stirring to see me go. It was still dark under the trees and the needles sighed as I walked on them going up to the truck stop. I had a gun in one coat pocket and in the other the little metal tracer box Guthrie had given me to tag the 'hopper with. It was about as big as a match box, but heavy. I paused at the edge of the clearing to look back.

In the silent trucks the silent cast lay sleeping. I owed them an apology, of course. I'd stolen the show last night from under their noses, cut Polly's part, shifted the pivot character from Roy to myself. They'd gone along with me magnificently, but still I owed apologies all around. I would have to make them later. I was on my way to something bigger than the play this morning, and I knew I wouldn't see this grove again.

Already it looked empty. Under the trees the pattern of our rehearsal stage lay deeply grooved in the needles. The wind had scuffed over the patterns last night, but you could see them still. And in my mind's eye I could see the ghostly shapes of all of us, too, still endlessly rehearsing under the hanging light. A lot had happened to me here in this clearing. A different Rohan went out of it.

A confident Rohan. Last night's tremor of the old deadness had gone again. The warm certainty that nothing could go wrong had come back in the night like a flooding tide, filling all the inlets and hollows of my mind up to the brim. In my pockets the gun and the tracer box balanced each other, both heavy and hard. I walked between them through the darkness, chilly and a little awed by the mountain dawn, but warm in the center with happy confidence.

I got coffee and eggs and hot cakes from a waitress moving in her sleep behind the counter. I hitched a ride with a trucker going toward San Andreas. I got off at the right spot and struck out through the fields toward the brown barn. It was that simple.

This was the day when I couldn't make mistakes. The episode with Cressy last night had somehow dissolved like a dream out of my mind and it seemed to me I had never lost the full flood of my confidence. If there was a guard stationed in the fields around the old barn he was asleep or looking the other way. The door creaked with a melancholy sound when I slipped inside. The 'hopper still sat in the musty, cow-smelling dark just as I had known it would. I couldn't make mistakes. Not now.

I touched the 'hopper's flank and it quivered like something nervous and responsive, glad of company. The tracer box was heavy in my hand. I slapped it on the underside of the 'hopper's frame and felt it leap the last half inch out of my palm and smack eagerly onto the metal surface. Magnetized, I supposed. Anyhow, it stuck.

I seemed to hear Nye's acid voice saying, 'For God's sake stop trying to be a hero and follow orders.' I laughed, gave the 'hopper a farewell pat (it shivered gratefully), and went out into the rapidly paling dawn. I had no intention of following orders.

From Nye's viewpoint I was now finished. From my own I hadn't even started yet. This was a lead I'd bought with my own sweat and blood. I'd risked my neck for the rebel contacts and the 'hopper. Out of what I'd done, somebody was going to make discoveries, trace leads, collect credit. I intended the somebody to be me.

The 'hopper itself was nothing. It might or might not lead into something. I needed a very important something to buy my theater with. I stood there in the thin darkness, breathing deep, testing my intention cautiously against reality. Could I do it? Would the world stay firm and docile under my feet? It would. Confidence brimmed in me like a deep, still tide. I was on the right path. There would be no turning back.

I hadn't a doubt in the world I could do what I meant to do.

The world was awake and rustling around me as I toiled up the mountain slope above the fields where the barn stood. Birds shrilled in the leaves. The sky glowed bright gold in the cloudless east and the morning smelled new-minted. I sat down under a tree to wait. It was wonderful to be alive.

If I had guessed right, whoever came for the 'hopper would have to bring it up in this direction. He wasn't likely to return the way it had come. He was even less likely to drive through San Andreas. From my vantage spot up here I could tell which way he was heading. I could get there first.

He didn't show up for so long I had begun to get sleepy again. The woods were alive around me and the warming air that rose from the meadows breathed upward still and peaceful and fragrant. But after a while I heard a faint buzzing far off and woke from a half doze. At first I couldn't see any motion, but then the high grass began to thresh in a diagonal across one of the meadows and the 'hopper with one man in it showed briefly before it dived again into cover and came invisibly toward the mountain in a heaving of grass, its buzz no louder than a bee's. It seemed to be alone. My luck still held.

I dusted myself off and set out to cut across its path. I had plenty of time. I didn't know exactly what I was going to do, but it didn't worry me. The magic had come back and I knew I couldn't go wrong. I heard the humming deepen as the 'hopper began to climb, and I pulled the gun out of my pocket and ran, bending low, the branches whipping my face. The driver was headed for a gap in the mountain ridge, and I wanted to get there first.

I made it with not much time to spare. On the way I ran into a broken branch that dragged a long scratch across my forehead, and even that was luck, though I didn't know it then. I felt blood begin to trickle and swiped it angrily with the back of my hand as I labored up the slope. The buzzing below swelled like a hive full of bees, and I topped the ridge and looked down on the oval top of the 'hopper bouncing briskly across the side of the hill, the legs on one side bent up tight and the legs on the other long. The driver sat low in the bucket seat, his knees bent high. I was close enough so I couldn't miss.

I took very deliberate aim and shot him through the calf of his left leg. The crack of the gun sounded crisp and loud in the woods, the echoes bouncing off from tree to tree like the sound of many guns firing. Maybe that's where I got my next idea.

I saw the driver double up to grab at his leg, and the 'hopper veered in a downhill semicircle and heaved to a stop. The idea bloomed full size in my mind and I spun away and scrambled over the slope in the gully I'd just emerged from. I rolled a little way downhill, and then I yelled as loud as I could three or four times, changing my voice between yells. At random I fired the rest of the shots in my gun among the trees, still yelling. One bullet whined off a rock. The echoes of them all resounded between the gully walls and diminished among the pines until my little gun fight with myself sounded like a brisk battle among half a dozen. I reloaded fast and fired off three more shots, yelling in several voices. And then I went calmly back across the hillside to the 'hopper.

My man was flat on the ground behind a rock, a gun nosing at me over the top and his eyes looking wide and surprised behind it. I dropped my gun in my pocket and held up both hands.

'It's okay,' I called to him. 'They're gone. Are you all right?'

'Who were they?' he countered, not stirring.

'Comus, I think. Or renegades. How can you tell? I didn't get a very good look.' I smeared the blood trickling down my face to improve things as much as possible. 'I was lucky,' I told him modestly. 'All I got was this. How about you?'

'Never mind about me,' he said, still watching me over his gun. 'Who are you? What are you doing here?'

I gave him a candid look. 'Name's Rohan. My troupe put on a play last night in San Andreas. Also I'm the guy who swiped that 'hopper. Harris's orders.' I smeared my bleeding forehead again and started to turn away. 'If you're all right, I'll go on back,' I said.

'I asked what you were doing here.' He tapped the gun barrel on the rock slightly to remind me about it.

'Tell you the truth,' I said with candor, 'I wasn't so sure just what Harris was planning to do with that 'hopper. After all, I stole it. My prints are all over it. If Harris wants to get me shot all he has to do is have it driven into the nearest Comus station. I got thinking about it last night and I couldn't sleep until I'd checked on it. When I saw you take off over the mountain I figured it was worth a little climb to see what's on this side. Maybe a Comus outfit, for all I knew. Then I heard shots and—' I gestured at my smeared forehead. 'There were only two of them and they're probably a mile away by now.' I paused. 'All right if I go now?' I added plaintively.

He heaved himself up from behind the rock, putting his gun away. 'Lucky for me you were here,' he said grudgingly. 'Thanks.' He looked down at his leg. The cloth was soaked and blood had begun to trickle down the rock he lay on.

I said quickly, 'That doesn't look too good. Let's see.' The bullet had gone through, leaving an unpleasant-looking hole on each side of his calf, and he was bleeding pretty freely. I didn't believe it was serious, but I wanted him to think it was. I gambled on the hope that he was as little used as I to this kind of derring-do. 'Got a handkerchief?' I asked. 'You're losing too much blood. Maybe you'd better get on back to town.' I let him think it over and then added, 'I could drive. I don't think you should.'

He looked pale, but he didn't say yes or no just yet. 'Let's tie it up,' he said. 'Maybe the bleeding will slack off. I want to get on if I can.'

I was very helpful.

CHAPTER XIX

Fifteen minutes later we were bouncing along in the 'hopper side by side, me at the wheel. We were going ahead, not back. I'd brought it off exactly as I'd known I would. I couldn't go wrong today.

The mountains rose in big wooded ridges on both sides. I took us northeast, heading as my new-found victim directed me. His name was Cliff. I asked no questions. I didn't need to. Under the 'hopper I knew the little box was hugging the metal and sending out its invisible, inaudible beeps of signal. Somewhere on a Comus map a little dot of light was crawling as we crawled. Maybe on the map they could see where we were heading. I couldn't. But it didn't matter. Cliff knew and so would I, eventually. Twice I heard the beat of a distant helicopter hovering after us. Both times I talked fast and Cliff was too preoccupied with his battle wound to notice.

I thought of the troupe far behind me, waking, packing, wondering what had become of me. I let the images of them move through my mind – Guthrie and his conflicts, Polly and Roy with their knot of commonplace trouble, Cressy the focus of so many kinds of desire from all of us, the Henkens with so little of life left. How long would they wait on me?

I felt a little sorry for Guthrie, in an agony of indecision by now, not sure whether he still had a show with Rohan missing. Let him sweat, I thought. Douglass Flats isn't too far away. I'd looked up the next stop on our itinerary and I could make it before opening time. Or if I didn't, I'd have a reason.

But I knew in my own mind I'd be there. The troupe would

know it too. They wouldn't be really worried. Wild horses couldn't have kept me off my stage last night. I'd make it if I had to tear down mountains to get there. Meanwhile there was another kind of work before me, and that looked promising too.

About half an hour later we topped a ridge and rolled downhill through high, streaming grass into one of the prettiest little mountain meadows in the world. A blue stream snaked through it and the floor of the valley was shoulder-high with flowering reeds and grass.

Cliff leaned forward, pointing. 'There,' he said.

You had to look twice to see it. The building was wide and low, with a roof thatched with growing grass so the reconnaissance planes that can tell the difference between green paint and chlorophyll couldn't spot it!

I said, 'What is it?' and Cliff said, 'Distribution center,' and went back to the careful nursing of his knee, which had a large, bloodstained bandage around it. I stared eagerly at the place, my heart beginning to thump a little heavily. So much depended on the next few minutes. And minutes was all I'd have. What I could accomplish before the helicopters closed in on us might determine success or failure for me, whether Rohan went back to the Croppers or rose to the top again in New York. And I had no idea even what I wanted to do. I'd have to snatch the moment as it came.

The grass streamed like water against the glass as we went rocking along the marshy valley floor. Twice sentries stopped us and demanded our business over the muzzle of a shotgun. We left the 'hopper under a tree at the corner of the building and Cliff, leaning heavily on me, progressed with painful hops toward the door. I could hear a busy hum of voices from inside now. I kept telling myself that every minute counted. I had to get as good a look as I could at the inside and pick up some kind of lead – any kind – before hell broke loose.

The inside was like a hive. I had time for one quick look too confused to tell me much before anyone noticed us. This was more like a factory than a building clear back of beyond, hidden in a mountain meadow. How all these people had got here without leaving more traces I had no time to wonder. Comus must have been hunting hard for places like this. There were long tables with people working in assembly lines packing boxes with ammunition and food. There were shelves and racks of clothes, boots, blankets. There were stacks of combat ration packs and first aid boxes.

And off in a corner behind a screen somebody was operating a machine that gave out long, muffled shrieks of metal on metal now and then. A smell like burned iodine came from behind the screen, and several people appeared to be moving around a table on which something absorbingly interesting was being assembled back there. I could see two or three of the bent heads from where I stood, and one of the heads was a woman's, with a dark, braided coronet of hair I seemed to remember.

At this point somebody near the door looked up and saw us. From then on for a few moments we had a minor riot, everyone wanting to know immediately what had happened to Cliff, and if this might be the forerunner of a raid. Several voices in overlapping sequence called for Elaine and Dr Thomas, who happened to be the same person. The crowd opened for her, cool and efficient, wearing a blue shirt and slacks today that did a lot more for her than the white coat I'd last seen her wearing. The black eyes went suddenly round and alert when she recognized me.

A gray-haired man with a scar across his cheek seemed to be in charge here. Elaine Thomas broke out a first aid kit and went to work on Cliff's leg while I told them my simple story. It was, perhaps, lucky for me that Elaine had been present at the scene of my induction to rebellion back in San Andreas.

'I ran the lie-box test on him myself,' she said, glancing up briefly as the gray-haired man shot questions. 'Unless he's had a complete change of heart since, he's still on our side.' She gave me a quick upward look. 'Or are you?' she asked.

'I'm on my own side. I told you that from the start.' I returned her look. The black eyes were managing to convey that she still thought there might be something interesting and exciting between us if we ever met away from the crowd, but she went on bandaging with quiet competence.

The gray-haired man was intensely interested in the alleged raid by two men on the 'hopper back there on the outskirts of San Andreas. I found it hard to keep my story plausible. I talked fast, making a good production of it, knowing all I had to do was keep talking for a matter of minutes, because Comus was on the way and coming fast. I told him about the 'hopper parked outside by the tree. I described the two men who were supposed to have jumped me. And all the while I was trying desperately to pick some lead out of this busy hive that could help me lever money out of Nye. I had to have something. I couldn't go back now without information of value, something to sweeten the reception already waiting for me.

I think just about then was the time I heard the first buzz of the helicopters. I heard it because I was listening. For the others, no heads rose. Elaine finished off the bandage and straightened, holding her bloody hands away from her, palms up with the fingers curled in, and gazed at me with a faint smile. 'Now what are we going to do with you, Rohan? This is a private place here. You aren't really supposed to know about it. Makes things awkward.'

'You might just shoot me,' I suggested, smiling at her. The black eyes, grave and considering, flickered at me with that readiness in them for the time when we might find ourselves alone together and free to explore whatever might come next. How much we might enjoy it, and how little chance there was that the time would ever come. But there was confidence in the look, and a kind of wary trust, and it occurred to me that nobody had looked at me like that for a long time.

It made me think of Miranda. A woman with warmth and beauty, a woman skilled in her profession, looking up at me with expectation. Miranda had looked at me like that. Miranda had thought – for a long time, perhaps – that the expectation was based on something real. That I had something in me to give. I don't know what. Something besides the fierce drive

I always focused on my work, something under the savage temper and the hard control. But for Miranda there hadn't been anything there at all.

Suddenly all the warm confidence that had been brimming through me in bright, hot waves cooled and receded. Suddenly I felt again like the hollow man I had been so long. I looked down with hatred at Elaine Thomas. I wanted to yell at her, 'You think I've got what Miranda thought I had, and not getting it from me killed her. And killed me. But I don't know what the hell it is you want, and whatever it is I haven't got it. All I know how to do is drive straight at what I want the hard way, no matter what it costs anybody. Me or anybody. No matter if I have to shut Miranda out of my life. No matter if I have to play the rebels here who trust me against Nye, who knows me for what I am, and double-cross Nye with the rebels to get the thing I'm after. I don't know any other way. I can't do it any other way. If I could I wouldn't. I'm Rohan, nobody else. I'm Rohan, and I do things my way!'

It all went sizzling through my head in the click of an instant while the black-eyed girl stood there with her bloody hands palms up, faintly smiling at me. While I stood hollow and shaken, hating her, a sudden crackle of gunfire made flat, slamming noises just outside the door. Somebody's yell of warning flatted upward into a scream.

After that everything went wild.

For just a moment longer I was hollow. Everything had drained out of my life again. I'd lost my chance too fast to accomplish anything. Here it ended.

But there was order in his sudden wildness. It took them only seconds to get organized. And out of that order I saw my chance. The warm, bright upward waves of confidence came welling back and Rohan was himself again.

I saw men and women jumping for the gun slots in the wall, grabbing up weapons as they went. The rest of the workers went into purposeful action, organizing under my eyes into a well-rehearsed drill they must have run over a hundred times, in readiness for the Day Comus Finds Us. The gray-haired man swung away from me, yelling orders over the tumult from outside, where gunfire still slammed deafeningly. The Comus men and the sentries out there were having a brisk battle. Nobody inside had yet fired a shot, though at the gun slots everybody with weapons stood tense, waiting for – something.

I jumped into action with the rest. I had it all back again, the happy confidence, the good luck. I couldn't miss. Even this was good. Because the things they salvaged were the important things. They were telling me plainer than words what to follow up.

I played it straight. Two women were struggling to rip the lid off a crate of rifles, and I grabbed the chisel out of their hands and levered the boards apart, nails shrieking. People at the antibiotics shelves were cramming their pockets with little boxes, and I dragged up a stool and handed down supplies off the higher shelves into their hands.

That was how I happened to see the box with the rings in it. Up on a top shelf, with DANGER – POISON in big red letters cross the front. I flipped the lid open while I was reaching for more packets of antibiotics, and two rows of neat gold finger rings looked up at me out of their nests, each with a round blue set like an innocent eye. They came in graduated sizes. Inside the lid of the box my quick glance had time to read the one matter-of-fact line of typed instruction pasted to the lining.

'Crush glass between teeth. Cyanide – Instantaneous Death.'

I stood motionless for a moment, letting that information sink it. The rings looked up at me, blue-eyed and full of instantaneous death. My mind felt very still in the midst of all this hubbub as I thought about it. I closed the lid quietly.

Shoveling down the boxes with automatic motions, I tried to remember why the rings hadn't looked entirely strange to me. I'd seen one on somebody's hand here in this building in the last few minutes. Just a passing glance, hardly noticed. Who? Whoever it was, he had to be important. You don't wear a cyanide ring for fun. You have to know important things that you don't dare risk talking about, even under narcosynthesis. Who?

Then I had it. The gray-haired man with the scar.

I was standing there thinking it over when the uproar from outside slackened and ceased. My ears drummed with the silence for a moment. Then an enormous metal voice roared through an amplifier outside.

'On the count of ten,' the great voice bellowed, 'we fire sleep bombs. You have a ten-count to come out with your hands up. One! Two . . . !'

I felt an instant of panic.

I'd never been on the receiving end of a sleep bomb, but I knew a percentage of the gassed victims just don't wake up. How big a percentage no two people ever agreed on.

If anybody else was scared, no one showed it. I heard rapid orders in half a dozen overlapping voices, confusing like crowd voices on stage.

'All ammunition carriers this way – meet Pedro at Eleven Eighty.'

'All food carriers scatter and meet at the Olsens' after sundown.'

'Diversion crews, work from the southeast corner. Cover the 'hopper getaway.' This last time was from the gray-haired man, who got up on a table to make sure everybody heard him. I looked at his hand and saw a blue ring glint briefly. He was shouting over the hubbub, waving his arm for attention.

'Cover the 'hopper getaway!' he was repeating. 'Pull attention away from the 'hopper! Have you all got that? Do it any way you can, but do it!'

From outside the vast metallic voice counted ominously, 'Five! You have a five-count now to come out with your hands up. You inside there! Six! Seven!'

The man on the table glanced around the walls at the people standing ready by the gun slots. He lifted his hand ready to signal. 'Here it comes,' he called. 'Brace yourselves, everybody. All right – fire!' And he dropped his hand.

All around the walls I heard the simultaneous crackle of the shots. The enormous noise from outside came so sudden and so loud I had the strange feeling I'd missed hearing how it began. One moment all was comparatively still. The next my head was reverberating like a gong and the whole room was solid with the crash of sound, and I had no memory of just when it started.

Some reeling element of reason told me the rebels must have set off some kind of buried mines in the area outside, around the building. Maybe by the simple expedient of firing at prearranged trigger spots. But all of us inside, even those who knew what to expect, were stunned for a moment by the noise.

Then the rumble of heavy doors sliding open sounded all around the walls of the building. Light gushed in blue with smoke and seething with dust, and out through the clouds of it the rebels went scattering. Everybody but me knew exactly what to do.

I had one brief second of hesitation. Then I found I too knew what I was going to head for. The 'hopper. Make for the 'hopper. Whatever they load into the 'hopper is the big thing. That's what you're here for. Don't miss it.

Outside, blinding in the sunlight, I saw the Comus helicopters sitting heavily in the flowery meadow a little way off. All around the building a ring of blackened grass and raw earth lay smoldering heavily. Bodies lay among the embers, and what Comus men were still on their feet looked dazed and unsteady. But they were recovering fast. Not quite as fast as the rebels scattered, but almost fast enough.

Now an outburst of yells and shots rang out noisily from the far corner of the building, and a series of minor explosions burst out toward the river. I wanted badly to turn and look, but I thought it was cover-up action from the diversion crews. I knew the 'hopper was the really important spot.

The scattering crowd ran like purposeful rabbits for the forest. They ran in all directions. But a few converged toward the tree where the 'hopper sat, and I was foremost among them. I was second on the spot. But in moments I was the center of a busy, silent throng loading boxes into the seat beside the driver's. Elaine Thomas was shoving packets this way and that to make room for a big, flat, square bundle about two feet across and wrapped tenderly in blankets like a baby susceptible to draughts. The way she handled it, and the way everybody here seemed to touch it with respect verging on awe, made me look at the thing with gathering excitement.

I wondered what it was. I wondered if this could be wishful thinking, or was it what I thought it was . . .

The gray-haired man was giving orders in a quick, firm whisper. 'All right, that's it,' he said after a fast thirty seconds of work that seemed a lot longer. 'In with you, Elaine. Don't argue. Quick! Keep to the high grass and try to cross the ridge at the gap. The rest of you, scatter out and run alongside through the grass. Thresh around. Make it wave. All right, get going. Good luck!'

We went. We spread out and ran blindly, I running with the rest, the reeds whipping my face, the marshy ground sucking at my shoes. Behind me scattered gunfire broke out as the Comus men began to get their wits back. All around me I heard feet thump, reeds lash, men breathing heavily as they ran, and to my right the beelike humming of the 'hopper carrying Elaine and the unknown treasure away from me faster than I could ever hope to run.

I wasn't getting anywhere this way. I'd had one glimpse and no more of something that might be, could be, just possibly was the biggest thing in California. Or a part of the biggest thing. But in minutes the 'hopper would take to the rising ground and go heaving up the slope and over into the woods. And after that I was finished. Somebody else would trace the 'hopper by its signal box still clinging to the metal. Somebody else would get the credit. Unless—

The gunfire from behind us picked up in volume. I heard the deep, heavy throb of a helicopter engine starting and realized that whatever I did I'd have to do fast. And anonymously. I was playing both sides against the middle and if either of them caught me at it I was done.

Underfoot the ground seemed firmer. It didn't cling to the feet any more and a slope was beginning to rise under the thick grass. I heard the 'hopper's buzz quicken as its wheels got better purchase and its laboring motor heaved it upward with a sudden burst of speed. Then the reeds thinned and through them I saw the little machine swaying and grinding up the slope, Elaine bent low over the wheel. She had outdistanced her escort already. In a moment or two she'd be over the ridge and out of my reach.

I stood still among the reeds, pulled the gun out of my pocket, and took careful aim. I waited for another burst of gunfire from behind us. When it came – and none too soon, for now the 'hopper was topping the ridge – I pulled the trigger steadily.

The 'hopper gave a violent lurch. Fire sprang out in brief, bright sparks from its underside where my bullet struck. I was glad they didn't ignite anything. That was pure luck, for an instant after a gush of heavy black oil burst out of its transmission chamber and poured sluggishly over the rocks. I had been holding my breath without realizing it, expecting an explosion. For one vivid moment it seemed to me I was looking into Elaine's bright black, expectant eyes that asked of me something I didn't have to give her. Protection? The thought that I should spare her from danger if she stood between me and what I wanted? I never spared myself. I knew now I never spared Miranda. No, if Elaine expected that from me then she expected too much.

But when I saw the black oil come panting out of the nervous little 'hopper's vitals in thick gushes I had a moment's foolish grief for the machine that I could not let myself feel for living creatures.

All this happened in a split second of action and response. The moment I pulled the trigger I had dropped flat on my face to the ground, and not a moment too soon. Three or four bullets whistled over my head among the reeds. I'll never know if they were Comus bullets or rebel. The threshing and thumping around me in the reeds paused suddenly, and then when nothing happened resumed its cautious advance. Voices called softly. I called too, asking with the rest what had happened. Nobody seemed to know.

Moments later, exchanging suspicious looks, we came out of the underbrush wiping mud and sweat off our faces. The helicopter was laboring to get off the ground back there in the meadow. Gunfire rattled sporadically around the building we had abandoned and now and then a stray bullet went wailing thinly over our heads. I looked up in time to see three or four men scramble to the disabled 'hopper and heave it over the ridge and out of sight.

I started up the slope after it. A bullet sang past my ear and smacked the rock six feet ahead of me, sending up splinters of stone in my face. Over to the left I heard a solid, thudding sound and didn't know it for what it was until a man beside me coughed and pitched forward and began to slide gently down the slope in a little avalanche of pebbles. I felt adrenalin pour fresh energy into every nerve and muscle I had as I hurled myself upward and dropped over the top of the ridge, landing on my bruised side. I slid a dozen feet before I could stop myself.

The gray-haired man was wrenching the 'hopper door open and I saw Elaine scrambling out backward, dragging the blanket-wrapped bundle across the seat. Even now, in all this stress, it seemed to me she handled it with awe, as if it might be the Grail. And maybe it was. Maybe it was a part of the biggest thing in California. Bigger than the biggest redwood. Bigger than San Francisco Bay. Bigger than Los Angeles. Bigger than the world, at least to Nye and to me and to all the rebels in the whole country. If it was what it might be . . .

There was an outburst of gunfire from the slope I'd just left, echoed by firing from the canebrakes below. It was loud at first as the guns of the rebels sounded in full chorus, and then it got ragged, because the slope was in full sight from the reeds and there wasn't any shelter out there. We had only minutes more of safety here.

I saw the gray-haired man look around with fast, considering glances, sizing up the situation. I jumped to help Elaine. My hands itched to feel the outlines of whatever it was she had wrapped in the blanket. Not that in my ignorance I could tell anything, but at least there'd be that much to report to Nye even if this whole project fell through from this point on. More eagerly than a bridegroom reaching for the bride, or a father reaching for his first-born, I took the bundle in my hands. For one tantalizing instant I felt its irregular and mysterious form beneath the blanket, intricate, blurred, indescribable.

Then an outburst of shouts and the crack of firing exploded from the far side of the little clearing where the 'hopper sat. I was too absorbed to think what it meant. The gray-haired man was quicker. He grabbed my shoulder and spun me around, snatching the blanket-wrapped Grail away from me. He heaved it back onto the 'hopper seat. He seized Elaine's arm and whirled her away. 'Stand back!' he said. 'Elaine, get away from the 'hopper.'

She knew what he meant if I didn't.

'Oh no!' she said with anguish. 'Tony, we can make it some-how. This is almost the last unit. Tony, we *can't*—'

'We've got to!' he yelled at her. 'We're surrounded. I have to do it. Stand back.' He dragged the gun from his belt, shouting, 'Scatter! Scatter!' to the nearer men. The firing grew stronger from both sides now, coming up the slope from the meadow and closing in on us from the trees beyond the clearing. The gray-haired man leveled his gun at the bundle on the 'hopper seat.

Elaine cried, 'No, Tony, don't!' and tried desperately to throw herself between him and the bundle. He didn't speak, but he gave her a heavy backhanded blow across the face that sent her staggering. And then he pulled the trigger.

The explosion seemed enormous. The Grail itself must have had its own potential destruction built into it for just such an emergency as this. Flying bits of glass or metal hissed by us in the shaken air. The clearing was blinding-bright for an instant, then invisible as our eyes reacted to the flash. When I could see again there was nothing but smoke, the twisted wreckage of the 'hopper, and a blue-violet afterimage of the explosion that swam on the surface of my eyes and half obscured everything I looked at.

I heard a familiar voice still yelling, 'Scatter, scatter!' from just behind me, and I turned blindly and stumbled toward it. The haze in the clearing seemed filling up with struggling figures and the flash and noise of gunfire. I saw the gray-haired man running through the trees away from me. Comus had caught up with us at last.

And everything was over. I had nothing to show for all my efforts, all my risks. I'd touched the precious mystery, but no more. Like What's-His-Name and the Grail, I could feel it but never see it. It *had* to be a part of the Anti-Com. In my daze it seemed to me not only that it had to be, but that I'd been all but led here, guided by forces out of a dream and my own compulsive behavior. I had touched the precious thing, and then, like the Grail, it had vanished in a flash of light seven times brighter than day.

I looked around wildly. Elaine wasn't anywhere in sight. I saw rebels whose faces I recognized either down in the dust or running. I saw a gray-headed figure disappearing among the trees. And sudden blinding rage flooded through me at the sight of him. The man who had snatched success out of my hands in the instant I touched it. The man who had smashed the Grail.

In the midst of my anger I heard a still, small voice. Quite coolly it suggested, 'If you can't take back the Grail itself, why not take back the man who knows about it?' I spun with the dust slipping under my feet and lurched after the running man...

I remember a bullet sang by me and slit my shirt sleeve neatly as I turned. The next thing I remember is a man's running back just ahead of me, and hurling myself at him, almost missing, catching him around the knees so we crashed down together across the rocky slope. I heard the breath go out of him in a grunt of surprise and pain. I had a rock in my hand as I scrambled to my knees, and I hit him with it across the back of the head, praying as I struck that I wasn't hitting too hard. He grunted again and went slack.

I grabbed for his limp hand and wrenched at the blue

cyanide ring. It wouldn't come off. He must have been wearing it a long time, I thought, almost wonderingly. I looked at his gray head and marveled at the secrets he must have stored away in there that I'd give so much to know. So much, so much!

The blue glass set wasn't very hard. It couldn't be if the wearer had to bite through it when the time came. I tapped his hand on a rock until the glass broke and the colorless liquid ran out onto the stone, bitter-almond-smelling, deadly. I held my breath until the breeze blew it away.

Then I lay down beside him in the dust and waited. It seemed like a long time. The noise around us slowly died away. Finally somebody's foot against my shoulder turned me over and I looked up into the disciplined face of a stranger.

'Get up,' he said. 'You're under arrest.'

I sat up stiffly. 'I think I've got a rebel leader for you here,' I said. 'Take us to headquarters.'

He gave me a skeptical look.

'That's a new one. Don't worry. Headquarters is where you're going.'

CHAPTER XX

Nobody knows how big a bite of the tax dollar Comus draws, but it isn't a small one. Comus doesn't stint itself. The local captain's office had thick carpeting with a rich, raised pattern and gold thread curling through it. The furniture was all glass. The captain himself looked green and yellow because of the stained-glass insets in the window behind him.

I sat in a black glass chair with gold fringe under it and argued fiercely across the gilt glass desk with the captain. He was a dapper man who looked uncomfortable out of uniform, and he didn't like me.

For a while I thought I'd have to go clear through to Ted Nye before they'd let me out of custody. I felt arrogant and self-confident. I think it may have been my confidence that tipped the balance. They listened to my story, looked over my ID cards, checked my photograph with my face, and finally with sour reluctance, agreed to talk to Guthrie. I told them no more than I had to.

'The man I captured for you is one of their top brass,' I said over and over in various versions. 'For God's sake look after him even, if you don't believe me.' Grudgingly they said they would.

They had to get through clear back to Washington to find Guthrie's call number, but after that it didn't take too long. On the wall screen above the captain's desk Guthrie, after a while, dawned glowering. The whole image kept jiggling, and behind Guthrie I could see the inside of the sound truck from the front end toward the back. The rear door wasn't quite shut and through the slit I could see a sunny road unreeling as the caravan jolted toward Douglass Hats. They must have waited a long time for me.

Guthrie blew up.

I let him blow. He said he hoped they'd hang me. He said he hadn't known where the hell I was or what the hell to do, and if I didn't get to Douglass Flats in time for the evening performance he would—

I said briskly, 'Oh, shut up, Guthrie. Listen, I've got news for you. Things have been happening. I want to talk to Ted Nye as soon as I can do it privately, so I wish you'd make an appointment for me. It shouldn't be hard – he expects me.' I put that in for the benefit of the captain. Guthrie started to interrupt and I shouted him down.

'I'll be with you as quick as a helicopter can get me there,' I said. 'You haven't got a thing to worry about. Just talk to the captain here and tell him who I am. I don't want to lose any more time.'

Guthrie glared at me, drummed on the table, and counted ten. The red flush that had suffused him receded slowly as he got himself under control. With great reluctance he started talking to the captain.

Half an hour later, bathed, shaved, and with all my abrasions medicated, I stepped into a helicopter and rose into the bright, hot noonday sky heading south. Half an hour after that I stepped out again onto the street of Douglass Flats.

The three trucks of our caravan sat side by side in a little grove of light-leaved trees around a stone camp stove just like the one we'd left in the redwoods. The same grease-stained plank table sat beside it. Public camps must be pretty much alike all through California. Beyond the flickering leaves I could see the roofs of Douglass Flats under a clear sky.

Pod and Eileen Henken were playing cards at one end of the table. Roy Copley, looking very young and boyish, was practicing a variety of inflections in his 'red-hot coffee' speech while Polly watched and listened critically, her red head on one side. I didn't see Cressy, and Guthrie was out of sight too.

Polly was the first to see me. I don't know just what I'd expected from them – angry reproaches or the complete freeze-out seemed likeliest. What actually happened surprised me. Polly looked up and said almost casually, 'Well, *there* you are. It's about time. God, you look terrible. Listen, Rohan, how do you like this for a reading? Go on, Roy, give us that half turn again and stutter a little before you start talking.'

And Roy stepped back, swung round in a half turn, faced me, and stuttered spontaneously into his speech as fresh and new as if he'd never spoken the words before. I gave my head a little shake and my mind took a half turn of its own, rotating back into the world of the Swann Players as if I'd never left it. For part of my mind it was a hard shift to make. But for another part the change was the easiest thing in the world. I felt as if I'd really never been away from the troupe. A part of me never had.

'Put more bite into it,' I told Roy critically. 'It's good. Let's have it once more.'

Polly gave me a grudging smile. 'Had lunch?' she asked. 'I'll open something.'

I nodded casually. 'Thanks. I wish you would.'

No, I'd never been away. And yet in a very clear sense I had been, and my absence had wrought some change in the troupe. I wasn't sure what. And it didn't matter. They'd known I'd come back. After last night they'd known no power on earth could keep me off the stage in Douglass Flats. I felt thankful for small favors. Life would be simpler now with the Swann Players.

I asked about a permit to open tonight, and Polly, setting a freshly unsealed plate of what looked like beef stew before me, said Guthrie had seen to it on the way in. She handed me a fork. Roy dipped his finger in spilled coffee and drew an oval on the tabletop.

'The rebels aren't very strong in Douglass Flats,' he said, giving the oval eyes, nose, and mouth. 'Guthrie saw the local mayor and he says it's okay.' He added a band across the forehead, and a padlock. Then he wrote 'Rohan' instead of

'Comus' as a label for the padlock, and gave me a wry grin. 'Rehearsal this afternoon? God, how I hate the stage.'

I took a bite of the stew and shook my head at him. I felt fine, confidence was warm in me, but exhaustion had begun to shiver under the confidence and I knew I was going to fold up if I didn't get some rest between now and tonight. The Cropper years had left me tough, but there's a limit to what any man can take.

'You might run through it once from about twenty-one on,' I said. 'Just to make sure. We skipped some of it last night. I'm sorry about that. We'll play it straight from now on. But I've got to get some rest. Maybe Guthrie would read my lines for you.'

At this point Guthrie came to the door of the sound truck, saw me, and yelled, 'Mr Rohan!' in an arbitrary voice. I picked up my plate of stew and crossed over to join him.

Cressy looked at me, large-eyed and startled, from the window that opened into the body of the truck from behind the driver's seat. All I could see of her was her round folded arms on the sill, and her chin on her hands and the halo of silvery-yellow curls with the light behind them. I gave her a wary look. After last night who knew how she felt?

She said in a perfectly friendly voice, 'When did *you* get back? We were all wondering—' Here she paused and then asked, 'Anything wrong?'

I shook my head slowly. 'No. Nothing wrong.' But I hardly heard my own words. Seeing her there framed in the window like a three-dimensional portrait of herself, I thought again, automatically, Miranda – a copy of Miranda – not like her, and yet – Miranda.

And the strange thing was that not until this moment had I thought of Miranda since I left the camp that morning. It was the longest time I'd ever gone, waking and sober or sleeping and drunk, without the unquiet ghost that moved between me and the world. I felt strangely lightened and relieved, and strangely saddened. 'No,' I said again. 'Nothing wrong.'

Guthrie said to her in a gentle voice, 'Run along, Cressy.

Mr Rohan and I have to talk business awhile.' She raised her eyebrows at him, gave me an impersonal smile, and said, 'Okay, I can take a hint.' Guthrie stood for a moment watching her go, some of the old sadness returning to his face. It was curious how she made us both feel sad at this moment. But when he turned to me the anger came back, and in my own mind the bright, hot confidence which sadness had submerged came flooding up in response. I swung around to face the television screen as he switched it on with a loud, impatient click.

Space dissolved in front of us. We spanned the Rockies with a glance, swooped across the Great Plains, leaped the Appalachians, and without passing through doors at all were suddenly inside Comus City, New York, talking to unstable secretaries who kept dissolving as we talked to them into other secretaries just as unstable. The last one of all dissolved into Ted Nye.

He looked up across his littered desk, distracted and irritable. His eyes were sunken into dark hollows in his little pinched face. He didn't look as if he'd slept in a week.

'What the hell do you want?' he demanded. 'Talk fast. You've got one minute.' I could hear two of his intercoms buzzing and winking out of sight, and there were voices in the room talking with a note of hysteria in them. Things weren't going too well in Comus City. Above the voices I heard one distinct trilling cheep and grinned with the realization that one denizen at least of the heart of empire felt pretty good today.

'Anything new on the Anti-Com?' I asked casually. Nye scowled at me, punched something on the desk, and picked up his earphone cup, as I had thought he would. Unless there were lip readers behind him, whatever else I said would be fairly confidential.

He said snappishly, 'Go on. What have you got?'

'Good news. If you're worried about the Anti-Com getting completed too soon you can relax. I got one of the important units blown up this morning. It'll take a while to rebuild unless they've got replacements.'

His little tense face went slowly dark with a heavy flush. 'How do you know? Tell me what happened. Talk fast.'

I laughed. The careless confidence I floated on was intoxicating as liquor. Now I had him. Now I couldn't fail. I gave him the story. He listened, tapping a pencil against his teeth and watching me as if he could drag the words out faster by sheer concentration.

When I was through he said, 'But you don't *know* the package was what you think?' He was almost pleading with me to say I was sure, and the hand that held the earcup shook against his cheek.

'I know what I think,' I said. 'I know how they acted – how they handled it. How they felt when they had to blow it up. No, I couldn't swear it was an Anti-Com unit, but I know who could swear. That man with the gray hair I pinned down for your boys to arrest. He was in charge. He seemed to know all about the job. Run him through a psychoscreening under Pentothal and then you can tell me.'

Nye banged his teeth with the pencil again. Then without another word he reached out and switched off the screen. He was already turning swiftly away as he shrank to do a dot that receded at infinite speed to the other side of the continent.

I looked at Guthrie and grinned. 'Wake me when he calls back,' I said. 'I'm going to catch up on sleep. With any luck, I'll wake up a rich man again.'

I went out, walking confidently. I knew it would work just as I'd said it would. I couldn't fail. The cast looked up as I came by but I only nodded. They weren't important any more.

Dimly as I dropped off to sleep in my bunk the face of Elaine drifted across my mind. The face of the gray-haired man crossed it like a dissolve on a movie screen. Remotely I thought of what they would be thinking and feeling now. What all this might mean to the rebels in all the areas in the country. What it might mean to us all. It didn't touch me. I did what I had to do. I knew what I wanted.

Sleep sucked me down into a vortex of nothingness and all thinking shrank, like Ted Nye, to a shining dot that vanished.

CHAPTER XXI

Thirty seconds later someone shook me heavily. I looked up into Pod Henken's face. I couldn't figure out how he happened to be wearing make-up, hearty pink with black lines carefully worked in at the eye corners. There hadn't been time, for one thing. I'd seen him playing cards at the table less than a minute ago. But beyond him the truck door framed blue twilight with trees blowing in a gentle wind.

'Guthrie wants you in the sound truck,' Pod said. 'Got some kind of message for you. He says hurry. It's time to wake up anyhow. We open in less than an hour.'

I groped my way dimly across the campsite, foggy with sleep. In the sound truck for a groggy moment I thought Ted Nye had somehow teleported himself three thousand miles in less than a minute and was sitting here in the truck bouncing excitedly. But it was only his image on the screen flipping off intercom switches as soon as he saw me and beaming from ear to ear. He started talking before I got my mouth open.

'You've done it, Howard!' he cried. 'God love you, you've done it! The rebel spilled everything he knew, and he knew plenty.'

'So it *was* an Anti-Com part,' I said, not surprised.

'A big part. One of the last units. Howard, we've got them now. With any kind of luck, we've got them.'

'What do you mean, luck?' I asked, rubbing my face to clear the fog away. I couldn't help feeling this was part of the last talk I'd had with him only a few seconds ago. Time seemed to have taken a long jump and I wasn't caught up with it yet. 'Haven't you got the Anti-Com? Isn't everything over?'

A shadow crossed Nye's face. 'Well, not quite. Not yet. We still need your help, Howard. And, incidentally, I was dead wrong about the kind of help you can give. You can name your own price. You've done a job none of my trained men seemed able to do. I keep wondering—' Here he paused and looked at me with narrowed eyes. He sounded baffled. 'Howard, how did you know?'

'Know what?' I felt an uneasy stirring in my mind.

He shook his head. 'I'm not even sure what I'm asking. You went so straight to the mark – somehow. Right from the beginning. Right from the time you asked for the Swann Players and hit San Andreas instead of some other town in the area. How did you know San Andreas was the spot?'

'Is it?' I asked.

'You know what I mean. No, San Andreas was just the jumping-off point for you. But you jumped so straight. I – Howard, why did you ask for the Swann Players?'

Something in the back of my mind said, 'Be careful, Rohan.' I said, 'If I knew I'd tell you. Luck, I suppose. It had to happen to somebody and the somebody turned out to be me. That's all. What do you mean, you haven't got the Anti-Com yet? Didn't my boy know where it is?'

'No, he didn't. He knew only about the part he supervised. He couldn't tell us how the Anti-Com works or where it's being assembled. These rebels are playing it cagey. No one person knows very much. They're smart – but not smart enough. Not quite. With any luck, we've got them. That's where you come in, Howard.'

I rubbed my face again, gingerly because my cuts and bruises hurt. I was going to have quite a job of make-up to do tonight. I said, 'Go on, go on. Where do I come in?'

'You put your play on tonight exactly as it's written. Understand? Exactly. And tomorrow I'm changing your itinerary. According to what your man spilled, Carson City's a hotbed. We're going to screen it with everything we've got. I want you to get every rebel in the township into your grandstands tomorrow night. I'll leave it to you to figure out how, but it's important. Can you do it?'

I said, 'Sure. I'll think of something. But why, Ted? What's this about the theater? I don't see—'

'Forget it. Let me worry about that. I'll explain later on, after we've won.'

We looked at each other warily. What he was thinking I don't know, but there was a little riot of thoughts rushing around in my own head. I'd had to ask. It would have looked as if I knew more than I really did know if I hadn't. Naturally he wasn't giving anything away. Just as naturally he'd made it clear the theater was part of the screening process of California. I wondered if I should say, 'By the way, Ted, the rebels know quite a lot about what's in this sound truck and why. They know it's a gimmick for tracking down some of the Anti-Com parts. Does that make any difference in our plans?'

I didn't say it. I wanted to find the Anti-Com as badly as he did. I didn't care how I went about it. But that quiet voice in the back room of my mind, the one that had said a moment ago, 'Be careful, Rohan,' now said, 'Keep your mouth shut, Rohan. That's an order.' And I didn't speak. I didn't even question the voice. So far it had led me right. I was willing to play along – up to a point.

Nye peered at me, elated but nervous. 'If we pull in the right man tonight or tomorrow, you can ask for anything you want,' he said. 'I mean it, Howard.' He shifted uneasily. 'Well, I guess that's about it. See you later. Good night and good luck, Howard.'

I crossed my fingers at him as he faded out of sight.

I stood under the grandstand in the street of Douglass Flats listening to the shuffle of feet overhead, the creak of the benches, the voices pitched a little high with excitement. Something new had come to Douglass Flats and the audience sounded responsive already. I breathed in the night air as deep as my chest would take it. I felt wonderful. I felt the world turn underfoot and knew it was turning because I walked on it. I wanted to turn it faster. I wanted to hurry on that hour when I stepped out into the floodlights and brought the play to life around me. There isn't any more wonderful experience in life. Not any. Tonight I'd play it straight, but it would still be my part, my play. I knew it. I could feel already what those first moments would be like when I felt the act of creation spark to life inside me, reach out and flood the stage and the audience and the world and fuse them all to one single breathing unit, me at the center.

Roy and Polly stood beside me, a million miles away, wrapped in their little separate worlds, creating their new personalities around them. Cressy was smoothing her skirts with nervous, unconscious gestures, her gaze focused inward, turning herself into the Susan Jones she would be in another minute or two when she crossed the threshold from darkness into floodlight on her cue. She and Polly had not spoken to each other at all on the way here. I could guess why, but it wasn't any concern of mine.

Everybody looked stiff and scared. Second-night stage fright isn't quite as bad as first-night, but it takes a long while to wear off. For some people it never does wear off no matter how long they play. I was a little surprised to realize that for myself I didn't feel scared at all. This was new. It seemed almost unnatural.

Over our heads the girders creaked. I looked up, noticing for the first time that a streak of some dull-colored paint ornamented the undersides of the girders and benches, with a thin line of silver drawn down the middle of each streak. It was thick enough to make a little ridge on the metal, and I rubbed my thumb absently across the nearest streak, wishing the earth would turn a little faster.

I heard Eileen Henken's voice from beyond the bleachers, full and easy and carrying. 'Dad! Dad, you hear me? With all these people in town tonight, seems like you could find something better to do...'

I bided my time impatiently. In four minutes, three minutes, two minutes more I would feel my own personality reach out and take that familiar, easy, confident, infinitely satisfying grip on the audience, feel their warm response start flowing in. One minute more.

Cressy beside me lifted her finger and counted with careful beats, unconsciously nodded in time with her finger. On the last beat she drew a deep breath, smiled radiantly at empty air, and stepped forward onto the stage.

My cue came. I drew a deep breath of my own and stepped confidently out into the hot, bright pavilion of light . . .

The axe fell.

The axe that had been poised right over my head for twenty-four hours, except I'd never thought to glance up and see it, dropped with a soundless thud right on my head.

Cressy swung toward me, radiant in the lights, tipped her head back, and said in a voice pitched a little bigger than her own, because of the way the stage was encircled, 'I didn't think you'd come. I really didn't.'

I stared down into her face in paralyzed silence. My lines had gone out of my mind forever, stone-cold, totally forgotten. I couldn't even ad-lib. I didn't know what the play was about. I didn't know who Cressy was supposed to be. I didn't know my own name or what year it was or what planet I stood on. Everything had stopped dead with me dead in the middle, out on my feet. And the audience waited in silence.

The pause drew out agonizingly. Sweat formed like ice on me everywhere a sweat gland operates. The world had stopped turning forever, and if it was up to me to start things again then we were all frozen right here in this moment until time ran out to its eternal end and the last trump sounded.

Cressy looked up at me in dawning horror. She repeated her last lines, rephrasing them just enough to sound normal. 'I really didn't think you'd come at all,' she said. 'Did you know I felt that way?' She was throwing me a direct question that wasn't in the script, trying in any way she could to break my block. Clearly she thought if she could get me to speak at all maybe I could pass over the bad spot and ad-lib my way back into my lines.

I just looked at her. The cold sweat was running down my sides now and popping out through the make-up in big, obvious beads. My stomach was tight in an agonized knot and I was so sick with nausea that if I could have moved a muscle I'd have run for the wings. But I couldn't move.

Nothing like this had ever happened to me before in my life. I'd had stage fright, sure. But nothing like this absolute, paralyzed agony. It seemed incredible. It seemed impossible. But right then I wasn't even trying to figure it out. I was too frozen in the nightmare to think why.

Cressy laughed, a lighthearted ripple of sound, and rose suddenly on tiptoe to clasp my neck and brush my cheek with a kiss. Still clinging, she said, 'There! That's for not disappointing me. Surprised?' Then with her lips near my ear she whispered my next line fiercely.

I stammered it after her like an automaton, my voice flat. In the same moment the rest of the cast, paralyzed as I was with surprise, swept simultaneously into action. The hell with the play at this point. All anybody wanted now was to get Rohan moving.

Roy rushed on stage and grabbed Cressy by the arm, yelling angrily at me for having apparently kissed Susan Jones right here on the street. Pod Henken waded sturdily in to separate them. Roy, fighting him off, lurched against me and muttered my next lines in my ear.

I parroted the words in that strange, flat voice, imitating every inflection Roy had fed me whether it fitted or not. Cressy pulled me away from Roy, clasped my neck with both hands, leaned her head on my shoulder, and fed me the next line. God help me, if I could have spoken in falsetto I'd have done it, imitating her voice as I'd imitated Roy's. I was a machine that could give back only what had been put into it, exactly as it was put.

But a sort of mechanical life was returning to me. From a long way off I seemed to remember dimly what this scene was about. I could even perceive how far off base we had distorted it, and creakily my mind began to wonder how we could pull it back. I was moving stiffly now, but at least I was moving. I picked up the sense of the last line I'd heard and croaked something in answer. Probably it made no sense, but at least I'd spoken on my own.

There was a horrible familiarity about all this. I'd had the curtain rung down on me before, when I was incompetent to go on. When I'd been too drunk or too despairing to care. But never before had I gone as blank as this, or in just this stunned, frozen way. I felt as if all aliveness had been drained out of me and nothing remained but some mechanical puppet that could move and speak only when somebody turned the crank.

Somehow, and how none of us ever knew, we got the scene moving. Everybody was ad-libbing wildly. On any normal stage the curtain would have come down by now. But here there was no curtain. Guthrie could have cut the lights, but he was too inexperienced to realize quite what was happening. I could, remotely and indifferently, imagine his fury as yet again I ruined the continuity of the play, but there wasn't much he could do to me – yet.

Toward the end of the scene something resembling life came faintly back into me and I was able to pick up the latent meaning of the lines and carry my end of it after a fashion. My tongue was stiff and my mouth dry, but somehow the scene did move toward a close not entirely alien to the close we'd rehearsed so often. I felt the tension relax a little out of the cast around me.

When I went off for my three-minute break toward the middle of the play Polly, waiting under the grandstand, grabbed me by the shoulders and sniffed my breath. Then she shook her head in a baffled way and whispered, 'Here,' holding out a pint bottle. I grabbed it like a drowning man and what felt like half of the contents slid down my throat before the impact really hit me. I had a seizure of agonizingly muffled coughing. Then I thought the whole drink was going to come back up again. Then the warmth began to spread and

I leaned back and let myself go limp, feeling the relaxation of the alcohol take hold. It occurred to me dimly that this was the first drink I'd had in – how many days? – and I hadn't even missed it until now.

Polly wrenched the bottle out of my hand when I lifted it again. 'Go easy! You're on again in a minute. How do you feel?'

I wiped my mouth with the back of an ice-cold hand. 'Give me my next line.'

She whispered it. I tried it over a couple of times, feeling the scene come slowly and stiffly back into my mind. But it was a dead scene as I thought of it now. Peopled by the dead, enacted by clockwork men and women in a dead clockwork world . . .

And I thought of the last time this hollowness had come over me, when I took Cressy, warm and responsive into my arms in the moonlight and the strong, soft wind – was it only last night? Just twenty-four hours ago. And I'd swung insanely since then between upbeats of manic exhilaration and downbeats of dead despair.

I thought, Am I out of my mind? What's wrong with me? What's happening?

Polly said, 'There's your warning. Can you go on?'

I straightened my back and breathed deep of dead night air. 'Oh yes,' I said, hearing my voice hollow and flat in my own head, 'I can go on.'

And I did.

Somehow while I'd been off stage the cast had wrenched the scene around toward something near normality, and when I stepped in on cue I was able to pick up the line Polly had fed me with a minimum of changing to fit the situation. And painfully, creakily, we labored through to the end. It was a dogged business. I had to be prompted a lot. Time after time I went blank again. And when I wasn't blank, still I was dead. But somehow we made it.

The audience was kinder than we deserved. They sat with us to the bitter end. They coughed and squirmed a lot, they whispered in the flatter scenes, nobody laughed at the jokes. But at least they didn't walk out. Probably very few of them had ever seen the living theater before, and they must have gone home with the impression that it's a dreary business compared with television and the films. But at least they didn't mob us.

The stands emptied. The lights went off. I sat down under the grandstand and took the pint bottle away from Polly. She surrendered it in silence. She and the rest of the cast stood there looking down at me, too bewildered to talk very much. This was outside their experience. Or mine. Everybody goes blank on stage sometimes. We all knew that. We all knew the usual things to say and do about it afterward. But this blankness that had hit me was too abnormal for anybody to cope with. They were still muttering uneasily to each other and watching me finish the pint when Guthrie came around the end of the stands and walked over to me.

I didn't look up. I knew his feet and legs and I saw no point in taking the trouble to see what his face looked like. I didn't hear him speak, but the other feet and legs within sight began to move away as if he'd given silent orders. The whiskey was humming inside my head just above the ears in an obscurely comforting way. I sucked down the last of it, grateful to the man who invented oblivion. Over the upended bottle I looked at Guthrie.

He wasn't red with anger any more. He looked quite pale, and the sad eyes were stony. He'd stopped being a cracker-barrel philosopher and he looked like the Comus man he was, resolute and ruthless. In a quiet voice that didn't carry any farther than he meant it to, he said:

'You've fouled up every job since you joined us, Rohan. I've had enough. I don't know what kind of a deal you have with Mr Nye about other things, but I know you're through with this troupe. I've already sent for a replacement. You can pack up and leave right now. You're out of the Swann Players, Rohan.'

It almost seemed to me, in the haze of whiskey that hummed above my ears, that he was speaking not in words at all. He was speaking in letters of fire which I didn't have to read because I didn't want to. Because it hurt too much to understand what he was really saying...

I think I was in and out of more than one bar that night. I seem to remember a lot of yelling and singing. I can't be sure because my little buzzing room had rebuilt itself around me and through those walls nothing unpleasant can ever penetrate. I balanced it delicately around me like a big, humming bubble. I wasn't quite sure what went on outside any more. Sometimes it seemed maybe I was back in that Cropper bus jolting along the road between the Ohio fields. Other times I could almost think I was back with the troupe, also jolting along, but this time in the caravan trucks, a tight little working group talking over the play, heading for – where was it? – Carson City and a new performance.

Except that I was washed up for good as a performer. If tonight had proved anything it had proved that.

And I couldn't really imagine even in my buzzing magic room that I was with the troupe again. I remembered too vividly standing in the road with my travel pack in my hand, watching them diminish in the moonlight. They had said goodbye in subdued voices, not quite meeting my eyes. And the little world they were part of went spinning away down the dark road, leaving a hollow inside me too cold for liquor to warm and too vast for liquor to fill.

But I tried. I tried hard.

CHAPTER XXII

The sky was transparently blue far up straight over my face. Treetops leaned together up there, swaying with a slow, dizzying motion. There seemed to be pine needles under me, but I had no idea where I was, or even who. A flicker of warning at the back of my mind suggested it would be better not to remember who. No good could come of that.

I sat up slowly. The motion made my head open and close once like a thunderclap. I held it together with both hands, fighting nausea. A hangover? Then I must have been drunk... Step by step I retraced the immediate past, working backward from the hangover. Then the mellow sunlight went black around me as I remembered.

Everything was over. The dazzling future I'd thought I had secure had slipped like quicksilver through my fingers and I was right back where I'd started. Not an actor after all. Nothing. I remembered the dead, frozen hour on stage. I saw Guthrie again, standing over me, looking down, pronouncing the words of excommunication. And everything had ended.

And I had dreamed a strange dream again...

I looked around the little clearing in the woods where I seemed to have spent the night. The night and a good part of the day, if the westering sunlight that slanted through the trees was anything to go by. I was trying to remember the dream.

Miranda. What was it? The theater had been in it – how? Something ridiculous – the traveling theater was a ring of bombs ticking toward explosion, set up on end like a circular palisade and inside it Miranda, going through some scene of infinite importance to me, but quite soundlessly, her lovely mouth opening and closing without a word while letters of fire shimmered over her and her corn-silk hair blew softly about her face.

Wait. Corn-silk? Miranda's hair was dark. It was Cressy who had the corn-silk curls. Something had been wrong in the dream. Miranda and Cressy blended into one? I didn't like it. Miranda and Cressy had nothing in common at all. Miranda was love and loyalty and brilliance and beauty. Miranda was all of me that had been worth having. Miranda was the rock I had stood on and the fire that had lighted me and made me what I was. Without her the world was a quagmire and the light a darkness. And I nothing.

In the dream rage and frustration had bubbled up in me. Miranda was saying something I had to know, *had* to, but the letters of fire wouldn't stand still to be read, and some kind of roaring like a hurricane had troubled my dream, and I remembered dimly doubling my fist hard and hitting someone, some enemy who stood between me and all I wanted. I hated him. I felt my fist sink into him and I heard him grunt.

But then, in the midst of the hurricane roar, I had opened my eyes and found I was hitting the carpet of pine needles over and over, hard, angry blows. The roar diminished into distance and my hand hurt from beating my enemy the earth. And I had sunk again into a confusion of dreams, because waking was even worse than sleep.

I heard the roaring rise again as I sat there trying to remember. It rushed toward me in crescendo, shivered the leaves around me, and swept by fast into the distance. A truck on the highway. So I had somehow last night stumbled out of town and found this hollow among the pines beside the road the troupe had taken going away. Polly and Roy, Cressy and Guthrie, the Henkens diminishing down a long highway with all their plans and problems, leaving me alone with mine.

My head ached. I rubbed my bristling cheek and wondered what came next. A faint hopefulness flickered in me and I asked myself why, after all, everything had to be over. Guthrie had fired me, yes. But who had the final word? Nye was the man I worked for, not Guthrie. Would Nye care if I froze up in the play? So maybe the job of actor wasn't for me any more. I was here for more than acting. I was on the track of the Anti-Com itself and Guthrie had no authority to stop me. All I had to do was get in touch with Nye, finish up my job of finding the Anti-Com, and—

And what? And earn back the theater I couldn't use any more? Step back into the old life as an actor who couldn't act? What place would there be for Rohan in a world he couldn't function in? No, I'd been right all along, from a long time ago, from the hour of Miranda's death. Maybe that's what the letters of fire had said in last night's dream. Without Miranda I was nothing. I'd always known it. With her I was more than myself, strong and powerful and alive. Alone I was less than a single person. So that one good performance when I'd turned the world underfoot had been one last flash before darkness, and the bad performance was the true reflection of myself.

So what good was Nye to me now? What could he give me that I cared for? Miranda back again?

Still, I had to do something. I couldn't sit here forever. I got up stiffly and looked at the sinking sun. A few hours from now the Swann Players would be setting up their grandstands in Carson City. Where would I be? Did it matter? Of its own accord the memory of the dream came back urgently into my mind. The theater was a ring of bombs minute by minute ticking toward the blowoff. And it did matter that I should be there. Why, I didn't know. But an anxiety trembled in me for something I couldn't name. Something furiously raging to be heard in my mind, and an inward force that said 'No, no, be quiet, I don't hear you.'

Moving stiffly, I toiled up the slope toward the sound of passing traffic.

The heavy truck rumbled to a halt in the twilight. 'Here we are,' the driver said. 'Carson City.' He slanted a look at me. 'You all right, bud?'

I got my chin off my chest and forced a grin. I'd been bad company all the way from Douglass. There was too much on my mind. I said, 'Sure, I'm fine,' and got painfully out of the cab. He watched me, taking in my scratches and bruises, the rips in my clothing. He shook his head at me. I said, 'Well, thanks for the lift.'

He hesitated, looking me over. Then he reached into one of the dash compartments and tossed a package at me. 'Here, catch,' he said. It was a ration pack, one of the food boxes drivers carry on long hauls. I wondered if I looked that hungry, but I caught it gratefully. There was no knowing how long I'd have to make my money last from now on. The driver was still looking at me as he pulled away, and just before the motor downed out all other sound, I think he spoke. I think what he said was, 'I used to like your pictures, Mr Rohan.' But I'll never know now.

I got some coffee at a stand near the highway. It helped a little. Carson City isn't very big. There's a park near the center of town, with a pool in the middle and big trees deep with summer leaves that have a rich, rolling motion when the wind blows. I found a bench and ate some of the food in the ration pack, not wanting any and not liking it much, but knowing I'd feel better when it was down. I did.

By then darkness had fallen, and now all I had to do was follow the crowd. *Crossroads* pulled very well in Carson City. This was the town which Nye had told me was important. This was the place where he wanted a big audience with all the rebels in it he could get. Looking up at the bleachers from outside, hearing the first familiar lines sounding in familiar voices, I wondered in how many other towns in California tonight *Crossroads* was being played. And whether there was something really special about Carson City. And what.

All the voices from inside the magic ring were familiar except one. The one that spoke my lines. I felt like a ghost.

I waited until I was sure Guthrie would be busy doing whatever it was he did do in the sound truck and the cast was all on stage. Then I slipped between the girders and the wall and climbed up the stands to a seat high up, near the top. Almost every seat had been taken. I fell over a few feet and dropped into a vacant spot.

Sitting there looking down at the lighted stage, I felt very strange. I was part of the play and not part of it. I couldn't quite believe I was sitting here as an onlooker, because I knew the play so well. And the oddest thing of all was watching the man who played my part. The man pretending to be Howard Rohan in the role in which I'd hit such heights and such depths. He handled it well. Well enough. He was about my size and coloring, and he played with a clean, sharp accuracy and no life at all. For the first time *Crossroads* was going to be seen in this theater exactly as it was written.

The cast was nervous. The man in my part was just a little off in his timing because he'd rehearsed with a different group. More than once he wasn't quite where he should have been when somebody turned to speak to him. Once I noticed Polly's face draw tight and a little bleak at a moment like that, and it seemed to me that she was seeing me, Rohan, a ghostly presence in that vacant spot exactly as I was seeing myself there. I thought with some wonder, watching her face, Maybe they miss me after all.

My hangover had receded a long way by now. I felt almost willing to cope with being alive again. I looked at the audience and wondered what they made of this exotic thing, a live play in the street of Carson City. They were laughing responsively in all the right spots, the kind of audience the people on the stage love and appreciate.

I found, rather to my surprise, that I was thinking about the Anti-Com.

I noticed that Cressy's pale gold hair needed retouching along the part, seen from this high up. I noticed that Roy had used too much eye shadow, so his deep-set eyes looked small and haggard. I made mental notes to speak to them both, and brought myself up with a shock, remembering that I and the Swann Players had nothing to do with each other any more.

I saw a familiar head down there a couple of rows ahead of

me and leaned forward to look with surprise. I had seen her in San Andreas bending over the lie box I was hooked to. I had seen her in the mountain valley above the rebels' distribution center, with the 'hopper exploding before her and the Comus forces closing in. Dr Elaine Thomas. She sat composedly on the bench below me wearing a yellow dress with a blue sweater thrown across her shoulders. The black hair was drawn tight in its usual coronet of braids, and the slightly tilted eyes were intent upon the stage. I looked quickly at her hand and saw a ring upon it with the big blue stone intact.

Cressy in the strong lights below us swung her bright pink skirts in a half circle and put out both hands to the man who was playing my part. They stood there laughing at each other, radiant in the brilliant light. I felt a twinge of curious jealousy. Cressy was putting more intimacy into the part than Susan Jones had to put. She was Cressy Kellogg, too, the little opportunist, playing up with all the sparkle that was in her to the new man in the cast. Because, who knows, there might be something in it for Cressy Kellogg.

She tipped her head sidewise and the corn-silk curls swung out. A shudder of anxiety without any cause I could name went through me coldly. She was Miranda suddenly, the Miranda of my dream moving in the circle of ticking bombs. For some reason my eyes moved to Elaine Thomas there on the bench below me smiling and watching. And it seemed to me death was in the air around us, chilly and smelling of dust.

Something strange was happening in my mind. The old, violent clash inside me between the thing I had to remember and the thing I could not endure to know. Miranda, I thought. Miranda...

Why did I hate to see Cressy in the role I had cast for Miranda in last night's dream? Because Cressy and Miranda were women at opposite poles in my mind and I didn't want them confused? Cressy wasn't Miranda. Miranda was light and life, loyalty, security, love.

Miranda?

I felt a kind of thunderclap in my head.

Somehow so many things fell neatly into pattern with a series of soundless clicks. Elaine Thomas and the blue ring unbroken on her hand, the thought and the smell of death, the dream of bombs ringing the theater in, Cressy imitating Miranda, and my mind rejecting their likeness...

For an instant I saw the thing in my memory I tried so hard not to see, only let float to the surface when I was very drunk or very despairing, too despairing to care. I saw again, clear and vivid, Miranda lying dead in her bright kimono on the bright green hillside, her cheek upon the grass and her hair stirring in the breeze, the only thing about her that moved at all.

And lying a little way beyond her I saw the man who had been her lover.

The man I never knew. The man I had never guessed existed. Whose very name I had told myself did not matter. And it didn't. Not as a name. But whoever he was, he was the man she died with and went away with into infinity, leaving me behind.

Miranda was *not* loyalty and love and security.

How strangely the mind works to deceive itself. How totally I had shut off that unbearable thought, walling it securely behind the memory of Miranda as I wanted to remember her. A Miranda who never existed. How fully I had convinced myself of the lie.

Why did I see the truth now? Something had happened in my mind to let this much of reality come through. Some gate opening because of – what? And why did the desperate anxiety well higher and higher like a tide that was going to spill over the brim any minute and inundate me?

Miranda was not loyalty and love.

I needed to think that over in solitude and silence. As I sat on the hard metal bench, it seemed to be there was nothing around me but the blinding glare of what I just come to realize, the paralyzing silence of the pain. I had a thought to examine too private and too shattering to share the same enclosure with any other human being.

I got up almost without knowing I was moving and went

down quietly along the side of the stands, slipped out between the building and the girders into the still street beyond. I was thinking of the little park with the pool and the big, quiet trees.

That was what I needed. The grassy place, the solitude.

Nobody seemed to be in the park tonight but me. I sat down on a bench beneath one of the big trees near the water. I leaned my back to the trunk and looked at the stars shining in the faintly troubled pool. I let my mind remember.

What was the real Miranda? Not the goddess I had made her into. Only a woman of beauty and talent and no faith. A woman who found me less than she wanted and who went elsewhere for the love I had not succeeded in giving her. No goddess. No talisman whose faith and love were the foundation of my success. She gave me neither faith nor love. She was a woman who must have smiled just as easily and invitingly at any likely man as Cressy had smiled at me.

I leaned my back against the tree. There was an immense stillness around me and through me. Far off I heard the voices from the stage, the laughter and response of the audience. In the dark street an occasional car went by. Over me the leaves rustled. But the stillness in my mind hushed every other sound. I could not think or feel. Not in that long silence.

Then feeling came back. I didn't want it. I couldn't face it. But I couldn't evade it, either. I felt the impact of that full knowledge of what Miranda was smash into me with paralyzing clearness. I tried to stand up, but my legs wouldn't hold me. For the first time physical reaction hit me like a hammer. All the small muscles of my shoulders shivered, and the muscles at the inside of my thighs shook until I could hardly stand. I dropped back to the bench and threw my arm around the tree trunk to keep the world from tilting.

I could see so clearly the bright colors of Miranda's kimono on the green eastern grass. The beautiful dreamer who would never wake again. This final loss was worse than the first shock of her dying, because until now I had kept so much of her with me, part of me, very precious and very safe in my mind. And gone now out of reach, out of time.

There let your sweetheart lie, untrue forever. Who said it? Never mind. Never mind. The tree was rough against my cheek. I hugged the hard trunk to keep my arm from trembling and felt the tears slip down my face between me and the insensate bark. The night was infinitely still.

Without opening my eyes I could feel its quiet presence. I heard the water making its faint, troubled sounds upon the shore. I heard the leaves heaving softly above me. I thought I could feel the tremor of their motion transmitting downward through the solid trunk I clung to, tugging at the deep roots spread out and clenched solidly far underground. The tree had stood here a long time, withstanding the shocks of all its lifetime. As I had to withstand the shocks of mine.

I felt the life of the tree against me. I felt the water lapping on the shore and the motion transmitting from molecule to molecule of the ground that upheld us both. The water and the wind, the living tree, the earth and I were all knit together in a single unit that breathed and was one.

And I wasn't alone. Miranda wasn't lost. Nothing is lost. Miranda was no goddess, but neither had she betrayed me – not in any way that mattered now. She did what she had to do. There is a term set on marriage, and beyond that I had no claim on her or she on me. I had to let her go.

I had been trying all this while to hold her closer in death than I had ever been able to hold her in life. But now I could accept what she was and wasn't and love her, and let her go.

I wasn't alone. I was the tree and the pool, the stars shining in the water, the wind in the dark. And Miranda was with me, everywhere and nowhere, a part of the tree and the earth and me. *Now may all clouds . . . of sorrow depart . . . beautiful dreamer, wake unto me . . .*

It was all right now. She could wake or sleep. I didn't need her any more. I was myself again.

After a while I stood up and wiped the smeared dirt from my face where I and the tree had shared that strange communion. Everything was very calm and clear now. Miranda had been lovely and corrupt, as Comus was beautiful and strong and corrupt. I couldn't have her back. I didn't want her back now. Not as she had really been. Not any more than she would want a return to me. All those memories, all that life, rich and lustrous and unstable, were a long way off now. A part of Comus. I had a sudden flash of memory in which the renegade with the swinging necklaces moved before me as clear as life, the glittering jewels, the human ears – Comus, beautiful and terrible, too dangerous to live.

I knew where I stood now. I had sorted things out. I knew what I valued and wanted, and what the cost would be, and the risk. But I didn't care any more.

When I went out of that dark garden into the lights again I knew I was a rebel. And I knew the work I had to do.

CHAPTER XXIII

I stood for a moment outside the grandstands listening to the smooth onward flow of the play, watching through the slatted horizontals of the seats the dark lattices made by scores of feet and legs. I was waiting for one of the big laughs. The play was building toward it. At the right moment I slid under the girders and began to work my way toward Elaine.

My timing was good. The wave of laughter broke over the whole audience just as I stooped over Elaine's shoulder and whispered in her ear. A gaunt man beside her turned to look coldly at me.

'There's no room here,' he said in a loud whisper, his glance registering my ripped shirt and the stubble on my face.

I said, 'I'm just staying a minute.'

Elaine was looking up at me in quick surprise. She whispered, 'I didn't think – why aren't you in the play? I expected—'

I said, 'I'll tell you later. Are you alone here?'

She nodded and moved over a little on the bench, making room for me. I shook my head at her. 'No, I want you to come with me.' I leaned closer and whispered in her ear, 'Get out of here fast!'

She gave me another quick look. 'Not now. Wait till it's over.'

'There isn't time,' I said. 'Wait for the next laugh. Then get out!'

After a moment she nodded, her eyes still fixed questioningly on mine. I waited, listening to the dialogue. 'Now!' I said.

Elaine rose quietly just as the laughter began to swell. Down on stage I saw Polly glance up at the unexpected center of activity here in the audience, and I think in spite of the lights she knew me, but after the briefest little break in her lines she went on smoothly. I followed Elaine down the narrow aisle at the end of the benches and out between the girders and the wall. The back of my neck was tingling. I thought, Someone will stop us. Someone will have to stop us. And then I thought chillingly. Maybe they don't need to. Maybe by now we're marked.

Actually no one seemed to notice our going.

Once outside in the quiet street, Elaine turned to me with bright, questioning eyes. 'What happened to you, Rohan?' she asked in a low voice. 'What are you doing here? I thought you were with the players.'

I rubbed my stubbled chin. 'A lot's been happening since I saw you last. Never mind now.' I wondered briefly how much she really knew. I had turned in her friend to the Comus forces and by that act brought the theater to Carson City, and the trap that came with it. But it was too late now to think about that.

'Stand still a minute,' I said. 'Listen to the play.'

Puzzled, she obeyed. After a moment I said, 'Now. Are you thinking of the Anti-Com?'

The flash of astonishment in her face as she turned to me told me the answer before she said, 'But how did you know? How could—'

'I'll tell you that later, too,' I said. 'If there's time. The theater's a trap. A lie detector – hunting the Anti-Com.'

In the silence a burst of laughter rose again from over the bleachers. Elaine looked up at me, her eyes anxious and searching.

'Are you sure? How could it be?' She didn't want to believe me. I saw the life and color draining out of her face as she stared, trying not to believe and yet, in spite of herself, beginning to realize I was right. 'How do you know?' she asked in a tight whisper.

I shook my head at her. 'It's a long story. If you can do

anything to counteract the trap you'd better do it fast. Or do you need to? Is anybody in the audience who knows anything?'

She said, 'Oh God!' in a stunned whisper.

'Shall I break up the play?' I asked impatiently. 'I could do it, but—'

Suddenly and violently she spun away from me without a word and began to run. I hesitated a moment, watching her go. Then I started after her, trying to make no more sound of running on the street than she did. She gave me one glance over her shoulder and then ran on, paying no attention.

I was panting before she stopped at a low two-story office building and fumbled a key out of her handbag. She got the door open and slid inside in one motion, vanishing into the dark. I went after her. She called breathlessly, 'Shut the door!'

I heard the lock click as I closed it. A dim light showed stairs leading up and Elaine already at the top and unlocking another door. I caught up with her in time to see her cross the office room inside, push aside a picture on the wall, and press two buttons set flush with the plaster under it. She stood there leaning her head against the wall, her eyes closed, her fingers on the buttons. She was breathing through her mouth and trying to listen.

I heard the distant shriek of the town siren beginning low and then wailing to full volume. It rose and faded and fell, and rose again in a pattern of sound like a code. Over and over it wailed out its staccato messages to the town and the quiet countryside. I imagined the whole of Carson City sitting stunned for the first few wails, not understanding. I imagined men and women in farms far out in the dark, people on the roads, birds and animals waking from sleep, all of them listening. And I had a moment's wild thought that Carson City was like a sinking ship in mid-Atlantic shrieking its message of disaster as it went slowly down in the black waters.

Elaine sighed and opened her eyes, stepped back. The picture swung into place again, covering the buttons. She looked at me, still pale but calmer now. The wailing siren died away.

'The riot call?' I asked.

She smiled faintly. 'H and C in Morse – for *Hey, Charley*,' she told me. 'That's the signal. Listen.'

Even from here we could hear the low, rising murmur of voices from the streets and houses, people calling to each other, doors opening, feet running.

'It means break up,' Elaine said. 'Stop what you're doing, get to your headquarters. Drop everything and move! By now your play's losing its audience – I hope. It means—'

Now it was my turn to say, 'Listen!' She was quiet. We both heard the staccato sound of gunfire from the way we had come. I said grimly, 'Maybe some of the audience isn't leaving so fast. What do you think?'

She started for the door. Then she seemed to take a tangible grip on her own emotions, and she turned back deliberately, pulled out a chair from one of the desks and sat down in it, closing her eyes again for a moment. Then she looked up at me, the bright black gaze very questioning, very disturbed.

'Sit down, Rohan,' she said. 'We've got to get things clear. What is it you know?'

I was glad of a chance to sit. I'd been through a lot in the past hour. I could feel random nerves and muscles jumping when I tried to relax, and my head ached savagely. I drew a deep breath.

'It may take a while,' I said.

She nodded. 'We've got about ten minutes. Let's have it.'

I said, 'About a week ago I was working out a Cropper contract—' Here I paused, marveling at myself. A week ago? It seemed like years. 'Comus picked me up,' I said. 'Ted Nye and I used to be friends when I was on Broadway. He needed an actor. He offered me the job. Before he offered it he had me run through the usual brain searching to make sure I wasn't a subversive. I mentioned this to you when we first met, back in San Andreas. Remember?'

She nodded, watching me. 'You saw my brother in New York at the psycho-search center.'

'You look a lot alike.' I hesitated. 'Is he – all right? I'm not sure how much I remember, but—'

'You remember,' she told me somberly. 'Joe – died quite suddenly just a week ago. Some kind of overdose, the newscast said.' Her mouth was grim.

I said in a quiet voice, 'He knew it was coming. He sent you his love – I think. And a message about the trap the traveling theaters are – I think.' I rubbed my eyes. 'I was drugged. They pump you full of stuff in those brain-searching sessions. That night – well, I thought I had a dream. All this while it's been bothering me – the message your brother sent, the things he told me. In the dream they were so garbled they didn't make sense. I began to realize it couldn't have been a dream after a while. But I still didn't understand.' I stopped and thought in silence about the dark garden and the still waters and the new knowledge about myself I had wrestled with tonight.

I said, 'I couldn't remember until – a little while ago. I *couldn't*. There was something else that kept getting in the way. Something about – myself and some things that happened a long time ago.'

I paused, thinking. Remembering the letters of fire I couldn't read for so long. I could guess now what happened back there in New York as that other Dr Thomas ran off the routine personality checking which Nye had ordered for me. Whatever it was he saw in the pattern of my reactions had made him believe I'd carry a message for him to the rebels in California. And he was right. Essentially I *was* a rebel even then, born to rebel, living in rebellion against the world.

But what he had told me was frightening. In essence he must have said, 'I'm working with a rebel organization that's going to destroy Comus with the Anti-Com. I've just discovered the traveling theaters are a lie-detector trap to spot rebels who know too much. You've got to carry the warning. You've got to help.'

But I'd protested. I wasn't ready to take up arms against a sea of troubles, his or mine or anybody's. And then he'd said – what? That I didn't need to remember what he'd told me, that I would when the time came – post-hypnotic suggestion? Something like that, I felt pretty sure. He'd been right about picking me out – not that he probably had much choice. His pursuers may well have been right at his heels or he wouldn't have taken such chances with such a broken reed as Howard Rohan.

It had taken me a long time to come round to his way of thinking. I'd had to clear away all that murk of confusion about Miranda before I knew what it was I really wanted, which side I was really on. It took me a long time to see the truth. Maybe too long.

Elaine said, 'What was the message exactly, Rohan? Can you remember?'

I shut my eyes and tried. 'Your brother wanted me to join the Swann Players because they'd been assigned to the area where you and Harris were, and the—' I paused, looking at her. 'The Anti-Com is here too, isn't it? In Carson City? I know Nye's looking for it here.'

She gave me an expressionless glance. 'No, it isn't here. Go on.'

I shrugged. 'He told me the Anti-Com would destroy Comus – make it commit suicide was the way he put it. He wanted to warn you about the traveling theaters. There wasn't any time to send a message directly to you and he had to take a chance on me.' I grinned faintly, seeing again the unreadable letters of fire circling before me – unreadable until now. 'It was a long chance,' I said.

'Don't worry about it,' Elaine said. 'I expected he used post-hypnotic suggestion on you. If he wasn't sure you were fully in sympathy with our side he had to implant certain mental blocks to make sure you wouldn't remember until it was safe to. Does that mean you haven't been really convinced about us until tonight?'

'I've had some problems,' I said with restraint. 'But—'

Elaine said, 'Wait,' and turned toward the door. I heard the sound of feet on the stairs, subdued voices talking excitedly, very low, and then a key in the lock.

Elaine said to me, 'I didn't tell you this. This is the Carson

City headquarters. Now we'll hear what's been happening. Whether you left things until too late.'

Two men came into the office, one of them disheveled and the other still buttoning his shirt as if he hadn't had time to finish dressing. A woman followed them closely, and then three more men. They looked at Elaine and me.

'Where's Beardsley?' someone asked.

'He was at the theater,' Elaine said, her voice under heavy restraint. 'What happened there? Does anybody know?'

The disheveled man said, 'I was there. When the alarm sounded we all tried to scatter. I don't think they expected anything like that so soon, because at first it was easy to get away. But they moved fast. Before Beardsley and Ferguson could clear the stands, the Comus cops closed in.'

'Not both of them!' Elaine said, her voice flatting a little. The man nodded somberly. Elaine got her voice under control and said calmly, 'What about the gunfire?'

'Comus, stopping some runaways,' the man said. 'None of ours, as it happened. But it shows they're not fooling.'

'You think they know?' somebody in the background asked.

'Rohan,' Elaine said, 'tell them about the theater.'

So I stood up and told them. While I was talking more and more people came into the room, most of them hurrying, looking shocked and a little exhilarated, as if now that things were starting life had somehow taken a turn for the better.

I told them about the play itself, the insistence on giving it verbatim, without changes in pace or action. I told them about the sound truck with its intricate, unnecessary apparatus. I remembered the line of silvery circuits painted along the insulated undersides of the benches. And I thought how often, sitting there preoccupied in the bleachers tonight, I had found the words, 'Anti-Com!' springing into my mind without any real reason I could think of.

There had always been something a little wrong about the play. I'd sensed it without knowing why. Thinking about *Crossroads* with detachment, I could see now that it was two plays. It had two levels. If you knew anything about the Anti-Com you responded on both levels. For people who knew a lot about it, Guthrie's instrument panel must have blazed with constant reactions. That maze of electronic equipment in the truck, intricate beyond any possible need of the play itself, had been triggered to catch the last subliminal responses of people who knew more than they should.

The word was never mentioned in the play. There was no reference of even the obliquest sort. And yet time after time I had found the one unspoken name coming up irresistibly in my mind as cues kicked off thoughts and responses centering around the one unspoken word.

Somebody said doubtfully, 'But could it work? Without any direct physical connection?'

I shrugged. Somebody else answered for me. 'Oh yes, it could work. It's the same principle as a lie jacket with a larger field. The body's own electromagnetic field could trigger it.'

'But how could he locate one person in the whole crowd?'

'How do you locate a disturbance in any electrical field? Hell, that's no problem. How they meant to follow them up afterward is anybody's guess, but you can be damn sure they'd thought of it.'

Someone else said, 'What about the rest of the traveling theaters? They must have picked up a lot of our people already.'

'Expendable,' Elaine said shortly. 'Nobody outside this area knows enough to be dangerous anyhow. But Ferguson and Beardsley aren't expendable. Neither am I. If Comus gets any one of us—'

'Alive,' somebody added.

There was a pause. Elaine glanced from face to face.

'They took Beardsley and Ferguson,' she said. 'Well?'

Silence for a moment. Then, from the rear of the crowd, 'Both alive when we saw them,' a voice said. There was another silence, briefer this time.

Elaine said, breaking it, 'We'll hear. There's time yet. Any more questions?'

'Yes,' a voice said. 'What about this theater? It's given two or three performances already. This isn't the first time the lie detector's been used in this area.'

I said, 'It's the first time it's worked. I loused up the only two performances we gave. Tonight was the first chance Guthrie had to screen the audience.' I was silent a moment, realizing clearly for the first time a possible explanation for my shattering freeze-up of last night.

Was it simply that the levels of censorship in my mind been shifting all along? I knew, down under, what the play *Crossroads* would do if it went on as written. I'd blocked it once by a brilliant performance that threw the emphasis off. I'd blocked it a second time by a total freeze.

A dazzling light sprang into full bloom in the middle of my mind. Had that compulsive freeze been nothing worse than the unconscious censor clamping down? Was that the only way it knew how to stop the trap from snapping on the rebels I had come to sympathize with? Could it mean that my ability to act, to hold an audience, to live the part I played, wasn't gone after all? I stood there speechless, a blaze of tentative joy beginning to pour through me in a warm flood. Maybe, then, there was still a chance—

Elaine said sharply, 'Rohan, what is it?'

I looked at her rather sheepishly. 'Nothing. An idea I had about – my own work. I didn't know it showed.'

Elaine said, 'Something did. You looked so happy I thought maybe you had some ideas about Comus. God knows we need ideas.' She glanced around the room. 'With Ferguson and Beardsley gone I think I'm next in line of command. George, will you see what you can find out about the captures? Johnny, get up to the top of the monument and see what the situation is. I think—'

Somebody came up the stairs running. Everybody turned. A breathless young man leaned against the doorframe and said, 'They're stopping anybody who tries to leave town. Somebody said they'd seen Prowlers on the road coming in. Where's Beardsley?'

Elaine said, 'Johnny, get started. Beardsley won't be here, Tony. I'm in control so far. What happened to you?'

'When I heard the siren I started out,' the young man said. 'A couple of blocks away two men closed in on me. One of them had a hypodermic. I slapped it out of his hand just in time. Some of the boys saw us fighting and got there just in time.'

Elaine nodded. 'Brewster, take charge of rounding up as many as you can to patrol the streets and watch for arrests. Try to recapture our people if you can.'

A thickset man said, 'I'll try, but I'm afraid it's too late.'

'Well, try!'

He nodded and turned quickly to the door, beckoning to people as he passed them. I had a sudden thought.

'Wait a minute,' I said loudly. 'Hold on. About the theater troupe – nobody in the play had any idea what they were doing. You've got to understand that.'

The words seemed to fall very flat. Nobody spoke. There was a small silence and then Brewster said, 'Come on,' and went out with his own group. I looked at Elaine.

'What about my troupe?'

She shook her head. 'I don't know. I've got a lot to think about, Rohan. They can look after themselves.'

Before I could protest a commotion near the door resolved itself into a woman with her hair wildly wind-blown. She was talking in gasps, as if she had been running.

'Johnny says you want to know – about the monument,' she said. 'I was just – up there.' She paused to catch her breath. 'All around the outskirts – in the fields – I've never seen so many machines. Tanks. Prowlers. Hedgehoppers. A ring of 'em, right around the town. A mouse couldn't slip through. They must have been waiting in the woods. They've got – radar set up, too. We're – locked in.'

I said, 'What about my troupe?' Nobody paid any attention.

'What are the machines doing?' Elaine asked. 'Just sitting there?' The woman nodded, pushing the wild hair off her forehead.

There was a muffled shout on the stairs. Footsteps thudded. An elderly man came in, his face grayish. He pushed directly through the crowd to Elaine.

'Ferguson,' he said. 'Dead. He got the ring to his mouth as they took him up the steps to the Comus Building. But Beardsley—' He paused, shaking his head. 'Sam couldn't make it,' he said. 'They've got him.'

'Alive?'

The old man nodded.

Elaine said, 'Couldn't he reach his ring?'

'He had it up to his mouth. I saw him. And then he – I don't know – he just let it drop again. He couldn't quite make it when the chips were down.'

Silence. Then Elaine said, 'Where is he now?'

'They're questioning him at Comus headquarters.'

'Under direct television hookup with Nye's office, I suppose,' Elaine said. Her shoulder sagged a little. 'Well, that's that.'

'How bad is it?' someone asked.

Elaine said softly, 'I was sure Sam would use the poison if he had to.' She looked down at her own ring. 'I guess we never really know,' she said, 'until we have to do it ourselves.' She was silent a moment longer.

'It's bad,' she said. 'Sam knows what town the Anti-Com's in. Not the exact location, but the town. It could be worse.'

'Isn't that enough? As soon as they mind-scan Beardsley can't they just move in on that town—'

Elaine said, 'Maybe. Remember, though, Nye wants the Anti-Com intact if he can get it. As long as he doesn't know what it is or how it works he's vulnerable. Even if he blew up this one, we might still build another.'

'But he won't risk our turning it on!'

Elaine laughed shortly. 'We aren't going to turn it on. That's something Beardsley doesn't know.'

There was a dead silence. Somebody said thinly:

'Why aren't we going to turn it on?'

Elaine said with sudden fierceness, 'Because it isn't safe! Because yesterday Comus raided a distribution center and we had to destroy the only safety device we had for the Anti-Com. That's why we won't use it.'

A voice said after a moment's shock silence, 'I thought it was all finished. All ready to operate.'

'It is,' Elaine said less angrily. 'It's finished. It'll work. It'll knock out Comus. But we got to one of the calculators for the first time last week and we found out it'll do something else, too – something we hadn't realized. There's going to be tremendous amount of energy released. It'll knock out Comus, all right, but it can bounce right back on us, too. It could blow the state clear off the map and gouge another bay out of the Pacific.'

'It could,' somebody said, 'or it *would?*'

Elaine shrugged. 'There's a chance it wouldn't. I'd hate to take the chance. We did have a safety device that would channel off the energy harmlessly. Since we lost it yesterday morning we've been working right around the clock on a new one. It's nearly done. But it isn't attached to the Anti-Com. If it were—' She shrugged delicately. 'If it were, Comus would end. Right then, at that moment.'

We all looked at each other, I with wild speculations. What was it that could put an end to Comus in the wink of an eye?

'Where is the safety?' someone asked.

Elaine shook her head. 'I'd better not say. There's still a chance. A pretty slim one, but a chance.'

In the silence as everyone thought that over, the distant trickle of gunfire sounded from far off, near the edge of town. Someone near the door said stolidly, 'If it was me, I'd take a chance. I'd use the Anti-Com and let it blow if it wanted to. We're done for either way. We might as well take Comus with us. If we've got any chance at all, I'd say take it.'

There was a brief babble of talk, most of it in agreement. Elaine said, 'We'd never know what happened if that's what they decided at the Anti-Com when the time comes.'

'*If it* blows,' the stolid voice insisted.

Elaine nodded. 'If it blows.'

'What's going to happen then?'

'Right now,' Elaine said, 'Nye is probably questioning Beardsley on the Comus channel from New York. As soon as he talks they'll know what town the Anti-Com is in and they'll start a house-to-house search for it. Sooner or later they'll find us. If we're lucky, the Anti-Com will go on, Comus will—' She hesitated. 'Well, Comus will end. And all over the country rebel groups will rise and take over.'

'How will they know?'

Elaine smiled. 'They'll know. If the Anti-Com goes on, nobody in the country will have any doubt what's happened. At best, it'll work fine. At worst, the explosion might light up half the continent for a minute or two. Oh, they'll know, all right.'

'But what are we going to do?' a voice demanded impatiently. 'There must be something we can do!'

'There is,' Elaine said. 'We're doing it. I ought to hear from the workshop where the safety fuse is being finished within the next half hour. Then it'll be a matter of getting the fuse to the Anti-Com before the Comus forces find it. There's just one thing to remember now – be sure you're all armed and be sure you put up a strong resistance if Comus tries to take over Carson City. I know those are standing orders. I just wanted to remind you it's more important than ever now.'

I said mildly. 'Why?'

'That's how we drove Comus out of California,' Elaine said. 'It's how we'll keep them out as long as we still have a chance to turn on the Anti-Com.'

A man with a torn shirt and a scratched face said, 'After all, Andrew Raleigh's still President. The old man could still kick Nye out – and he would, if we raised enough trouble. If the lid blows off here, it'll blow all over the state, and Nye can't hush that up even with the Comus walls. He's still afraid of Raleigh.'

'Comus will have to move in on the town where the Anti-Com is,' I reminded them.

'And there'll be fighting. We've got strong forces there and lots of ammunition and weapons. But Nye's got a good excuse for that kind of trouble. After all, if he knows the Anti-Com's there not even Raleigh could object.'

Elaine added, 'Nye won't do anything drastic. That's why we're waiting this out. If Comus can infiltrate the Anti-Com town he'll do it. Remember he wants the Anti-Com in one piece, so his technicians can find a defense against it. There's only one thing we've got to do now.' She glanced around the room.

'Johnny, get your group together and find some way out of town. We've got to get past the Comus ring.'

Johnny shook his head doubtfully. 'They're only passing out their own cars,' he said. 'But we'll try.' He beckoned to several of the bystanders and they went out together.

I said to Elaine, keeping my voice quiet, 'Have you thought why the town's boxed in like this? Do you know what they're still looking for?'

She met my eyes calmly. 'Yes, I know.'

'They're looking for you,' I said.

She spread out her hand as if she were admiring the blue stone of her ring. I knew she was wondering if when the moment came she, like Sam Beardsley, might falter in doing what had to be done. But in my own mind I knew she would not falter.

'Not only me,' she said. 'Anyone who knows more than Sam about the Anti-Com. We've got to find some way out of town.'

Somebody was running up the stairs outside. For no reason I found myself thinking again of the Swann Players, isolated in the besieged and probably hysterical town. I started to say, 'The troupe ought to be looked after, Elaine. They didn't know what they were doing. I wish—'

But then the door burst open and a young man came in, breathless, saying before he had fully entered the room, 'They're through with Beardsley. I heard most of it. He spilled everything he knew – you'd better clear out of here fast. They know this is headquarters. They're on their way.'

The crowd eddied wildly for a moment. Then Elaine's voice, pitched high, sounded over the brief uproar. She was giving orders quickly and calmly. Looking at her, I saw the way the pulse beat in her throat, and her hands were trembling, but you wouldn't have known how scared she was by anything in her voice. I hoped her thinking was straight. She was telling them where to scatter and naming the next meeting place. And in the next few minutes the room filled with orderly regrouping and then the quick tide of their dispersing swept me down the stairs with the rest.

Outside the streets were almost dark. Glass from the street lights gritted underfoot. Somebody had decided against too much illumination, and he had been quite right. It was easier to scatter here in the dimness.

Elaine's hand was on my arm. 'I want to finish talking to you, Rohan,' she said. 'Wait with me. You know too much now and I don't want you picked up—'

Down one of the dark streets the sound of purring motors came swelling, nearer and louder by the second. 'Hoppers, I thought. Or even a Prowler or two. I hadn't seen a Prowler's big crimson bulk since I crossed the border into this rebel land. It made me chill a little to remember how their great swollen sides loom over you as they come.

Somebody said, 'That's them! Run! Scatter!'

And we ran.

When I stopped at last, out of breath, in a pocket between two old wooden buildings in a dark street, I found I was alone.

I stood there quiet, fighting to get my breath back, listening. Far off I could hear outbursts of shouting now and then, but no footsteps sounded near me. I could smell dust and old wood and the damp scent of dew-wet, trampled grass from some unseen lawn. If there was anyone in these buildings he was as still as I was, listening and waiting. I couldn't see any motion in the street at all.

After a while I lit a cigarette and asked myself what next. But I knew the answer to that one without thinking. Until I was sure the troupe was safe I couldn't relax enough to take the next step, whatever it might be. There was no reason at all behind this feeling I had. The troupe had disowned me. At least, Guthrie had. But the sense of responsibility I had taken up for the little group I'd worked with wasn't something I could lay down again at will.

I studied street signs to orient myself. I looked up for the Dipper in the starry dark and found the North Star weakly blinking. The theater had been set up at the south side of town. I started off cautiously, keeping in the shadows.

CHAPTER XXIV

I had been walking for maybe ten minutes when I heard the first church bell begin to toll. It startled me. It didn't sound like an alarm, but seconds later another bell began to sound, and beyond that another, far off at the north edge of town. One bell was big and deep, one rang slightly flat, the third had a tenor note to its tone. They didn't ring very well together, and probably they weren't trying. All they meant to do was fill the night with the solemn sound of their tolling. I wondered if somewhere men were pulling and releasing the ropes that turned them, or are church bells rung mechanically? And either way – why? Why tonight in this besieged and frightened town? I walked faster.

I passed furtive pedestrians now and then, and stayed out of their sight when I could. I didn't want anything to do with either rebel or Comus forces yet. The bells tolled on. I knew there was probably a big public-address screen somewhere near the center of town, and there might be news on it I needed to know. But it would have to keep.

I passed the little dark park where I had spent my bad time alone. I passed the pool and the tree and turned the corner into the street where the theater had been set up. In the faint light of the nearest unbroken street lamp I could see the bleachers still standing, looking gaunt and deserted in the empty street.

On the far side of the bleachers the big square bulk of the round truck sat silent. Its round loudspeakers yawned up at the sky. The cab was empty. The troupe – had it gone? I stood there feeling foolish in the deserted street, the church bells knelling slowly in deep eddies of sound that filled the air around me. Naturally the troupe would have taken shelter somewhere, and fast, when the sirens first began to blow the *Hey, Charlie*, and the crowds scattered. But where would they have gone?

On the verge of turning away, I paused to listen. Voices? A muffled sound, curiously resonant, but voices speaking, and not very far off. I laughed suddenly at myself and started across the street toward the sound truck. The pavement at the edge of the grandstands was littered with the debris of the escaping audience – dropped handkerchiefs and hats, one shoe, several handbags turned inside out by provident looters. I kicked through the litter and reached up to tap at the door in the flat rear of the truck. I could hear the sound reverberate inside, and there was a sudden hush of the muffled voices, except for one that spoke on imperviously. I couldn't hear the words.

After a moment there was a sound of footsteps inside and Guthrie's voice said, 'What is it?'

'Rohan,' I called. 'Let me in.'

A pause. Then, 'You alone?'

'Yes. Open up.'

Very cautiously the door opened a narrow crack. I could see Guthrie's cheek and one eye, and just below his face the single eye of a Comus pistol looking straight at me. There was another pause. Then Guthrie grunted and pushed the door open. 'Come in,' he said.

The inside of the truck looked cavernous without the tightly packed and folded grandstands taking up most of the space. Standing up in the middle of emptiness on one side were the banks of instruments that had operated the lie-detector devices. At right angles to them, flat against the front wall, stood the television apparatus. The screen was lighted and a man was speaking portentously. The rest of the troupe, gathered at the screen, turned to look at me in surprise, and as I glanced from face to face, seeing Polly and Roy together, the Henkens and Cressy, I also saw Ted Nye's little dark excited face in the group and for a moment of surprise that rocked me back on my heels I thought again Ted was here in the truck.

Then common sense took over. It was Ted on the television screen. It was Ted speaking in the portentous voice. He wore a black band around his sleeve and his face looked self-consciously grave, but I knew the elation that shone just behind the gravity of his look.

'...the period of national mourning,' he was saying. 'Messages are already beginning to arrive from the heads of foreign states, and it is good to know that the world mourns with us the loss of the greatest man of modern times. The President's body will lie in state from...'

The realization of what had happened hit me belatedly and not with great surprise. Ever since I heard the church bells tolling I must have known with a part of my mind what that knell was sounding for. But the jolt was strong just the same. For a timeless moment I stopped hearing Ted Nye's voice at all. I stopped perceiving anything around me.

So much was going on in my mind. Awe and incredulity. The unthinkable idea of a nation without Raleigh. I couldn't remember a time when that strong, calm face hadn't dominated the whole continent. The nation itself was the very shape and substance of the man Raleigh, and it didn't seem conceivable that we could continue without him. And along with the solemn personal loss, because he was so strong when we needed him, a long time ago. Because he did so much for us that no other man alive had been able to do.

I looked at the faces turned toward mine. On all of them the same look of stunned incredulity was strong. This was an idea that would take getting used to. All of us had known it was coming. But when the moment really came, its impact was hard.

I looked at Guthrie, and then looked again, closer, shocked at the gray, desperate blankness of his face. He didn't look like a man sharing a national loss with two hundred million fellow countrymen. He looked like somebody with a stunning private shock and grief he had not shared with anybody. At first I thought the death of Raleigh had just hit him harder than most. But then I realized there had to be more to it than that. I saw his gaze move to the group by the television screen and fall upon Cressy's softly curved cheek turned away from him, the pale curls shining in the colored light of the screen.

'Where's the man who took my part?' I asked over the sound of Ted Nye's voice. I had to know where we stood, what had happened. I had the feeling that time might be running out on us.

'He left,' Guthrie said shortly.

'Ran like a rabbit,' Polly added with obscure satisfaction. 'What happened to you, Rohan?'

I started to answer, but the scene on the television screen changed then and we all turned to watch. Nye had gone off camera briefly, and a long, panning shot moved with impressive slowness from left to right above the roofs of night-time New York. I could see the lights in solid, glittering banks. Everyone was aroused and listening and stunned by the news of the nation's bereavement. Across three thousand miles I could hear the solemn tolling of church bells as the east coast mingled its knell with the tolling in the town around us. The nation was awake and all through this summer night history was on the turn.

Polly said again, 'Where were you, Rohan? I thought I saw—'

I shook my head at her sharply. If Guthrie didn't already know the part I'd played in breaking up the play he didn't need to know now.

I said, 'I just got here. What happened?'

Cressy smiled up at me. 'The show broke up, that's what. There was a lot of yelling and we made it into the truck just in time. They bounced stones off the sides until Guthrie took a few shots outside. Do you know what happened?'

'Whatever it was, it's all clear out there now,' I told her. I didn't look directly at her when I spoke. The likeness to Miranda was too poignant.

Guthrie put his hand on my arm. 'Rohan, I want to talk to you.' His face was haggard in the dim light from the television screen. 'Come outside if it's safe to. What do you think?'

'It's safe right now,' I said, 'but—'

The panorama of New York flickered sidewise off the screen and a voice said with enormous solemnity:

'Ladies and gentlemen, Mr Robert Dudley, the Vice-President of the United States, has an important announcement. Mr Robert Dudley.'

The Vice-President's pale, unfamiliar face looked out at us unhappily. A nerve twitched under his eye and television make-up couldn't entirely hid how wan he looked. He said in a voice that shook just a little:

'Ladies and gentlemen, I – pending action on the part of Congress, I—' He swallowed and then got it out in a rush. 'I feel it my duty to surrender office in favor of Mr Theodore Nye, recently named Secretary of State and coordinator for Comus.'

Guthrie's hand on my arm pulled stronger. His voice was shaking a little too. 'Outside,' he said, reaching for the door. 'Come on.'

It was cool and still down in the street except for the continuous heavy tolling of the distant bells. Guthrie looked around nervously. 'I thought for a while we were set up for a lynching,' he said. 'They've gone to the big news screen to listen now, but they'll be back. Rohan, things are bad. I want you to do a job for me.'

'You can't trust me,' I said. 'Remember?'

He brushed that aside. 'Hell is going to pop,' he said. 'Right here in Carson City. Any minute.' He jerked his head toward the truck and the sound of the voice from New York. 'I knew this was coming,' he said, 'but I didn't expect it so soon. I—'

'You knew Raleigh was going to die?' I heard my own voice going thin with disbelief. 'You knew—'

He said wearily, 'Rohan!' There was infinite cynicism in the way he said it. I felt a flush of sudden embarrassment at my own naïveté hot in my face. Maybe it takes a Comus man to know when Comus is lying.

I said, 'So they've found the Anti-Com.'

'Not quite, from what I'm told,' Guthrie said. 'But they know the town it's in. A place called Corby, about twenty-five miles from here. They may have the thing by now.'

I stood there hardly listening, staring up at the stars that twinkled through the naked girders of the grandstand and thinking what a fool I was. What a fool the whole nation was if it believed that Raleigh had died tonight.

Guthrie knew better. I wondered how many others knew, or had leaped to the same conclusion Guthrie had. It was much too pat. How long ago had the old man really died then? Days ago? Weeks? But Nye hadn't dared release the news until he thought he had his hands on the Anti-Com. If Raleigh had been a safety fuse that held Nye in control Raleigh too had been a safeguard for Nye. As long as the President lived the nation would respect his government. Nye was part of it. If Raleigh died *before* Nye could be sure Comus could hold the nation steady, then Nye might be done for.

But now Nye felt secure. Now he could announce the death. Now he could shove Vice-President Dudley out and seize the power in name that he had held in fact for so long. Now there was nothing to restrain him. Now—

'You get it?' Guthrie said urgently. 'While Raleigh was alive Comus didn't dare clamp down hard on California and risk an open rebellion. This means Nye's ready to strike. It's coming, Rohan. Any minute it's going to break.'

'What is?' I asked. 'What's going to happen?'

'For one thing, I think Nye will blow Corby right off the map. If he has to. He's got to stop the Anti-Com one way or another. I think the Comus forces are closing in now on Carson City. We know there are rebels here who know things we still have to find out. There's a lot of rebel ammunition and a lot of rebel forces right here in this town. We're going to see the kind of fighting in California tonight the country hasn't seen since the Five Days' War. Rohan—' He leaned forward and shook my arm urgently.

'Rohan, I want you to help me. I want you to get Cressy out of town before the trouble starts.'

I looked at him blankly. 'Cressy?' I said.

He grimaced in the thin darkness. 'Cressy is – she's my responsibility,' he said. 'I told you. I've got to stay. This is my job and I'm going to follow orders the way I always have. But

Cressy – she deserves something better. My wife and I never had a daughter, Rohan, but I – I kind of feel if we had she'd be just like Cressy. She's a good girl and she's going to have her chance. She needs help. I want you to see she gets it.'

'Nobody can get out of town,' I said.

'With the right pull, I can manage things. They're passing Comus cars in and out. I think I can work it.'

I said, 'Wait a minute, Guthrie. Use your head. I'll go if you can get a pass for us. But I'll take the whole troupe with me.'

He looked at me suspiciously. 'The whole troupe?'

'I can't leave them here!' I said. 'They'll be lynched. Besides, once we're outside Carson City, what then? The country's full of renegades. The more of us there are the safer. You'll have to get us some guns. Pod Henken and Roy can use them. I'll bet Polly can too. And we'll need all the defense we can get.'

Guthrie said doubtfully, 'I don't know, Rohan. I'm not sure I can—'

'It's the whole troupe or nobody,' I told him.

He hesitated a moment longer. Then he gave in quite suddenly. 'All right, have it your way. There isn't time to argue. Get back in the truck and wait for me. I'll have to move fast. It shouldn't take more than half an hour at the most. Be ready to move when I say so.'

He turned and ran off heavily down the dark street.

I watched him go. My heart was pounding with deep, uneasy thuds and my hands had begun to shake again. I was as scared as I'd ever been in my life. Because I knew what I was going to do – or try to do – and the risk was so great I didn't dare think about it.

I remembered the meeting place Elaine had assigned for the rebels to gather next. I wondered if there was time enough to do what I had to do. I heard the heavy tolling of the church bells. I looked up at the stars winking in the dark. I asked myself how much longer before the white glare of explosion would light up the nation from the spot where California used to be.

CHAPTER XXV

The schoolhouse had a big ornate AR for Andy Raleigh over the door. The schools, like almost everything else in the nation, were a part of Comus. They're Communications, aren't they? Looking up at the big AR as I went up toward the unlit building, I wondered how the Anti-Com could possibly knock out anything as diversified and as powerful as the thing Ted Nye had made of Comus. I didn't think it could be done. But the gamble had to be made.

A classroom with knee-high chairs and kindergarten tables seemed like a very strange, incongruous place for the meeting of revolutionaries. Or maybe appropriate, after all. Here where the first seeds of acquiescence had been planted in the minds of the newly schooled, maybe the fruits of rebellion were about to be harvested. It was anybody's guess at this point.

In the dim room lit only by street lights shining through the window walls I couldn't at first pick Elaine out of the crowd. There was a lot of going and coming, quite orderly. Everything seemed superficially under control, but the air of hysteria was building in the room, and I knew they were finding out how tight the ring had been drawn around Carson City. Maybe they guessed as Guthrie had guessed what was about to happen next.

I got Elaine by the arm as Guthrie had taken me. When she saw who it was she came willingly, with just a flash of that old, intensely personal look which had passed between us before now, when times were not so ruinous. But the flash went by and was past, and everything was strictly business out there in the hall that smelled of chalk and children.

'I got to talk fast,' I said. 'Don't argue. First – you said the Anti-Com isn't in Carson City. I wasn't sure before. Now I believe you. Is it in a town called Corby, about twenty minutes from here?'

The look of slightly dazzled dismay she turned to me was answer enough. 'All right,' I said. 'Next question – is that safety fuse here in Carson City? I need to know because I think I'm going to be able to leave town in the next half hour. Don't fence with me. If the thing's here – if it's finished and if it's portable – I'll take it to Corby for you. Yes or no?'

She gave me a look of desperation. 'I can't answer you, Rohan! I haven't the authority. Even if I had I wouldn't dare. I—'

I said harshly, 'Face it, Elaine! How could things be worse? Comus is searching Corby right now for the Anti-Com. What have you got to lose? There's nothing you can tell me now about the Anti-Com that Comus and Nye won't know within the next hour anyhow, when they find it. The worst I could do would be to take your safety fuse and run to the nearest Comus cop with it. How could that hurt anything now? The best thing that could happen would be to get the fuse to Corby before the Anti-Com blows the lid off California. I'll do it if you'll let me. How about it?'

She looked up searchingly into my face, hesitated a moment longer, and then sighed a very deep sigh and said, 'Wait.' I saw her dark outlines merge with the outlines of the shifting crowd. I saw her stop a passing man, speaking urgently in a whisper, and measure something large and square in mid-air between her outstretched palms.

When she came back she took me by the arms, her hands cold and unsteady, and stood looking up into my face again, still with that anxious, uncertain stare. She drew a deep breath and began to speak quite fast in a very low voice.

'The Anti-Com's in Corby. In the basement of the Methodist church. You can't miss the stone tower from anywhere in town. I've sent for the safety fuse. If you can get it to the Anti-Com crew they can wire it into the circuit in less than a minute.' She paused. 'You know the chance you're taking,' she said.

I nodded. 'If I think about it I'll get too scared to go,' I told her frankly. 'How soon can I start?'

'Five minutes,' she said. 'Maybe less. They're boxing it for you now.'

I said, 'What *is* the Anti-Com, Elaine? How does it work?'

She started to shake her head. Then she laughed unsteadily. 'I'm so used to keeping it a secret,' she said. 'Actually it doesn't matter now. Either we get the fuse to Corby in time or we don't. Nothing else matters. Rohan, all the Anti-Com has to do is operate thirty seconds, and every Comus mechanism that uses a transformer goes dead all over the nation.'

'Thirty seconds!' I said.

'It's awfully simple. We've found a way to induce permanent resonance in practically every transformer in the country.'

'Permanent resonance?'

'I don't understand it completely, of course. The Anti-Com will broadcast two particular frequencies in a certain order that will set up a sort of circular process in the transformers. Energy input and energy output rates will be identical, and no outside force can break the cycle. When it happens the transformers are no good at all. And that means that everything using electricity will stop dead.'

I said, 'Everything? But—'

'I know. Hospitals and homes, planes in the air – there'll be casualties. But not for long. Our people all over the country are ready and waiting. Comus is spread pretty thin in manpower because it's so well organized. You know how intricate its system of communications is. And all its power depends on the network of communications and transportation. Knock out that organization and – well, there's a lot more of us than them.' She drew another of those deep, unsteady breaths. 'That's the story,' she said. 'Now you know.'

I started to say, 'Elaine—' but I stopped again, because she couldn't hear me. She had closed her eyes and she was shivering uncontrollably from head to foot. I closed my arms around her and she leaned her forehead against my shoulder and let the deep, strong shudders go over her unresisted. I stood there holding her fast.

The fit didn't last long. Then she laughed with a sound more like grief than amusement and pushed herself back from me.

'It's just reaction,' she said. 'It's such a relief, Rohan, to pass the responsibility on!'

'You've done a fine job,' I told her. 'Now your part's done. I'll get the fuse to Corby if anybody can. If I can't – what's your guess, Elaine? Will the crew turn on the Anti-Com anyhow and take the chance of its blowing?'

The bright, dark eyes met mine levelly. 'I think they will. I think maybe I would if I had to make the decision. There's never been a chance against Comus before. There may never be again. Either way it's a terrible decision to have to make. But I think they'll turn it on.'

Down the hall the sound of hurrying feet came nearer. Two men rounded a corner, carrying between them a square case about the size of a portable typewriter box, with handles on two sides. I looked at it dubiously.

'How am I going to smuggle that thing into the sound truck?' I asked Elaine. Then I realized I hadn't explained to her how I expected to pass the Comus cordon, and I told her the story in quick sentences.

She frowned a little. 'It isn't really heavy,' she said. 'But it's clumsy. And conspicuous, unless there's someplace you can put it in the truck where it might seem to fit in. Will they search the truck?'

'I don't know. Maybe not. So far I don't think they know there's anything vital to search for. You say Beardsley didn't know about the safety fuse?'

'That's right.' She thought it over briefly. 'Go on back to the truck then. Some of the boys will go with you. We'll manage a diversion just before you reach the line-up at the check station.

Be at the back of the truck and we'll hand the box in to you. I can't think of anything better, can you?'

I said, 'It ought to work. Okay then, let's go.'

She held out her hand. It was cold and still unsteady in mine. I said, 'Elaine there's going to be a bad time in Carson City tonight. Now that Raleigh's dead the safety controls are off Nye. You realize that?'

She nodded.

'Keep under cover, will you?' I said. 'If we ever come out of this—' I paused, smiling at her. 'I'll come back and find you.'

'I'll expect you,' she told me quite impersonally.

We let it go at that. Maybe it was as far as it would ever go. Who knows?

CHAPTER XXVI

Guthrie glanced around the anxious faces in the truck for one last time. His eyes lingered for a moment on Cressy's face.

'You'll be okay,' he said reassuringly. 'Rohan, I've made all the arrangements. Once you're outside, head for Truck Station 33, north on the highway about ten miles. They'll be expecting you. They're fortified well enough and you'll be safe. Okay?'

Cressy smiled at him. 'Stop worrying,' she said. 'We'll live to tell our grandchildren about it.' She was sitting on the floor with her feet tucked under the bright pink skirts of her last-act costume. The make-up was smeared a little on her face and the mascara had run down to streak her cheeks, so I thought she must have cried. Maybe when the mob bombarded the truck and a lynching seemed like the next thing the troupe might expect. Whatever it was, she had got her courage back now.

Polly said, 'Guthrie, you're sure we'll get our pay and the bonus? We only gave three performances, but—'

'You'll get it,' Guthrie told her. 'We did our job. Don't worry.'

Polly nodded and gave Roy a cold glance. He sat beside Cressy, examining the pistol Guthrie had handed him, and he didn't meet his wife's look at all. They were not, apparently, on speaking terms this evening.

Pod Henken said, 'Good luck, Guthrie. Look out for yourself. You sure you won't come with us?'

'I've got my orders,' Guthrie told him.

Mrs Henken, sitting on the floor beside Pod, her feet out straight before her, reached up and removed from her wild tangle of white curls a single carnation which she must have picked from somebody's garden on the way to the theater tonight. She twirled it between her fingers and in some perfectly mysterious way managed to rivet every eye in the truck upon it. Her old scene-stealing techniques were flawless, as usual, even when there seemed neither need nor point.

She said to me calmly, ignoring everyone else, 'Rohan, do you remember *The Mouse-trap?*' and before I could answer, went smoothly on into the familiar lines from *Hamlet*.

> 'I have heard
> That guilty creatures sitting at a play
> Have by the very cunning of the scene
> Been struck so to the soul that...'

She broke off. 'How does it go, do you remember?'

Guthrie said hastily. 'You'd better get moving. I'll see you all later on. Good luck. Goodbye.' He swung down to the ground and the door closed behind him.

I grinned at Mrs Henken and shook my head. I wondered how long she had known the theater was akin to Hamlet's *Mouse-trap*. It didn't matter now, but I wondered.

'Pod,' I said, 'will you drive?'

The distraction I'd been expecting came right on schedule. A block away from the tail of the line-up at the check station a thrown rock bounced thunderously off the front wall of the truck. An outburst of yells and flung stones drew every eye to the road before us. Pod threw on the air brakes and stopped us with shattering suddenness. I never did know why. Maybe a log thrown across the street.

The moment we stopped I opened the door at the rear of the truck very quietly. Hands out of the darkness held up a square case, the handle ready for my grasp. I had it inside the truck and set down in the spot I'd picked out for it while the shouts and reverberations of rocks on the metal walls still echoed deafeningly in our ears.

It was over in thirty seconds. Pod started the truck again.

The shouts faded behind us. We all let out the tightly held breaths we had drawn and looked at each other with shaky smiles.

At the check station we all showed our regulation Comus passes. They matched us up carefully with the photographs on our cards. Someone came in and cast a very cursory series of glances around the truck. What they seemed to be looking for was stowaways. Nothing else interested them much. The whole thing was over in less than five minutes.

Pod swung the truck up the ramp toward the highway. He turned right, swung into a suitable lane, and set the controls for automatic. Then he leaned over the back of the cab and grinned at us.

'We're on our way,' he said.

'Look in the map compartment, will you?' I said. 'I'd like to see what the layout is. I've got something to tell you.'

The highway ran straight between Carson City and the Corby turnoff. The truck stop where we were expected lay about five miles beyond the turnoff. Corby was at the end of a winding twenty miles of mountain road. I looked at the map. When we came to the spot where the Corby road left the highway we would stand at the branching of a Y, down one leg of which the troupe might find safety – of a sort. If the Anti-Com didn't blow California sky-high. But there wasn't going to be time enough to spare for that trip down the far leg of the Y.

I had to get to Corby as fast as the truck would take me. Every second counted from now on. The troupe was going to need the truck to reach their refuge. I was going to need it to get to Corby. We couldn't both have it.

I stood there balancing against the swaying of the floor and frowning down at the map. This was a problem I hadn't thought of. Back there in Carson City it had seemed enough to get the Swann Players out of town before the fighting began, before the townspeople returned to their lynching. But what was I going to do with them now? I couldn't take them with me, I couldn't leave them to walk the five dark miles through renegade-infested country.

'Set her at high speed, Pod,' I said. 'We're in a hurry.' I looked from face to face around the familiar little group. I thought how well I'd come to know them in the past week. I remembered how willingly they'd worked under my harsh direction. I remembered how they'd backed me up on the night when I got my old magic back again, and how they'd rallied round to keep the show going the night I froze. The responsibility I felt for them was a very real thing. But I had a bigger responsibility now.

They would have to know what we were all up against. They'd have to make their own decision. I couldn't do it for them.

'Pod,' I said, 'watch the road, will you? I want to know when we reach the Corby turnoff.' I glanced around the group. 'All of you,' I said, 'there's something you've got to know. We aren't out of the woods yet, cast. I think there's a bad time ahead. Here's the setup.'

I told them briefly, keeping my voice calmer than I felt. I told them about the Anti-Com and the probability of a blowup. 'If that happens,' I said, 'we'll never know what hit us.' I told them where the Anti-Com was. That had stopped being a secret now. 'And Nye will bomb Corby right off the map the minute he decides it's that or risking the Anti-Com's knocking Comus out,' I said. 'Corby has two chances out of three of going up in a cloud of smoke within the next hour. So now you know where we stand.'

They had been watching me with frozen attention all the time I spoke. There was a deep silence when I finished.

Then Roy said, 'What's the third chance, Rohan?'

'Comus gets knocked out for good and the country moves into a whole new phase,' I said. 'The rebels take over.'

'The Second American Revolution,' Roy said. 'Is that it?'

I nodded. 'That's about it.'

Silence again. I measured them with a quick glance. I dropped my hand casually into my coat pocket and closed my fingers around the little gun. Still casually I moved toward the back of the truck until I had my shoulders against the far corner and faced the rest of the troupe gathered toward the front around the television screen. Pod watched me without blinking from the driver's seat. I couldn't see his hands.

'There's one thing more,' I said. 'I'm going on into Corby. I've got to get there fast. That means I've got to take the truck. I'm sorry, cast. I'll have to drop you at the Corby turnoff.'

It took a moment for the import to sink in. Then Pod Henken said sharply, 'Rohan, you can't do it!'

I took the gun out of my pocket and rested it across my left wrist.

'I've got to. Believe me, if there were any other way—'

'But it's only an extra five miles,' Polly said in bewilderment. 'I don't see—'

'An extra ten, there and back,' I told her. 'I haven't got the time.'

Pod Henken said, 'But Eileen can't walk five miles, Rohan. And it isn't safe! We don't know what kind of men are on the roads tonight.'

'I can't help it,' I said stubbornly. 'I've tried every way I know to think of an out, but—'

Pod looked at me over the seat back. 'There are five of us against one,' he observed in a mild voice.

I jerked my gun a little to remind him. 'I thought of that,' I said. 'Maybe you could jump me, but I'd get two at least before—'

Pod Henken said, 'Sorry, Rohan,' still very mildly, and over the back of the seat a star of blinding light seemed to explode right in my eyes. I heard a singing sound and the gun in my hand gave a metallic wail and jumped with paralyzing violence backward out of my grip. I thought for a moment it had taken my fingers with it. I felt a line of ice-cold force rip straight across my forearm, and the double impact sent me back hard against the truck wall. My head struck with a hollow-sounding thud.

Everything in front of me blurred. All the faces swam in a haze of gray. Very dimly I saw Polly swoop to snatch up the fallen gun. I thought, *I can't black out now. I can't! Everything's done for if I do.* I felt my knees sagging and the floor of the truck seemed to tilt upward.

Very fast, before I could fall forward, I pressed my back to the wall and skidded to a sitting position. I bent forward until my head was between my knees, and with my good hand I hit my forehead, little jolting blows to keep the blackness from settling over me. *Stay here, stay here!* I pleaded silently with myself.

It wasn't easy. My head was ringing and I couldn't be sure whether there was an interval of black-out after all, but the next thing I knew I was looking up into Polly's astonished face as she stood over me holding the gun. Pod was speaking from the cab.

'. . . mentioned I used to run a sharp-shooting act before the carnivals shut down, did I?' he seemed to be saying.

I blinked at him witlessly.

'Guess I'm losing my grip,' he said. 'All I aimed to do was knock the gun out of your hand. I never went for your arm. That was an accident. How you feeling, Rohan?'

I straightened and leaned my head back against the jolting wall to keep from folding forward again. 'Was I out?' I demanded.

Polly, still more bewildered than hostile, said, 'I don't think so. How's your arm?'

I looked down, aware for the first time of a heavy, throbbing pain. Blood was spreading bright red across my shirt sleeve in two rapidly broadening wet spaces that made the cloth stick to my arm. Shakily with my left hand I pushed the sleeve up. On the underside of my forearm and in the middle of the back of it two neat bullet holes pumped bright blood.

Polly said in exasperated voice, 'Oh, for God's sake, Rohan!' She dropped to her knees, laid the gun on the rumbling floor of the truck, and took my arm in firm, competent hands turning it to look.

'No broken bones, anyhow,' she said. 'But I think you got the artery, Pod.' She glanced over her shoulder. 'Roy let's have your shirt. Cressy, come over here and hold your thumb tight where I've got mine. Good. Keep it there.'

Over their bent heads I looked up at Pod Henken. I drew a deep breath. 'Pod, where are we now?'

He glanced out at the dark road. 'Coming toward the Corby turnoff,' he said without expression.

Polly was ripping cloth into strips with long tearing sounds. I said, 'Pod, are you a Comus man?'

There was a little shocked pause. Pod said indignantly, his red face redder than ever, 'Hell, no! What do you take me for?'

'You've done a Comus job,' I said.

It was Roy, pulling his coat back on over his undershirt, who said, 'What do you mean by that, Rohan?'

Cressy was looking into my face from very near, the stains of mascara and recent tears giving her a childish look. Polly paused with two ends of half-torn cloth in her motionless hands. Even Eileen Henken, the carnation between her fingers, gazed questioningly at me. It was Pod I looked at.

'The odds just dropped on the chances of a Second American Revolution,' I said. 'I can't give you orders now. But I'm asking you. Get out at the crossroads and let me take the truck on into Corby.'

After what seemed like a long pause, Roy said, 'Why?'

'*Crossroads*,' Eileen Henken murmured in a meditative voice.

'That's right,' I told her. 'A bigger crossroads than you know. I can't explain it, cast.' I hitched myself a little higher against the wall. Automatically Cressy's hands moved with me, maintaining the pressure on my artery. I pulled myself together inside, throwing all the persuasion I could find in me into my voice. 'You've got to do it,' I said. 'I know it's dangerous. Maybe you'll get robbed on the road. Maybe you'll get killed. But you've got to go. And I've got to have the truck.'

Polly said in a strained voice, 'I think you'll have to explain, Rohan.'

But before I could speak, Roy spoke for me. I looked up with astonishment at the sudden violence in his voice. His sullen look had lightened amazingly. For the first time I saw life and excitement in his face. He was reacting hard.

'Explain what?' he demanded. 'That he's been working with

225

the rebels? Damn you, Rohan, why did you have to keep quiet about it? I'm with you. What do you want me to do?'

I felt my jaw drop as I looked at him. Polly said, 'Roy?' in a small, thin voice.

'You think I've just been sitting around with my eyes shut?' he demanded angrily. 'I know what's been going on out here. I like what I've seen. I like the feel of it.' He wiped the back of his hand across his cheek with a violent motion, smearing the make-up. With a sort of savage contempt he held out the streaked hand. 'You think I like being an actor? You think I *want* to act? I hate it. I always did hate it. But under Comus I act or starve. I want out of this rat race.' He swung back to me. 'Rohan! Have we still got a chance?'

I tried to read the truth in his eyes. How much could I trust him? How strong a tool would he be in my hands? He wiped his palm across his thigh and then held out both hands to me, shaking with tension.

'Give me a job to do! I'm willing to gamble if you are. What's going on?'

I found I was shaking again, too.

'It's too dangerous,' I said. 'No.'

'Yes!' Roy yelled at me. 'I'm not afraid! I'm sick of Comus. How much of a chance have we got?'

I looked around the jolting truck. I looked at the dark trees whipping by outside. I looked toward the east, where at any moment, for all I knew, the white glare of explosion might begin to rise.

'I don't know!' I yelled back at him. 'Damn it, I don't know! I think there's a chance but I don't *know*. I'm so scared I can't think ahead. I'm so scared I'm shaking. Look!'

'But you still want to go into Corby?'

'I've got to!'

'You can't make it alone. I'll go too.'

Cressy said seriously, 'I can't hold the bleeding back when you yell like that, Rohan. Calm down or you won't do anything at all.'

I looked down at the freshly welling blood. I leaned back against the rumbling wall and drew a long, unsteady breath.

'All right,' I said. 'Over there behind the control panels is a square box. Inside it there's a safety fuse that belongs with the Anti-Com. My job's to get it into Corby before the Anti-Com crew gets desperate enough to go ahead without it. So now you know.'

Roy said, 'With it everything will go through without a hitch? Is that it?'

I nodded. 'The Anti-Com will knock out Comus – *if* we get there in time. If we don't, it may just knock California off the map.'

From the corner of my eye I saw Pod Henken turn around in the driver's seat. I felt the floor under me begin to slow in its vibrations. The darkness outside flowed slower too. Then brakes sighed and the truck rolled heavily to a halt. Pod Henken's voice called calmly back to us.

'All out that's going out,' he said.

CHAPTER XXVII

In the sudden dead silence Polly finished ripping the strip of shirt she held in mid-air. It made an angry sound.

'Who's getting out?' she demanded. 'I'd just as soon get blown up trying as blown up running. All right, Cressy, your thumb, will you? Let's get this bandage on.'

Pod grinned at her from over the back of the seat.

'I can remember the old days,' he said in a conversational tone. 'Before Comus. I'm with you, Rohan. Eileen?'

She gave him a placid smile. 'We're not gambling much at our age, are we? What are we waiting for?'

Cressy looked up. 'Me?' she said. 'You mean me?' She flashed me a make-up-smeared smile, opportunist to the last. 'Maybe we'll all be famous,' she said. 'It's worth a chance.'

I sat up straight. Suddenly I began to feel much better.

'Hurry up with that bandage, can't you?' I said to Polly. 'I'm going up front with Pod. It rides easier, and I want to get to Corby in one piece. We've got a rough trip ahead, cast. Hang on!'

The pavement poured past under us like a curving, uneven river that swung us rhythmically from side to side. There seemed to be an unusual amount of traffic on the Corby road tonight. Ahead of us and behind lights swung in and out of the steep, climbing curves. I was glad of the company on the road. It made us less conspicuous. I wondered how many other travelers toward Corby knew what it was they were racing into. Probably Comus was pouring in troops, by air as well as by road. Probably they'd find the Anti-Com long before we got there. Probably by the time we rounded the next curve, or the one beyond, we'd see the blinding flash start to burst outward from the exploding town, spreading fast toward us and eastward across the continent.

I didn't believe it. I didn't care. My arm throbbed and the blood kept seeping in a wider and wider stain through the bandage, but that didn't bother me either. I felt cool and confident. The whole night world around me seemed strangely alive, and I was responding vividly to every random stimulus. The stars glittered against my very skin and the sound of a night bird calling clearly in the dark was a sound my own mind had made. I felt as if the last walls had fallen away around me and I was alone and free. It made me a little sad without knowing yet just why, but very fresh and clear.

In the rearview mirror I saw the lights of following traffic jolt up and down. We were going much too fast and it didn't seem to matter. I had the wild, irrational idea that we couldn't go wrong tonight. The world was turning obediently under my feet again and history was turning too. History of our own making, new-minted, fresh as the mountain night around us.

Pod said suddenly, 'Look over there to the right. Wait a minute – there. Those lights. That must be Corby.'

The road was topping a rise, and for a moment we could all see the winking clusters far off. Then the road sank again and all we could see was the rushing river of the highway and the bursts of light and sound that were passing traffic. But the glow of Corby hung above it in the sky now, and over the glow a star winked red, white, and blue over and over. I thought of Charlie Starr and the San Diego Massacre and I wondered in that formless way we all must have when we think of the dead whether he could possibly know what was happening tonight, ending the thing he had begun. Ending it one way or another. But that was a thing too big and dim for the mind to cope with long.

Pod Henken said with a sound of sudden alarm, 'Look back,

Rohan. I thought I saw something – something behind us that was red.'

My heart gave a lurch before my reason did. Something red? I leaned out futilely, trying to see the road behind us. Something the color of Comus following us along the Corby road? 'Not necessarily following us,' I told myself. 'Corby is the center of the nation tonight. Everything on this road except us is bound to be Comus.'

We rounded a curve. I could see down the way we had come, and something brilliantly red flashed suddenly into sight five or six headlights behind us. I caught my breath.

'You were right, Pod. There's a Prowler on the road. Coming this way.'

'After us?' Pod asked quietly.

'I don't think so. I don't see how anybody could know. Unless—' The thought jolted me. Unless they picked up Elaine ... But I couldn't believe that one either. I remembered the blue ring on her hand. I didn't think they could keep Elaine in their hands long enough to make her talk. She had her own infallible way of slipping between their fingers and I knew she would have used it. No, they couldn't be looking for us ...

Pod said, 'Brace yourself. I'm going off automatic. We've got more maneuverability on manual, and we couldn't outrun a Prowler anyhow.'

I felt a strange little wrench somewhere in my mind as the truck lurched and we broke, maybe forever, the bond with that humming artery which had been guiding us down the highway. The artery of Comus. We were on our own.

Pod said, 'Listen.' And after a moment I heard it too – a siren that wailed high and then low, shrill and demanding. In the rearview mirror I saw the distant spot of red swell with terrifying speed as it swept toward us down the road, radiant in its own crimson light. The noise swelled as the teardrop shape swelled. A sight to make the heart hesitate and the breath come faster. Already I'd begun to forget how intensely red they are, how big, how fast.

It swung wide around the set of headlights just in front of

it, screamed peremptorily, and crowded the two shining eyes to a halt at the edge of the road. Then the little tableau leaped backward and dwindled to a dot as Pod put on more speed. The truck groaned and boomed hollowly. The road poured past like a river in flood. The stars burned white above the treetops. I heard a heavy buzzing overhead even above the truck's thunder, and a moment later we saw the lights of a laboring helicopter sinking toward Corby like an overladen bee buzzing in bass. And another. And a third.

When we topped the next rise Corby was much nearer. The whole town was brilliantly alight, and I thought I could hear the sharp crack of gunfire, though the noise around me was too heavy now to be sure. The town couldn't be more than five minutes away, I thought.

But maybe we didn't have five minutes to spare. The voice of the Prowler rose again in that terrifying, high, undulating scream that sounded bright red like the creature that voiced it. In the mirror I watched it swing contemptuously around two sets of headlights and come roaring after us down the road, swelling, crimson, glaring with light and color.

Pod's foot was on the floorboards and the truck heaved and rocked, booming in protest. The lights of Corby rushed toward us and the trees rushed backward along the road in continuous hissing streams. The stars winked above Corby, quiet and cool.

The Prowler cut in on a car two places behind us, herding it in toward the roadside with an ear-destroying wail of the siren. Again the tableau of Prowler and captive leaped backward and dwindled in the dark.

But this time something else happened. One of the enormous Comus trucks behind the Prowler swung wide around the halted tableau and came thundering after us, closing the distance with appalling speed. I saw the wheel fighting Pod Henken's grip like something alive, terrified and struggling to escape. He swerved toward the edge of the road, cutting across the humming power lanes, trying to lose us among the line of rushing trucks and cars.

He couldn't do it. The pursuers were coming too fast behind

us, and it was us they were after. A quarter of a mile behind us the huge Comus van swung into a lane paralleling ours and came roaring down on us like a cyclone, blinking its lights on and off furiously. Pod stamped the accelerator hard on the floorboards and the whole vehicle shuddered under us, but still the big pursuer gained and gained.

Now it was drawing level with us in the next lane. It didn't try to pull ahead, but went thundering along neck and neck in a high-speed tableau, hunter and hunted alike roaring down the road together. I saw Pod give it one quick glance and then stare straight ahead, his jaw set, fighting the wheel to keep us on our course. Very briefly I realized how little I had known of the old man until tonight. He had come a long way from the red-faced nonentity I'd met back there in the redwoods. Or maybe I'd come a long way. Maybe it was I who'd changed.

The enormous truck towered over us on juggernaut wheels like a moving factory that thundered along the road. Now it was moving in as the Prowler had done to other cars, crowding us toward the edge of the pavement. The relief driver on our side was leaning out of the window, yelling and waving.

'Pod!' I shouted. 'Your gun! If we could hit their tires—'

Pod rolled sideways in the seat. 'My pocket!' he yelled, not taking his eyes off the road. I groped in his coat pocket with my left hand. And then, with the gun in my grip and halfway lifted to take aim, I paused suddenly, straining my ears. Had I heard what I thought I heard?

'Hey, Charlie!' a thin voice was yelling in the whistling dark between us. *'Hey, Charlie – can you hear me?'*

A flash of bright excitement glinted in my mind. I leaned back across Pod's bent shoulders and waved furiously.

'Charlie?' I yelled in answer. 'What's the word?'

The wind whipped his answer to rags in the space between us. All I could hear was a thin sound that seemed to say, '—block ahead—'

'What?' I shouted. And this time it came clearer through the roaring of the wind.

'Roadblock ahead! Take it easy – we'll crash through! Let us get – ahead...'

Time seemed to stretch out like elastic. Time stopped entirely. We would go on at this racking speed forever with the huge bulk of the truck pulling ahead of us, lengthening the distance between our lights and the great, rumbling, shaking galaxy of lights that outlined its rear.

Now I could see the barricade set up across the whole highway just outside the lights of the Comus check station at the edge of Corby. But trucks were parked nose to tail in a solid wall across the road, and an enormous Prowler sat waiting at the narrow gap through which traffic was being passed. I thought, watching the traffic slip through the barrier:

They know about us. Somehow they know. The trap's set up for us and nobody else. And it had to be true that the word was out about us, or how had our friends in the truck ahead known we needed help? Someone had talked. It was the only answer. I wondered painfully if the someone had been Elaine. And I wondered if I'd ever know the truth about that one.

The Prowler at the barricade began to howl high and shrill as the huge truck hurtled toward it, not slowing down at all. The truck added its own hornblast to the commotion, raucous and defiant. For one long last moment it thundered straight for the barricade with all its lights glittering and its horn screaming until the echoes rolled back from the hills around us. The noise was exhilarating and contagious. I leaned over to slam my wrist down on our own horn, hearing the hoarse bellow of it leap into life. The world was full of tremendous motion and the stunning sound of horns filling the road and the air and the sky.

The next moment the leviathan before us hit the barricade.

The sound was enormous – high, hollow, booming. All the horns stopped on the same note and the world was full of that tremendous booming and nothing else at all. We saw the trucks that made up the barricade hurtle left and right as the huge battering-ram thundered forward, plowing its path through their ranks and leaving a broad space open across the road. Then slowly, solemnly, it began to heave over toward one side. There was something awesome and deliberate about its overturning. It leaned, leaned past the balance point, leaned solemnly and crashed...

We hadn't time to pause or look back. The Prowler was already gunning into life as we hurtled through the opening the nameless rebels had made for us and shot straight toward the center of town at close to a hundred miles an hour, Corby streaming back on both sides of us like a town made of water.

Pod threw on the brakes. The sound truck skidded and shrieked, tires smoking on the pavement until we rocked at last to a standstill and the houses around us turned solid again and we had stopped in the center of Corby.

I looked at the street before us and blinked and looked again. All I could see was the color of Comus – bright red. Two of the three helicopters we had seen laboring over us above the road sat now in the middle of the main street of Corby, glinting crimson in the light. Drawn up before the helicopters were the men who had come down in them, red-coated men with guns in their hands, waiting for us. Comus knew. And Comus had got here first.

For a moment it seemed to me that after we stopped the world went right on streaming backward on both sides, and the ground still seemed to be heaving under us. Walking across the heaving ground came a familiar figure in a familiar checkered shirt.

Guthrie's face was as red as the coats of the men behind him. Anger made the veins beat in his temples.

He called up at me in a tight voice, 'All right, Rohan, come out with your hands up. I made a mistake with you, but it's not too late to catch it. Where's the Anti-Com fuse?'

CHAPTER XXVIII

Behind me I heard a sudden brisk motion inside the sound truck. I didn't turn my head. I was looking at the town of Corby and wondering where its people were. I was sure I'd heard gunfire from back there on the road. I was doubly sure there had been fighting here to slow down the house-to-house searchers. It came to me only now, in a sudden blaze of realization, that we'd made it into Corby and the Anti-Com hadn't yet blown up. I thought, Then they *can't* have found it yet. There's still time—

But was there? Time for what? Time to be arrested and searched, outnumbered by the Comus men before us. I wondered if Guthrie would shoot if we tried to run him down. Gunfire might rouse the local rebels, call them to the rescue. Alone, we'd shot our bolt. We couldn't do much from here on in without help that I saw no way to get. Guthrie said, 'You heard me, Rohan. Come on down.' For a moment I was acutely aware of my own weakness, the pain in my arm, the dizziness in my head. I drew a breath and started to mutter to Pod Henken. All I could think of was to start the truck again and force their gunfire. It was all I could think of. But behind us in the truck better wits were at work.

I heard from the roof of our cab a sudden, hollow, metallic coughing sound, loud and carrying. Then a voice amplified all out of recognition, a woman's voice that sounded a little flat with age, shouted to the silent town.

'*Hey, Charlie!*' the amplifiers on the roof of the sound truck roared. HEY, CHARLIE! The enormous scream went rolling into the dark. HEY, CHARLIE! The flat-faced houses around us picked up the words, flung them from echo to echo until they diminished down the streets of Corby in overlapping patterns of sound. HEY, CHARLIE! the housefronts seemed to be shouting. HEY, CHARLIE — CHARLIE — CHARLIE!

The whole town heard it. The sound soared up and made a dome above the rooftops, and even the stars must have been listening.

Guthrie's gun arm swung up and I saw his lips move, but I couldn't hear anything he said in the amplified screaming that filled the whole air. I did hear his gun bark, and then the twang of the bullet on metal, and one of the two amplifiers above us coughed and went silent.

For one last moment I heard Eileen Henken's defiant voice screaming the rally call in vast, metallic tones. Then the gun barked again and the sound amplifier gave a hoarse squawk and was silent. My ears roared with the stillness when it stopped.

From the row of flat-faced houses to our left and right I thought I sensed motion behind windowpanes. I wasn't sure, because a Comus sergeant in a brilliant red coat had jumped out before the line of unmoving men as Eileen's alarm began to sound, and I was watching him, ready to duck. His mouth opened and closed with some order nobody could hear while the amplifier horns still screamed. I wasn't even paying attention to Guthrie just now. I thought this man was our nearest real danger — now.

When the roar of the amplifier died the sergeant's voice bawled out with unexpected volume. He got some of the command out. 'FI—' he yelled.

A rifle cracked sharply, with a sound of brisk authority. The yelling sergeant never finished his command. Guthrie whirled toward the noise, and in the same instant I realized that all alone the street gun muzzles were poking out from upper windows with a sharp crackle of breaking glass. Their fusillade swept the scarlet ranks, whined from the helicopter sides, sang on the pavement. The Comus men reeled in a moment's wild

236

disorder before they broke for cover, firing as they ran. The focus of the fight had changed with amazing swiftness.

So the rebels had known we were on our way. They had held their fire until now.

But it was still up to us to take the next step.

I felt the shape of Pod Henken's gun solid and unexpected in my hand. I had forgotten I held it. Clumsily in my left hand I hefted the thing.

Then from behind us the wild, rising wail of the Prowler we had so briefly escaped came swelling toward us along the street. A burst of futile rifle fire rattled from windows above as it passed. I heard a dull boom and saw a flash of sullen reddish light reflected on the building fronts around us. The Prowler had fired a small bomb into one of the centers of rebel resistance as it passed. And it must be a building Comus had already searched, I told myself. They still wanted the Anti-Com and wanted it intact, or all of Corby would by now be rocking with explosions. I glanced apprehensively at the quiet stars. There might be bombs or bombers on the way already, poised to strike if all else failed.

Over the wild shrieking of the Prowler and the rattle of gunfire a voice was shouting in my ear from the back window of the cab. Roy's voice, pitched to carry. He was almost at my ear but he sounded as if he were shouting over windy miles, the noise around us was so heavy.

'Where – we headed?' he called. 'Where's – Anti-Com?'

It brought me back to life. The tremendous noise and the numbing effect of all I had been through had dulled me briefly to the need for more action, and fast, while the rebel firing still gave us time to move. It occurred to me with a kind of impersonal interest that I was losing blood and had been for the past half hour – or was it less? Time had little meaning now. The loss of the blood had little meaning. It was somebody else's blood reddening the bandage on my arm.

I leaned to look through the windshield at the skyline of Corby. Elaine had said you could see the church tower from anywhere in town. And after an instant I saw it, high and gray, underlighted from below by what might be the glow of an unseen fire somewhere near it. The belfry shone pink-lit and pale against the sky, and I could see one star shining through the arches.

A hand came through the window of the cab at my side groping for the inside handle. An arm with a checkered shirt sleeve. I looked down at Guthrie's red, determined face, dark with anger. My gun was in my left hand and I swung it up and looked straight down the barrel at him, the gun sight centered between his eyes and the rest of his face so near my own hand blotted it out. He looked up at me, his eyes on mine, waiting because it was too late for him to do anything at all but await the explosion.

I couldn't pull the trigger.

I tried. I couldn't do it. From a distance, yes, maybe. From an impersonal distance when it was his life or mine. But not now, not this close, not with his eyes calmly gazing into mine. I knew him too well. He was a tough old man doing a job he didn't much like, but doing it because he knew he had to. According to his lights, I was a fool.

I turned the gun barrel sidewise and struck him in the face with the back of my hand, heavily, knocking him backward into the street.

'Pod,' I said, keeping my voice as quiet as I could, 'get going. Turn left into that street there. We're heading for the gray stone church.'

The motor heaved into life before I finished speaking, and the truck rumbled into motion in a slow arc across the street. And not an instant too soon, either. The wail of the Prowler was all around us, bathing us in sound that made the viscera tighten. To our right just as we began to move an enormous crimson shape went hurtling by, so close its curved side shrieked against the side of the sound truck. They had meant to ram us. They had only barely missed. Next time they wouldn't miss at all.

Pod knew it as well as I did. He didn't try to straighten out of his arc and enter the street I'd pointed to. Instead he swung the truck broadside across its mouth, blocking the whole way.

'Outside!' he yelled. 'We can't outrun 'em! Maybe on foot we can make it. Hurry!'

He was down in the street before he finished the last words. I scrambled across the seat after him and dropped through his open door, hearing the thud of hurrying feet in the truck behind me as the rest of the troupe scrambled too. Pod caught me as I hit the street and staggered. The next instant the whole truck boomed and leaped as the Prowler, accelerating backward with enormous speed and accuracy, crashed hard into the side I had just vacated.

It crashed and rebounded. The street was fully blocked – for a minute or two. For whatever that was worth to us. For under the continuous wailing of the Prowler I felt rather than heard a heavier beating throb, and knew that the helicopters were heaving their crimson weight into the air.

Cressy was on one side of me, Eileen Henken on the other. 'You all right?' Roy asked anxiously, peering at me. I looked past him at Polly, her face strangely not haggard at all any more, but bright with a flamboyant freshness of excitement. Between them she and Roy were carrying the square box by its handles.

'I'm fine!' I yelled at them through the uproar. 'Come on. Run!'

Somewhere down a side street another of the dull explosions boomed and another fan of crimson light sprang briefly up. Smoke blew toward us, veiling the buildings. People were running in the smoke, turning to fire back the way they had come. From the hidden side street the wail of another Prowler shrieked to a terrible crescendo and swooped down again with a shrill falling sound. Behind us the stalled sound truck reverberated again as the Prowler crashed once more into its side. A fusillade of useless rifle fire burst from a row of windows above us, bullets spattering against the high crimson curve of the Prowler futilely. We could see its gleaming red brow above the top of the sound truck drawing back for another blow.

We ran, under a slanting curtain of the rifle fire down the street toward the church tower in the distance.

It was like running through chaos. My head felt light and my feet seemed a long way off, hardly touching the pavement. The smoke that blew past us seemed to swirl through my mind. I remember a bright red 'hopper rocking toward us down a street where men and women were running and falling, and I remember one man drawing back his arm to throw something bottle-shaped that gleamed in the 'hopper's single headlight and then crashed against its side. Oily liquid splashed as it broke, flashed into fire, and spread a film of unsteady flame over the whole side of the 'hopper. A homemade bomb, I thought. They're fighting back with all they've got.

But it wasn't going to be enough.

'Hoppers you can knock out. But not Prowlers. Not helicopters. The machines were closing in on us all and rifles are no good against the kinds of machines Comus was mustering against us.

Only the Anti-Com could knock these monsters out.

A heavy buzzing overhead made my very bones vibrate, and somebody's hand on my arm dragged me under the overhang of a porch roof just before the search beam from the sky came splashing down, outlining startled runners in the street. They turned up frightened faces bleached white in the strong light. Bullets rattled down along the high beam and an irregular zigzag line of people doubled up and dropped onto the dazzling pavement.

Comus was out of control. Ted Nye was out of control. The safety fuse we carried with us was a safety fuse for Nye as well as the powerful thing we carried it to. I remember thinking desperately, They won't take much more of this. They can't. They shouldn't. They'll turn on the Anti-Com, safety fuse or not, and stop Comus in its tracks or blow up California trying. I heard Pod Henken's voice wheezing in my ear.

'Guthrie's behind us!' he yelled above the noise. 'Look back!'

I saw the checkered shirt dimly through smoke. A swirl of people in the street moved between him and us, and when the view was clear again for a moment I saw red coats moving behind him. Not only machines were after us. Distantly I heard Guthrie shout, and a bullet spattered on the brick wall above our heads. Chips and brick dust rained over us.

Pod said in a firm, hurried voice, 'You go on. It's only a couple of blocks more. You can make it if I draw Guthrie off.'

I started to say, 'No, we'll—'

Pod cut me off. 'Eileen can't go any farther now anyhow,' he told me. 'Look.' I turned my head and saw the red stain spreading across the side of her aproned costume. Her face was as white as her hair in the intermittent glare of the searchlights, but she still held her single carnation and she smiled at me almost placidly.

'It isn't bad – I think,' she told me. 'But I feel kind of – giddy. I think I'd better – sit down.'

Pod glanced around the smoky street. We seemed to be standing in rubble in a haze of dust that smelled of old wood and burning. I had no idea how we had got here. It was no surprise to me to see the pillows of a couch spilled helter-skelter across a broken wall. Pod kicked them together into a pile.

'Sit down here,' he said.

Roy and Polly, carrying the square case between them, hesitated only a moment. 'We'd better not wait,' Roy said crisply. 'Good luck, Eileen. See you later.'

'Get moving,' Pod said. 'All of you.'

He glanced once at his wife. She smiled up at him and deliberately held the carnation to her nose, inhaling with delicate pleasure. Pod nodded as if she had told him something important. Maybe she had. Then he turned and lumbered heavily along the street, yelling at the top of his voice.

'Hey, Guthrie, Guthrie!' He waved an arm above his head. Bullets sang over him. Then a little knot of running people swerved between us. I saw a woman in the knot pause in her running when she saw Eileen on the cushions. I saw her stop, bend over the white head, call across her shoulder to a companion. Eileen waved me away with the carnation.

I ran dizzily after Cressy and Roy and Polly, my eyes stinging with smoke and pain and confused emotion I could not now stop to feel. Not yet. Cressy looked back for me and waited, taking my arm when I came within reach of her. It felt good and reassuring to let myself lean for a moment on her resilient young shoulder. I hadn't realized how weak I was until I touched strength. But I knew my own weight. She couldn't uphold me long. I straightened after a moment. I went on under my own power.

We had two blocks to run. We stumbled over rubble that blocked off half the street. Behind us suddenly rose the wail of another Prowler and we all looked back instinctively, seeing it loom above a welter of toppling walls and swerve up the street toward us, collapsing bricks and beams falling over it and sliding harmlessly to the ground. People scattered left and right as it came swelling and screaming down the long street. I saw another homemade bottle bomb glitter through the air and smash upon the broad red brow of the machine. Fire spread futilely and burned itself out across the undamaged hull.

The Prowler swerved again and vanished down a cross street with a fierce, diminishing wail. I had thought as I saw it come how beautiful it was, how perfect in shape and color and power. As Comus had been beautiful, once – perfect and powerful – before corruption took hold.

They were hunting us through the streets of Corby, but I knew they had lost us now. The chaos they had created was part of the force that defeated them, because the chaos was closing over us and we were only units of the mob, running and dodging and hiding when the Prowlers screamed or the helicopters roared overhead.

We had only one more block. At the end of the street the gray stone tower loomed against the stars. Once a bullet struck through the belfry arch and a bell sang out with a single startled clang that vibrated in my ears a long time after it had fallen silent again. And I had the curious feeling that Ted Nye was here in the roaring street behind us, searching frantically with fingers three thousand miles long. The Prowlers were his fingertips. The helicopters were his eyes. He *was* Comus, as Raleigh had been the nation, and with all the powers of omnipotence he was searching the streets of Corby for our four running figures and the box we carried.

A heavy roaring soared over us suddenly above the rooftops. A searchlight beam splashed down on a diagonal and for an instant bathed us all in its fierce white light that seemed to scorch the skin with terror where it touched us. Cressy and I dropped with a single motion under the shelter of a concrete wall. Roy jerked the box and Polly with it toward the nearest doorway. He made the cover himself, and the box was under the shelter too, but when the firing started Polly was still out in the white glare of the light. I think we all heard the bullet hit her, a solid, smacking sound.

She dropped as if the bullet had been a fist knocking her flat. The box thumped to the ground as Roy dropped his side of it and sprang out into the white moving beam. Bullets for a moment sang about him as he seized her under the arms and dragged her toward the doorway's dubious shelter. They bounced like spring rain on the pavement, missing the two by a series of repeated miracles in the endless moment before the searchlight beam moved impersonally on and the hail of bullets ceased.

When Cressy and I reached them Polly was sitting up and cursing with weak fluency, her hand to her side where blood had begun to spring out between her fingers. Roy looked at me, his face suddenly haggard with all the haggardness Polly had worn so long.

'You'll have to go on by yourselves,' he said in a flat voice. 'I won't leave her.'

Polly flashed one dazzling upward glance at him. She shut her lips for a moment over a curious look of weakness and warmth; she shut her eyes. Then she opened them again and said, 'Get the hell on with it, Roy. I'm okay. Don't be a fool.'

'Shut up,' Roy told her. 'Lie down and stop worrying. Rohan and Cressy can make it. We're almost there.' He gave me a resolute look.

'Don't argue,' he said. 'There isn't time. Get going.'

A remote part of my mind laughed silently, thinking of the

fresh-faced, irresponsible Roy of a week ago, who never made decisions because it was easier not to. I thought again about crossroads, and I gave him a brief grin.

'We're on our way,' I said. 'Take care of her.'

Cressy had already heaved the box off the ground. 'It isn't so heavy,' she said. 'I can handle it.'

I took hold of one of the handles with my good hand, squeezing her grip of it aside. 'We'll go faster together,' I said. 'It's awkward to run holding it in both hands. Let's go.'

It felt strange to be running without feeling the ground underfoot. Like running in a dream. We cut across the dark street, staggering a little because our pace was uneven. Smoke blew past but, curiously, there seemed to be nobody in the street at all now. From nearby and far off shots and yelling and the wail of Prowlers filled the night, but here we ran in a silence like a dream.

We were halfway to the church when I heard a sharp, cracking sound behind us and felt something hit me heavily in the leg. The impact made me stumble. I was aware of a penetrating hotness that was very cold – or was it a coldness that was very hot – drilling through my thigh. And my leg failed under me.

I saw Cressy's smeared face turn toward me with a look of appalled surprise as I fell, my leg folding under me. I felt grass under my hand as I caught myself. I had dropped on somebody's dark lawn across the street from the church.

I said to Cressy, 'Go on, go on!'

She caught the other handle, hefted the box with a two-handed grip before her, and ran without another word. I sat there watching her and trying somehow with all the power in my mind to evoke some magical wall of protection around her and the box. If she fell, the box would fall with her and crash upon the pavement. And the whole United States of America was inside the box. Every state and county, every city and farm and town, all packed neatly away and all the minuscule people going about their lives inside that crate. If she jolted it,

I thought everyone in the nation would have felt the impact. Even I would. Because I was in there too.

I was sitting on a patch of dark grass behind a row of trampled geraniums. The night around me reeked with the odor of their crushed leaves, strong and sharp, and the smell of burning and gunfire and blood. I felt my leg gingerly to see what had happened to me.

The sound of footsteps crunching loud on the rubbled street and coming quickly toward me made me look up. Then I saw a familiar checkered shirt.

My leg gave a sudden throb, as if the wound knew the gun that had made it. I was sure without reason that my leg was right. Guthrie didn't see me. He didn't even know I was there. His eye was on Cressy in her bedraggled pink ruffles, running through the smoke with the nation in a box in her arms and the church looming just above her.

Without a sound I slid my hand in my pocket, eased out the gun. I bent my good knee up to brace my good left wrist across. The blood was running down on my leg now, and there was a strange, high, increasing roar in my ears that sounded strange and new. I wondered if I was about to black out. But I had a job to do first. A job I should have done back there in the street when we first hit Corby. I should have shot him then.

He was close, slanting closer across the street. Even firing left-handed I ought to get him with any luck. But with my finger on the trigger, suddenly I paused, watching Guthrie.

He was in trouble. He stood all alone in the street, in bad trouble from some inward rebellion of his own.

This was Cressy he had to shoot.

I saw his gun hand rise and level the weapon at her. And I saw his gun hand somehow seem to rebel. Slowly the muzzle of the pistol sank and he stood watching her run, her hair blowing in the night wind, her skirts belling about her. In the dimness I couldn't see his face, but an anguish of irresolution was in every line of him. I remembered that other dark night in the truck station after we had fought off the renegades. I remembered Guthrie looking down into his glass and talking in slow, gentle tones about Cressy and his wife and his own past, the things he had hoped for and never had.

I thought, He won't do it. He can't. And I watched with a paralyzed fascination. I knew I ought to shoot. I shouldn't take any chances with him. But I had the obscure feeling that this was a decision Guthrie had to make, his own crossroads in the center of his own life. He had the right to choose for himself without interruption from anybody. It was very important that he should make his choice unaided.

He drew a deep breath and lifted his gun again, trying to take aim. Then he dropped his arm as if all strength had gone out of it. I thought, It isn't only that this is Cressy that bothers him – I think. It was more than that. Maybe he too knew that the whole United States was in the box she carried. If he fired and Cressy fell, the box fell too, and we would all fall with it and crack wide open on the dusty street.

He lifted his hand again, the third time. Again there was revolution in his mind and his muscles. I could hear him breathing hard. Then I saw him raise his other hand to brace the reluctant wrist. I saw his feet shift on the pavement, taking a firmer stance. I heard that strange roaring so loud in my ears I could hear nothing else at all.

Guthrie squinted along the barrel of his gun . . .

I couldn't wait any longer. I didn't dare. My finger was on the trigger. I felt it tighten without any orders from my mind. I felt the gun jolt, I heard the explosion. My shot cracked loud in the reverberating street, audible for an instant even over that increasing roar.

A fraction of a second after my bullet hit him his own shot exploded from his gun. But it exploded harmlessly upward into the roaring air, because he was falling as he fired.

Cressy didn't even look back. She only ducked her head over the box, hugging it tighter, and staggered up the steps of the Methodist church.

I let my gun hand drop to the wet grass. In spite of the roaring in my ears I felt as if an immense silence were settling around me in the empty street. I saw the church door open and

Cressy vanished through it to her rendezvous with history. I sat there alone on the damp dark grass with the smell of blood and geraniums strong around me. The stars were very bright and I felt very much alone.

The roaring in my ears was distant but so strong I wondered why I hadn't blacked out by now. I shook my head gently trying to make the noise stop. And then for the first time it dawned upon me that the sound wasn't inside my head. I wasn't in the town at all.

It was in the sky.

And it was coming nearer, converging upon Corby out of the black night of the continent. It was Ted Nye's last throw of the dice. I had expected bombers or bombs upon Corby long before now. Ted Nye at last had made his choice. He knew he had gambled and almost lost. Almost . . .

A strange, childish little rhyme sang through my head.

Ted – Dead.

Nye – Die.

I felt it circle around and around, following the walls of my skull. The town was full of the wail of sirens and the reverberations of gunfire, but the hollow thunder of the bombers was beginning to blanket all other sound. I felt very light, very dizzy. I felt somehow as if my whole life until this minute had been a long rehearsal for the real thing. For this moment on the dark grass with the stars winking over me.

Suddenly my ears ached with silence.

A silence that fell like a physical blow over Corby and the world. I thought I had gone deaf. I thought I was hovering on the verge of a faint. The sirens had stopped screaming. The gunfire had faltered to a ragged, astonished stop. No voices shouted.

And in the sky, wiped out as if with one enormous gesture, the heavy throbbing of the bombers had ceased to sound.

My reason caught up with my unbelieving senses. The Anti-Com, I thought. The Anti-Com just went on.

Comus is dead.

I felt one moment of anguish and loss for all the power, that wonderful, intricate, beautiful thing which had saved the nation in its day, before corruption touched it. For the lustrous world I had known and would never know again. The world had gone darker and grimmer and heavier in this moment while history turned around me in the silence and the night. A new world lay ahead. All I could be sure of was that it would be a harsh world, full of sweat and bloodshed and uncertainty. But a real world, breathing and alive.

'What's past is prologue,' I thought. 'Wait and see.'

I sat there on the trampled grass, dizzy and confused and somehow, strangely, very happy. Very calm.

Around me in the town voices were beginning to rise again. Gunfire broke out spasmodically here and there. But no sirens. No lights except for the light of fires. Comus lay dead across the continent like a vast, inert giant.

I sat quietly waiting for the crash beyond the mountains where the bombers had begun to fall.

Catherine Lucille Moore was born in Indianapolis in 1911. Prolonged illness when young meant she spent much of her time as a child reading the fantastic tales of the day, a background that no doubt spurred her on to become a writer of science fiction and fantasy herself. Moore made her first professional sale to *Weird Tales* while still in her early 20's: the planetary romance 'Shambleau', which introduced one of her best-known heroes Northwest Smith. She went on to produce a highly respected body of work, initially solo for *Weird Tales* and then, in collaboration with her husband, fellow SF writer Henry Kuttner, whom she married in 1940, for John W. Campbell's *Astounding Science Fiction*. Moore was one of the first women to rise to prominence in the male-dominated world of early SF, and paved the way for others to follow in her footsteps. Moore ceased to write fiction after Kuttner's death in 1958, concentrating instead on writing for television. She died in April 1987 after a long battle with Alzheimer's Disease.